Tired of vampires who are romantic figures who just happen to need blood to live? Or of vampires who were transformed against their will and desperately seek ways to survive without hurting others? If you prefer your vampires evil and disgusting, then this may be the book you're looking for.

MANAGANSETT PRESS

NIGHT RULES

Paul Alan Sheffield

Managansett Press Edition 2015

NIGHT RULES

CHAPTER ONE: SATURDAY

Four days before she was scheduled to finally graduate from high school, Rachel Darian felt almost ecstatically happy and certainly had not the least premonition that she would not live to wear the cap and gown which now hung in her closet. The same could be said of her best friend and current companion, Teri Chin, who had somewhat uncertainly agreed to go along on a one night camping trip in the woods of western Rhode Island. Rachel's assurances that they would never be more than an hour's walk from the nearest road and that the most dangerous animal they were likely to meet would be a stray dog had been less than convincing, but appeals to their long friendship and Rachel's relentless enthusiasm for the trip had won the day.

"Where are we anyway?" Like her companion, Teri was active in school sports, too short to play her favorite, basketball, although she had become a first string Lacrosse player, but she was a novice in the woods. She had realized that she was completely disoriented within less than an hour after they had left Rachel's car parked on a side street near the junction of the town lines of Scituate, Managansett, and the city of Providence.

"I don't know exactly," Rachel paused and half turned toward her friend, slipping her hands into the back pockets of her jeans. She raised her eyes in counterfeit alarm. "Maybe we're lost."

Teri rolled her eyes dramatically and took advantage of the momentary pause to shift the straps of her back pack. "Come off it, Rachel. Stop fooling around. You know how I get when I don't know where I am."

Rachel shrugged her shoulders with an exaggerated sigh. "Where's your sense of adventure, Teri? Here we are, alone in the mysterious wilderness..." In fact, Rachel did not know precisely where they were, but she knew the surrounding geography well enough to make a fairly accurate guess.

"How romantic," the other girl interrupted sarcastically. "I don't suppose you've got Andy and Kevin tucked away in your pack to keep us company?"

"Ick! I know you've got the hots for Kevin, but couldn't you pick a better choice for me than Andy?"

"I thought you told me Andy was pretty neat?"

"Yeah, well that was before I talked to Valerie and she clued me in about him." Rachel suddenly became uncomfortable with the subject and averted her eyes.

Teri recognized the change in her friend's demeanor. Although pretty enough in an unremarkable way, Rachel rarely dated, and then only as part of a group. She was uneasy when certain subjects came up in conversation, an only child raised in a very religious household, but she kept her opinions to herself. Her parents were much older than those of any of her friends; Marie Darian had been nearly forty when her daughter was born, and had previously abandoned hope of having a child of her own. The unexpected pregnancy seemed nothing short of miraculous, and she treasured her daughter with legendary single-mindedness. It was only her inability to resist Rachel's rare moments of determination that had made this overnight trip possible.

"So where are we really?"

Rachel's good humor returned immediately. "I don't know, really, not exactly anyway. Somewhere north of the reservoir, probably in Scituate. The border runs through here somewhere but it's not marked."

"Are you telling me we really are lost?"

Rachel laughed. "No, not the way you mean. Relax, Teri, I know what I'm doing. Look, the Upper Valley River is over that way. It runs into the reservoir. No matter how lost we get, all we have to do is follow it downstream until we start crossing the service roads. Or we could go the opposite way and sooner or later we'd reach the interstate. Trust me, it's easier to get lost on the highway than it is in the woods around here."

Although her expression remained dubious, Teri allowed herself to relax slightly. "All right, I guess. What time is it anyway?"

"It's only three o'clock. What's the matter? Sore feet?"

"As a matter of fact, yes. I stock shelves nights, remember? I don't get to sit down from the time I leave school until I get home at ten thirty."

Rachel dropped her bantering tone. "Yeah, I'm sorry, Teri. I guess I got carried away being out here. It's so, you know, wild and free, no telephone, no internet, no parents asking if you've done your homework or whatever. No boys. Look, we'll head off that way for a while." She pointed roughly to the east. "We ought to find the river pretty quick and we can set up the tent nearby. Another hour or so, tops. I promise."

"I think I can manage that."

Rachel remained motionless for a few seconds. "Are you sorry you came, Teri? Without the guys, I mean?"

The other girl pushed one cheek out with her tongue before answering. "No, I guess not. I mean, it's fun fooling around and like that, but there's always this, like, pressure."

Rachel nodded. "Yeah, I know what you mean. Okay then, let's get going."

Deliberately slowing her pace, Rachel forced herself to entertain her friend with a constant stream of small talk. She would have preferred to remain quiet and just enjoy the isolation but she was afraid Teri's second thoughts would grow stronger.

The found a path twenty minutes later.

It was clearly an old one, no longer in use, wide enough for a single vehicle and with some deep ruts which had long since lost any real detail. It was heavily overgrown, but not as much as the ground to either side, which was covered by an increasingly thick tangle of bull brier, wisteria, trumpet vines, and prolific thickets of sumac, all engaged in a relentless battle for access to the anemic sunlight that penetrated the canopy spread by larger oak and maple and ash trees.

"There's an old abandoned boat house down here somewhere," Rachel explained. "I've seen it from the other side of the river when we hiked along the bank but I've never been in it. It used to be part of the Sheffield estate."

"Maybe we could sleep in it tonight." Teri had been chasing images of creeping insects and slithering snakes out of her head for most of the afternoon.

"No way." Rachel shook her head emphatically. "It's half collapsed into the river, all rotted out underneath, and part of the roof is caved in. It's probably filled with rats and things. I wouldn't mind checking it out if we come to it, and if it looks safe, but that's as far as I go. I like to choose my own adventures, not fall into them."

"So where do we sleep?" Teri glanced to either side, frowning at the rocky, overgrown, and irregular terrain.

"Don't sweat it. We'll come out of this stuff pretty soon." But she was less confident than she sounded. Rachel had hiked extensively down near the reservoir and on the Managansett side of the river, but this was her first foray into the heavily forested west bank. "If we have to, we can cut down some of the brush and use it for a mattress."

"That sounds like fun." Teri directed a withering look at the back of her friend's head.

They followed the abandoned road in silence for the next several minutes, then crested a small rise and found themselves staring down at a rapidly flowing stream that stretched directly across their path. The watercourse had cut a narrow but deep bed for itself, exposing naked roots and half buried stones, all covered with a green slime. Skating bugs flitted across the quieter pools, and frogs and salamanders crouched in the cool shade.

"Looks like another road," Teri pointed to her right.

As with the one that had led them here, this was also heavily overgrown; bull briar had bridged the gap with tentative feelers, although the center of the path was comparatively free of vegetation. The intersection was just ahead of them, but it was almost impassible, undermined by erosion, the ground deeply gouged and crumbling.

Rachel examined their surroundings critically as they progressed. For some reason, the undergrowth had not yet consumed the crossroads area, which was in fact devoid of life except for patches of moss and occasional chunks of serrated fungus. The proximity of water made this a likely campsite; it was moving fast enough that she doubted they'd have much trouble with mosquitoes. In fact, even the tiny midges which had hovered around their faces for most of the day seemed to have abandoned this spot, where dead trees marked the edge of an irregular circle of bare ground. She was mildly concerned that something toxic might have been dumped in the water, resulting in the die-off, but the vegetation both upstream and down seemed unaffected.   "I'd like to be a little higher, but it's not supposed to rain, so unless you want to keep going, this looks like a pretty good place to pitch camp"

"Are you kidding?" Teri was already slipping out of her pack. "I've been ready to quit for hours."

"There's a level spot over there where the tent should fit

okay. Let's clear the rocks and stuff out of the way and get it up."

"Drinks first. It feels like I've been eating sand." She pulled a cup out of her pack and started toward the stream.

"Not there!" Rachel was surprised at how loudly she had spoken, but there was something about the prospect of drinking the water here that disturbed her. "Use the canteens, Teri. We don't know where this comes from or what's in it."

"Oh, yeah, sure." Teri stopped abruptly. "What're we going to do when they're empty?"

"There's Gatorade in my pack, and we'll run into apple trees in the morning. There used to be orchards just south of here, you know. They've gone wild but they still have fruit. And the stream there is supposed to be drinkable. It runs into the reservoir."

"Right." Teri was clearly not thrilled by the prospect of more hiking.

They scoured their campsite reasonably clean, clearing away stones and fallen branches. The ground was completely bare when they were finished, no grass or other ground cover, even the stones in the stream adjacent were free of moss. Rachel was pleased that they hadn't disturbed any gross spiders or insects, guessing that her friend would be put off by such a discovery. It never occurred to her that the complete absence of insect life was in fact distinctly unnatural. She'd spent enough time hiking in Vermont and New Hampshire with her parents and her church fellowship to know that there was something strange about the clearing, but she was tired and preoccupied and if a restless thought stirred at the periphery of her awareness, she managed to ignore it.

The tent went up quickly. After more than a score of camping trips, Rachel could have done it alone and almost with her eyes shut. Teri's help was largely a matter of courtesy, Rachel's attempt to make her feel that she was contributing to the effort. Once it was in place, the familiar security suggested by the open tent flap overwhelmed what remained of her uncertainty.

Unexpectedly, it clouded over as they were gathering dead wood for their fire; the air became noticeably cooler and the sky had become quite dark by the time the first flames came licking up through the pyramid of sticks Rachel had carefully constructed. She continued to add increasingly thicker bits of wood to the outside as the fire spread until she was satisfied that it had stabilized and could be fed more casually.

They sat beside the campfire eating sandwiches of ham and salami and provolone cheese, drinking Gatorade, and talking about graduation, the behavior and style sense of several of their classmates of both sexes, and their hopes for college in the fall. Rachel had been accepted at her first choice, Michigan State University, where she hoped to major in packaging design, and Teri had gotten into NYU by the skin of her teeth, her major as yet undeclared. Teri had been adamant about attending college in what she called a "real city", something bigger than Providence.

"I've spent all my life in Rhode Island," she often complained. "I want to see what it's like to live in New York or Chicago or Los Angeles, some place where there is always something exciting going on."

It was not quite full dark when Teri lifted her head and stared off past the edge of their campsite, so distracted that she didn't respond to her companion's next question. The silence suddenly became awkward.

"What is it?" Rachel felt distinctly uneasy, a sensation that had been creeping up on her for the past couple of hours, so slowly that she hadn't realized what she was feeling until just a few minutes earlier. She hadn't said anything; Teri would never have let her live it down if it had been she, the seasoned camper, who panicked in the darkness. But she'd had the strangest sensation, a growing conviction that they were being watched, or if not watched exactly, at least that they were no longer alone.

"I don't know. Just for a second..." She paused, half rose to her feet. "There! I saw it again when the fire flickered just now. Something glowing, over there in the stream."

Rachel squinted, trying to follow the line from her friend's pointing finger. "I don't see anything..."

"C'mon, I'll show you." Teri stood and walked quickly across the intervening space, then crouched beside the murmuring brook. After a moment's hesitation, Rachel followed her.

"I still don't see anything, Teri. It's just the fire reflecting off the water." The fog of uneasiness continued to thicken.

"No, look right there."

And this time, Rachel saw it too, a sharp, distinct reflection as if from a piece of polished metal. "I see it." Her voice trembled.

Teri leaned forward, one hand braced on the ground, the other reaching toward the reflection. "There's something buried here, Rachel. A box of some kind, I think. I can feel the corner. Damn, it's cold!"

Rachel reached across as well, using touch rather than sight. Now that they both crouched by the water, most of the light from the fire was blocked off. But even in the darkness, she was able to confirm her friend's words. There was something inside her that knew more than her eyes could see. "It's some kind of a box, all right. Wait a minute, I'll get us some light."

Rachel pulled a burning stick from the fire and propped it between two stones so that its flame illuminated the area where they had made their discovery. Using thin stones from the stream bed, they chopped away at the packed earth surrounding the box. Despite a growing uneasiness, Rachel was infected with her companion's enthusiasm, felt an irresistible compulsion to help unearth whatever it was that they had found. Its nature quickly became more evident. The sides of the box were made of wood, remarkably well preserved considering its present location, the corners and edges protected by bands of hammered metal, with other bands crossing and reinforcing the wood along its sides. Several odd symbols had been carved into the wood where it was exposed, and others seemed to have been etched into the metal -- crosses, ankhs, reversed swastikas, less identifiable glyphs that neither girl recognized.

"Do you suppose it's some kind of buried treasure?" Teri asked breathlessly.

"Oh, sure, pirates in Rhode Island. Galleons on the Providence River. You watch too many movies."

It took half an hour to free their discovery completely and when they did finally pull the chest loose, they almost dropped it into the water. Although the box was less than two feet in length and half that in depth and width, it was remarkably heavy.

"What do you suppose it is?" Teri was almost feverishly animated, convinced that they'd found some kind of buried treasure. Rachel was less hopeful, but equally curious about its contents.

"I don't know." She gave a tentative tug at the hasp, which showed no signs of rust. "How are you at picking a lock?"

"I took Introduction to Safecracking instead; it sounded more practical. Maybe I can pry it open with a stick."

Three broken sticks later, Teri admitted that they needed a more rugged tool. "How about your knife?"

Rachel carried a sheath knife on her belt, a present from her father of which she was inordinately proud. "No way. We'd just break the blade anyway." She licked her upper lip with the tip of her tongue. "Hand me that rock there."

She began hitting the lock at an angle, striking with the narrowest part of the wedge shaped stone. The metal dented slightly at the point of impact but showed no other indication that it had been weakened.

"Here, you try it for a while."

Teri accepted the rock dubiously and pounded away with considerably less coordination. She lost interest quickly, however, and let the stone fall to the ground. "How about dropping it off a cliff or something?"

"Right, Teri. First we have to dig a real deep pit so we have some place to throw it. Give me that rock."

Rachel leaned down and peered closely at the box, trying to determine its most vulnerable spot. Despite the earlier pounding, there was no indication of anything other than superficial damage. Drawn by a compulsion she could not quite understand, she reached out with the tip of one finger and traced the outline of the metal strap, up one side and down the other.

"What're you doing, making love to it?"

Rachel shook her head, more to rouse herself than as an answer. "Just trying to find a weak spot." She raised her hand and began hammering at the lock.

Apparently some damage had been done because this time, on her third attempt, Rachel felt something give. She paused, startled by her sudden success, then struck twice more, and the lock fell open.

""Great. Here, let me help." Teri moved quickly to grasp the sides of the lid, then used both hands to force it open. Despite the absence of the lock, it held for a few seconds, cemented with mud and the inertia of age. Teri was on the verge of giving up when it finally gave way with a low hiss, as though it had been air tight, the contents pressurized. The top popped open and fell back against the stops and an incredibly strong odor of sweet decay filled the air, so powerful that both girls retreated hastily, not even waiting long enough to look inside.

"Smells like something died in there," Teri complained when she could stop sneezing.

Rachel, whose eyes were watering uncontrollably, agreed with her. "Maybe someone buried a pet or something. God, that smells awful. We'll have to get rid of it or I'll never be able to sleep."

"You're right about that." Teri was waving her arms through the air, trying to fan the smell away. There was a fairly brisk breeze rustling the leaves, but their encampment seemed to be in a natural shelter. The air around them was stale and cloying. "Can't we dump it in the water or something?"

"Yeah, that might work." Rachel looked around, grabbed the longest piece of wood she could find from the pile they had accumulated to keep their fire going.

Despite the fetid smell, Rachel remained curious about the contents of the box, so she also picked up a short length of burning wood, then jumped to the opposite bank, so that she could look down into the interior of the now open box. To her disappointment, it looked as though there was nothing there more substantial than mud or dead leaves or possibly the rotting body of some small animal, certainly no coins or jewels or precious stones. She dropped the firebrand into the stream where it hissed and died, then wrapped both hands around the shaft of the longer stick and tried to push the box into the water.

It was too heavy and awkward to be moved easily, and Rachel was sweaty and irritated before she was finally able to nudge it over the bank and into the stream. When it finally fell into the water, she slipped and sat down hard on the ground, then wiped the back of one hand across her sweat slick forehead. "Damn it, Teri, why'd you have to find that thing in the first place?"

Teri just shook her head; the smell had upset her stomach and she didn't feel like talking. She detected the onset of a migraine and wanted to lie down quietly and calm herself until it eased itself.

The rancid smell still clung to the area and the air remained stagnant. Impulsively, Rachel stood up and approached the box, which lay half immersed in the water. Holding her breath, she used the stick as a lever to tilt the box further forward. As she did so, a thick, slightly fluid mass surged over the lip, hesitated for a second, then fell into the water. With its contents partially disgorged, the box's center of gravity changed and it drifted about a meter downstream before getting caught on a rock. Stifling her distaste, Rachel followed, prodding the box relentlessly, pushing it past the rock and toward the center of the stream, where it was suddenly caught by the current and whisked out of sight.

There was faint movement in the darkness, faint but recognizable. Rachel told herself that it must have been a trick of her eyes, an illusion caused by the uncertain light reflecting off the restless current. For just a second or two, it had seemed to her that the formless mass had moved a short way upstream toward her, defying the rushing water, and when she held the fire near, it seemed almost to recoil, move away from the flame and surrender to the inevitable. It was gone so quickly that she couldn't be certain, and after all, it made no sense. Her eyes must have been playing tricks on her.

The smell was still overwhelming. She gagged, breathing deeply to expel the last of it from her lungs. With the source gone, it diminished rapidly in strength, but never quite went away, lingering long after they realized they could not recapture their lighter mood and climbed into their sleeping bags, each trapped by her own thoughts. Teri had become unusually quiet, her head throbbing, the rancid odor still faintly burning the inside of her nose. She could almost taste it and the urge to vomit was so strong that all she wanted to do was crawl into her sleeping bag and escape into unconsciousness. Rachel was less affected, and when the air finally began to clear somewhat, she was reminded of exotic perfumes and the lure of romance. Wearing a secret smile that she would have been unable to explain, Rachel drifted off to sleep.

Teri woke to absolute silence. In fact, it may have been the quiet itself that roused her. The usual sounds of night in the forest had been suppressed from the start, crickets, frogs, the occasional night bird. At first she could not identify what had changed since they had gone to sleep, but now she realized that the faint, even breathing of her friend was no longer audible.

"Rachel?" She whispered. "Are you all right?"

Silence was her only reply. She reached out tentatively, found the edge of her friend's sleeping bag, explored further and discovered that it was flat, empty. She was alone in the tent.

Teri squirmed around and stuck her head out through the entrance flap. They had doused the fire, but the cloud cover had cleared off and a nearly full moon shone surprisingly brightly through the branches overhead, many of which were strangely denuded of leaves. There was just enough light to reveal that Rachel wasn't sitting just outside the tent, or anywhere in the immediate vicinity.

"Rachel!" She called slightly louder, but still not even at her normal speaking level, inhibited by the darkness. "Damn it, Rachel, where are you?"

Teri bit her lip indecisively, then twisted around, groping until she found her sneakers. Rachel might just have gone out to take a pee in private, but Teri wouldn't be able to go back to sleep until she knew for certain. Something might be seriously wrong. Rachel could have tripped and fallen, hit her head, be lying somewhere just out of sight. Teri was still dressed; the night had grown cool by the time they'd banked the fire and retreated into their tent. Outside, she stood up, tucked her blouse into the waistband of her jeans and looked around.

The night was loud with silence.

Despite her earlier complaints, Teri had actually enjoyed the hike. Kevin Randolph's ardent courting had recently betrayed a hint of desperation. He was clearly worried that she would find someone else once they were separated by her move to college. Kevin was still "thinking about" a trade school, but appeared content to keep his job pumping gas. He seemed perfectly happy to remain in Managansett despite the town's limitations, and Teri was smart enough to know that their lives were diverging, that she wanted more than Kevin was prepared to offer. Her parents had also been hovering uncomfortably close, and were openly unhappy with her college choice. Although they had adopted a veneer of American customs, they were still at heart a traditional Vietnamese family, and Teri understood their reluctance to allow their daughter to grow away from them.

For one reason or another, Teri had enjoyed little time to herself during the previous several weeks. A weekend away from the pressures generated by Kevin and her family was a welcome respite. She and Rachel had become increasingly close during their senior year, and when Teri was honest with herself, she acknowledged that she would miss Rachel a lot more than Rachel would miss her. She could say things to Rachel that would have shocked her mother, without being judged, without fear that her secrets would be broadcast to the world.

The woods were spooky, she realized, standing in front of the tent, but also rather pretty. A very tenuous fog had drifted up from the river, distinct tendrils insinuating themselves among the trees and lower branches, reflecting just the faintest hint of blue in the moonlight. They seemed to her like shy ghosts trying to touch the real world. It was utterly quiet; the air had cooled slightly but remained heavy with moisture, the leaves motionless, and even the brook seemed to have grown mute. There was only the faintest trace of the foul odor now.

Teri stood rubbing the palms of her hands along her thighs, reluctant to disturb the silence, but concerned that her friend might be hurt or sleepwalking or even just lost. She licked dry lips and was about to call out when she heard something, almost certainly a human voice, female, somewhere ahead and slightly to her left. It was barely more than a whisper, not secretive exactly, but indistinct, blurred.

"Rachel?" Her voice was barely audible but she couldn't bring herself to shatter the brittle silence by calling more loudly. She walked slowly to the near bank of the stream, straining to hear more.

The voice came again, a short string of indistinct syllables. The tone was conversational; there was no sense of danger or alarm. "Rachel, do you walk and talk in your sleep at the same time?" Teri whispered.

She began to move along the side of the stream, picking her way carefully in the darkness, one arm half raised to brush away any stray branches that might be invisible in the night. Approximately twenty meters away from the campsite, she heard the voice for the third time, still too fuzzy to understand, but recognizably Rachel's. At that point, she almost overcame her reluctance to shout, but even as she decided to call out, there was an answer, indistinct so that she could not make out the words, but undeniably male.

"You creep," she whispered under her breath. "I can't believe you arranged to meet a guy out here and didn't tell me." Teri hesitated, torn between conflicting desires. She felt an obligation to respect Rachel's privacy, but at the same time she was curious about her friend's unusual behavior. Whoever she was with, it hadn't sounded like Andy; his squeaky whine was unmistakable. One of the few secrets Teri had withheld from Rachel was the fact that she and Andy Kirschner had slept together twice the previous summer, and that she had found him to be almost comically inept. In the throes of what passed for passion, Andy's voice grew even more high pitched and nasal than it was already.

Teri crossed the stream at one of its narrower points, using a flat rock as a stepping stone, and made her way carefully along the edge of a crumbling hillside. At some time in the past, the stream must have been considerably more robust; the ground to either side was heavily undercut, large taproots lay exposed, protruding from badly eroded slopes. She used one of these to climb up and away from the water and found herself in a dense stand of white birch, squinting to see in the dim light.

Something moved in the distance.

Her curiosity overcame her scruples at last and Teri began to make her way forward somewhat circuitously, wanting to see but not be seen. Less than five minutes later, she noticed something shining pale white in the dim light, advanced cautiously until she recognized what it was.

"I'll be damned," she breathed. Hanging from slightly above eye level was Rachel's blouse, draped casually over the stub of a broken branch. Her bra lay on the ground close by. "I didn't know you had it in you, kid," she said softly, unconscious of the double entendre, now more determined than ever to find out who Rachel was entertaining in the darkness.

Her curiosity neared satisfaction a few seconds later. One of the birches had grown too heavy for the soggy ground in which it had grown and had uprooted itself, slowly collapsing until the surrounding trees provided enough support to hold it at a forty-five degree angle. Rachel was there, lying back against the recumbent trunk, her arms extended above her head.

Rachel had always preferred to wear baggy, formless clothing, which effectively concealed what Teri knew to be an enviable figure. She reacted with muted shock when she saw that Rachel was completely naked at the moment. She was moving her hips slowly while her mysterious companion ran his hands along her sides. When he touched her breasts, Rachel moaned softly but it carried through the still night air and Teri felt her own pulse quicken. It took considerable effort to move her eyes away from Rachel's pale form to examine her companion.

His back was turned and he was wearing indistinct, formless clothing so dark that he seemed more shadow than substance. Teri could tell that he was quite tall, but thin, almost spindly; his arms looked disproportionately long, although this might have been a trick of the shimmering, uncertain light.

Teri's desire to see his face was now so strong that she felt no further misgivings about spying. One careful step at a time, she advanced to her right, upslope, using a stand of birch to mask her approach should either of the lovers glance in her direction. A darker, blocky shape stood in the darkness ahead, and a few more steps brought her to a large, rocky upthrust, with a relatively flat top and one side slanted toward the ground. With continued deliberation, she crawled up the rough surface on hands and knees, hoping to reach a better vantage point.

At last she reached the top, where she took a few seconds to focus her eyes. She could see Rachel quite clearly now, but the other figure was oddly indistinct, and much to her surprise, still apparently fully clothed. He had shifted position slightly, frustrating her hope to identify him. She stayed where she was, hoping that he would move again. "Come on, you bastard," Teri mouthed the words, barely whispering. "Let's see your face."

As though he'd heard her, the dark clad shape below rose from his crouch and half turned in her direction. The cool moonlight washed across his upper torso but she still couldn't make out details of his clothing. It was almost as if his body was swathed in black cloth, wrapped around chest, abdomen, and limbs. Only his face and hands were free.

Finally he turned his head, far enough that a beam of moonlight fell across the long black hair that grew in scattered tufts covering only a small portion of his skull. His eyes glowed like the coals in their dying fire, noticeable even across a distance of several meters, embedded deeply in his chalk white flesh. Teri recoiled, sending a small avalanche of crumbled rock and sand down toward the ground. The man's face was lumpy, misshapen, asymmetrical. Even from a distance and in the poor light, Teri saw enough to startle her into an inarticulate cry of horror.

She knew she had given away her presence so she scrambled backward down the rock, no longer making any attempt to remain silent. Teri could think of nothing but to run. As soon as her feet were on solid ground, she turned and started back in the general direction of the tent, fortunately managing to keep her footing on the uneven ground. Consumed by panic, she quickly became disoriented and missed the campsite, plunging further into the wooded area beyond. Terror drove her forward blindly, one arm raised to protect her eyes, and when she reached the bank of the Upper Valley River, she almost ran straight over the bank and into the water. The current was very strong here and if she hadn't caught herself at the very last moment, she might have drowned or been battered to death on the rocks.

Either of those fates would have been preferable to the one that pursued her.

At the lip of the river bank, Teri froze, mesmerized by the sight of the barrier the river presented. Her breath was so labored that it hurt to draw in the stale night air. The worst of her panic receded and she realized she must move either upstream or down if she were to continue her flight. A glance over her shoulder made the decision more urgent. A tall, impossibly thin figure was standing less than five meters away, leaning forward like a praying mantis contemplating its next meal.

She took a quick step backward and spun to her right, but the dark figure moved effortlessly to intercept her, almost floating across the uneven ground. Teri drew back, balancing precariously above the rushing water. "Who are you? What do you want?" Her voice was a hoarse croak.

There was no answer.

Clenching her fists nervously, Teri glanced around, searching for an escape route. "Look, I'm sorry if I stuck my nose where it didn't belong. I was just worried about Rachel. I can see she's all right with you, so just let me go, all right? She's my best friend; I won't tell anyone."

Again, neither answer nor movement. Her heart was beating so fast that she thought it must burst. "I'm going now, all right? Just leave me alone."

Cautiously she took a single step. Most of the man's face was shrouded in shadow, but she was no longer interested in seeing him clearly. The brief view she had had earlier was more than enough, and a formless terror still quickened her heart. A sickly sweet smell flavored the air, as though something had died and decayed nearby. It was something she had smelled not long before.

Teri was about to take another tentative step when something changed, some subtle alteration in the other man's posture that told her to run. She tried, but he was in her path before she had taken three steps. When she tried to change direction, she ran into a tree, bruising her right shoulder and spinning her around, and then he was closer than ever.

She sensed rather than saw the hand moving toward her face, jerked her head away but not far enough to avoid the impact. Something hard and intensely cold struck her right cheek with stunning force. Teri's feet flew out from under her and she was floating for the split second it took before she hit the ground with her hip and shoulder, banging her chin hard enough to rattle her teeth.

She lay there stunned as something touched her body, rolled her over onto her back, then brushed roughly over her breasts and gripped the top of her blouse. Teri opened her eyes and tried to push the hand away as she was half lifted from the ground. Her attacker's face was close to hers now and she saw that the cheeks and forehead were riddled with pale red scars and running sores. A stubble of black hair covered parts of the unusually sharp pointed chin and the eyes were smoldering amber under chiseled eyebrows, bracketing a swollen, lopsided nose that had only a single nostril. The lips were thin and dry, pulled back from blackened gums and irregularly spaced teeth that looked not even remotely human.

Teri wanted to scream, but her body no longer responded to her brain. Something warm and hot was flowing down the side of her face and she realized without alarm that it must be blood. Mercifully, she was already slipping into shock when her blouse was ripped down over her shoulders and her attacker lowered its head, misshapen lips curling back to reveal rotted, irregular teeth.

There was a moment of incredible pain that gathered up and swept away everything that was Teri Chin. Her pallid killer crouched over her body for some time afterward, then threw what remained into the river. The corpse was swept off into the darkness, already forgotten as her killer turned back to where Rachel Darian still rested with her back pressed against the fallen birch, patiently waiting for the return of her lover.

Teri had seen a malformed, diseased face that inspired only horror and revulsion, but in Rachel's eyes was the image of a handsome, blonde young man in his mid-twenties, with a firm chin, perfect complexion, and a manner that was almost regal. She smiled as he approached, and when his hand brushed her thigh a hot wave of pleasure pushed her to the brink of fainting.

She cried out softly, turned her head to one side and closed her eyes, completely caught up in a rush of ecstasy.

The spindly figure stepped between her legs and crouched, placing one hand on each hip, then lowered its head past her breasts, the lower ribs, her navel, finally hovered just above her lower abdomen. If Rachel had glanced down at that moment, she might have seen through the handsome illusion to the monstrous form that dwelled beneath. The mouth opened, exposing the still bloody fangs for a brief second before they sank into her flesh.

Rachel convulsed but made no move to escape, spoke not a word of protest. Despite the cool night air, her hair grew matted with perspiration and the strength seemed to rush from her body like air from a balloon. A tiny voice in the back of her mind cried out that this was wrong, that she was going to die if it didn't stop, but the voice was wrong.

Teri had been an inconvenience, a victim to be drained and discarded. Rachel was to serve a higher purpose.

CHAPTER TWO: SUNDAY

Dan Scapelli preferred not to work on Sundays, but the nature of what he considered his "profession" was such that his working hours were generally dictated by outside forces. For the past three years, he'd been supporting himself by freelancing for the *Providence Journal* and *The Rhode Island Register*, more often for a few of the smaller circulation weeklies which had proliferated and then mostly died during the past decade, as well as occasional articles and short stories, one of which had been adapted as an episode of a half hour television anthology series. He wasn't getting rich, but he paid the bills regularly and maintained a satisfactory if not exactly comfortable lifestyle.

He stabbed at the police scanner automatically on his way to the bathroom where he showered and shaved, choosing not to notice that his hairline had receded visibly, even though he had turned thirty only a month before. His mind automatically filtered out the routine traffic news, waiting for anything that might provide a hook, an item that regular reporters would ignore but which might conceal a viable story. Wearing slacks and a lurid short sleeved shirt, he poked through his refrigerator, finally selected a Tupperware container of tuna fish salad, which he spread on wheat crackers for his breakfast, washing it down with warmed up coffee left over from Saturday. His table was a chaotic mix of dirty dishes, unshelved groceries, and tubes of paint he'd been sorting through a week earlier while trying to find just the right shade of green for the landscape he'd been working on since winter.

Someone knocked on the door at precisely nine o'clock, a quick double tap followed by a laggard third. "Come in!" Dan didn't even look up from the newspaper he'd been reading. "It's not locked, Kelly."

There was a click as the door swung open, followed by a cheery greeting from his visitor. "Good morning! Heard your shower running so I knew you were up."

He glanced in her direction. "There's coffee hot and not too stale. Or you could make fresh if you're finicky."

Kelly Marsh was, in addition to being Dan's next door neighbor, a year older and, in her opinion, far wiser. They had known each other for over a year now, and their relationship had gone from casual formality to close friendship, and was now teetering on the brink of becoming romantic, a realization which had made both of them somewhat tentative. Neither had a particularly extensive or happy history of close relationships, and both were wary of putting a strain on the status quo.

Kelly pulled a coffee cup from the overhead rack and poured herself some, sipped at it carefully. "I don't know how you do it, Scapelli. Every time I come here you have warmed over coffee, never fresh. Morning, noon, night-time, doesn't matter. What do you do? Buy it at the used stimulants store?"

"The story of my life, Kelly. Always the bridesmaid, ya-ta-ta ya-ta-ta." He closed the paper and turned in his seat. "What's new and interesting in the world? You said you were expecting some fresh assignments."

She took another sip of coffee and walked slowly across the kitchen. "Oh, more of the usual. Just not as much as I was expecting." Kelly ran a clipping service out of her apartment, as well as working sporadically as a research assistant, had in fact helped Dan on more than one story in the past, at first as a business arrangement, but later informally. Dan reciprocated when time permitted, helping gather, classify, and summarize the various materials she routinely indexed. Her income wasn't much better than Dan's, but it was steadier, although she had been complaining of a drop off in her normal business lately. The internet made research a good deal easier than it had once been.

"Any plans for the day?"

She nodded and Dan realized again how much his perception of her had changed since they had first met. Although he had liked her from the outset, his initial impression had been that she was unattractive. Kelly was almost a foot shorter than his sixty-nine inches, solidly built though by no means overweight. Her face was round with full cheeks and a wide, almost oversized mouth, as opposed to his narrow features and flat planed face. As they had grown to know each other better, he found himself responding to her infectious smile and the way it lit up a room. He had begun to dream of her when he slept and found himself thinking about her at odd moments during the day.

"Unfortunately, yes. I have to do those summaries for Dr.

Brodsky. She needs them Monday morning, early."

"How about supper later on? My treat."

"Maybe. I'll have a better idea once I get started. You going to be around all day or are you working?"

"Not today. This month's rent is already paid and I deserve a day off. I thought maybe I'd paint for awhile if the light is good." Art was Dan's informal therapy, a hobby at which he demonstrated no perceptible skill, but which focused his attention and helped him relax. "Things haven't been very lively on the new front lately. There hasn't been a mayor indicted in almost a month, Senator Winston and his wife have reconciled, at least publicly, and the nutcases picketing the Providence library got tired and went home. The routine stuff all gets written by the house reporters, so I find my services temporarily superfluous."

At which point, of course, the telephone rang.

It was Mel Hollins, a laboratory technician at Providence Hospital whom Dan occasionally appealed to for technical help. Hollins occasionally called Dan when something interested turned up in admissions, and Dan encouraged him with well received bottles of aged scotch.

"Listen, Dan, you got anything on for the day?"

Dan rolled his eyes but kept his voice flat. "As a matter of fact, I did have some plans, but they're flexible. What's up?"

There was an unusually long silence before Hollins spoke again. "We've got something here, a new patient, and I thought you might be interested."

"What is it, Mel? Another sick kid? Not much demand for human interest stuff when the unemployment rate is this high."

"Oh, this'll make the papers all right. But not all the details. Listen, I don't want to talk about it over the phone, but I think you'll find this one is worth your time. Some of the stuff I've heard...well, it sounds really strange."

Dan sighed, but his curiosity was piqued. "All right, Mel. I'll be there in an hour or so." He broke the connection.

"Hot lead?" Kelly was refilling her cup.

"Lukewarm, more likely. Mel lives in his own little world over at the hospital and sometimes he loses his sense of proportion. He got me out of bed at four in the morning once to tell me they'd found a new strain of some influenza virus. Wanted me to rush right down and start working on it." Dan found his wallet, a clean handkerchief, and his keys. "Called me another time because someone gave birth to a badly deformed baby. I've stooped pretty low in my time, but not to the tabloid level." He returned to the table and washed down another loaded cracker with the last of his coffee.

"Well, have a good time." Kelly leaned over the tuna fish, picked up a glob with the tip of her finger and put it in her mouth. "Needs more radish and less celery."

The hospital was on the south side of the city, just off the interstate and near the waterfront. Dan parked in the visitor's lot but avoided the main entrance, walking around the side of the building to the door used by employees and staff. The guard on duty looked up from his magazine and nodded neutrally; Dan visited often enough that the security people knew him by sight. Technically speaking, he was supposed to have clearance from the administrative section but old habits persisted.

He made his way through the bowels of the hospital to the laboratory area, passing a couple of people he knew by sight but no one whose name he remembered. Mel wasn't at his desk and Dan was looking around for someone to ask when he came up behind him and touched his elbow.

"Sorry, I was watching for you but I had to go to the can."

"No problem. So what's up, Mel?"

Mel Hollins was in his forties, nearsighted, the lenses of his glasses so thick that they gave his face an unfocused appearance, almost entirely bald, slightly overweight despite a tendency to be hyperactive. He looked around nervously before answering. "Not here. Come on."

Although Mel always exhibited a tendency for melodrama, the exaggerated caution he was demonstrating today aroused Dan's curiosity. He followed through a bewildering series of turns into a small room lined with filing cabinets, then waited while Hollins closed the door behind him, not bothering to turn on the overhead light.

Dan spread his arms wide. "All right, Mel, we're alone at last. So give."

Hollins licked his lips. "They brought a girl in this morning, a teenager. Some truck driver saw her walking naked along Route 13 just after dawn and radioed the police."

"Unfortunate, but hardly unusual enough to justify all of this secrecy. High on drugs or a rape victim. Or more likely both."

"No, not exactly." Dan noticed that the older man was perspiring heavily despite the air conditioning. "She seems to be in shock all right, but other than a few scratches and some dehydration, there was no evidence of physical injury or drugs."

"So she got away from her attacker. Or was dumped by a boyfriend, maybe."

Mel shook his head. "She was out camping with another girl, according to the mother."

Dan raised his eyebrows. "Sounds kinky." But not promising material.

"You don't understand. I mean, she's just a kid, a virgin. There's no evidence of any sort of sexual activity. And the other girl is missing. No one knows where they were camped exactly. I guess they're organizing a search party now." Dan couldn't remember ever seeing Hollins so animated before, and was at a loss to understand why this particular incident should so affect him.

"Sounds like they were attacked and one girl, at least, escaped. Bad business, but a case like this really isn't up my line, Mel. The papers will all put their crime reporters on it, whether it's rape, or assault, or even murder. There's nothing in it for me." Dan survived by exploiting the kinds of stories that other reporters considered beneath consideration or politically sensitive. He had done articles on extrasensory perception, censorship in school libraries, the subsequent careers of politicians turned out of office, and other marginal areas, mining the veins of information that his full time colleagues considered overworked or lacking in potential. Sometimes they were right and he just wasted his time. Sometimes they were wrong and he deposited a nice check in his account.

"You don't understand; the girl's pregnant."

"So?" Dan shrugged. "Mel, I hate to tell you this, but half the kids who graduate high school have already graduated from virginity, and a good percentage of them have had abortions or babies along the way. It's sad, but hardly news."

Hollins shook his head impatiently. "You weren't listening to me. I told you, she's a virgin."

Dan's face froze except for rapid blinking. "Run that by me

again. Slowly."

Hollins leaned against a filing cabinet. He was still sweating and his complexion was more pallid than could be explained by the dim light. "Listen, Dan, I'm a Catholic, you know. I've kind of fallen away the last few years, but I still believe, you know what I mean? The doctors here, they treat it like it's some medical puzzle they need to solve. They're looking at what's going on inside her body, but they're ignoring what's going on inside her head. There's something about this girl that's spooky."

"Look, Mel, I'm not interested in ghost stories. If there's something here for me, then you'll have to tell me what's going on, from the beginning this time."

Hollins sighed. "Sorry." He used the fingers of his right hand to squeeze the bridge of his nose before continuing. "Listen, they brought the girl in about seven thirty this morning, stark naked like I said, wrapped in a blanket. Her visible injuries were superficial other than a couple of nasty looking puncture wounds but she was in mild shock, answered questions once you got her attention but she was kind of vague. It was almost like she was talking to someone who wasn't in the room. No, that's not right. She was responding to the doctors, but it was if SHE wasn't in the same room with them. I can't explain it any better than that."

"All right. Go on."

"There was no evidence of any real physical trauma. The worst was the soles of her feet from walking in the woods. She told us her name and personal details, Rachel Darian, age eighteen, lives up north of the city. She claims not to be able to remember anything that happened since she and her friend pitched their tent for the night, but doesn't seem very concerned about it either. Temporary amnesia's not uncommon when someone's in shock and she might get her memories back, might not. Sometimes it's better if they don't."

Hollins moved away from the filing cabinet and began pacing slowly. "The mother showed up right after she was called; the father's out on the west coast. She confirmed that her daughter and a friend from school went camping up near the Managansett Reservoir, said her daughter goes up there all the time, hiking and stuff. I didn't hear all this direct, you realize, but I'm sort of invisible around here, and the doctors say things in front of me sometimes that they wouldn't if they'd stopped to think about it. And one of the nurses heard part of it while she was helping dress the cuts." He hesitated. "She was weirded out too."

Dan nodded. "Do you know the friend's name?"

Hollins shook his head. "I might have heard it, but I don't remember. Anyway, after they told the mother that her kid was all right and she had calmed down, they broke the news about the pregnancy."

"The mother, I assume, didn't know about it."

"Better than that. Or worse, I guess. The mother says it's impossible, says her daughter was in for a complete physical three weeks ago at this very hospital, so there's no way she could be early in her second trimester. Dr. Marin looked up the record, and she's right."

"So someone screwed up the test. Wouldn't be the first time."

Hollins shook his head. "No, Dan. I'm telling you, this girl is still a virgin, and she's going to be giving birth in about six months." He paused and licked his lips. "Right about December 25th, in fact."

Dan's expression didn't change, but his interest level went up a notch.

The search party had been arranged as quickly and quietly as possible. The most popular theory was that someone had attacked the two campers and that Rachel had somehow managed to escape. If the theoretical rapist did exist, the chance that he was still somewhere in the woods with the missing girl, one Teri Chin, age eighteen, was slim. The escape of one victim would almost certainly have caused him to leave the area as quickly as possible, with or without the other girl. But given the slight chance that he had been foolish enough to wait around, they had surrounded the area as tightly as possible to minimize the opportunities for escape. Rachel had been induced to provide the approximate route of their weekend jaunt, but it wasn't nearly precise enough to suit the authorities. Even after her car had been found, exactly where she had said she'd left it, there was still no way to shrink the search area. This part of the state was largely undeveloped and overgrown, but it was also sharply delineated by the river to the east, Route 13 to the south, an arm of the reservoir to the north, and Route 6 to the west.

Fifteen police officers were assisted by two dozen cadets

from the State Police Training School barracks and a National Guard unit that just happened to be on active duty that week. They stretched themselves in an uneven line that extended from the highway to the river bank. A small contingent from the Managansett police force was also sweeping the opposite bank, similarly equipped with brush cutters and walkie-talkies, while the main body of searchers would start from the town line and sweep to the northwest, more or less following the girls' route.

They had started to move in force a few minutes past seven on Sunday morning, hampered by the heavy undergrowth and plagued by flying insects that grew steadily more numerous as the morning progressed. Half their number started at the highway and worked their way north while the rest closed in from the west. The first wave moved with considerably greater speed than had the girls, and since the southern contingent had only half the distance to travel as their fellows, they reached the campsite first, shortly after noon.

Patrolman Arthur Krenkle was the first to spot the tent, and he almost fell into the stream in the process. He was actually several meters in advance of the skirmish line as a whole, because his position had led to the abandoned and now largely overgrown dirt road that Rachel and Teri had discovered the previous afternoon. Although he was an unusually conscientious police officer, his attention had begun to wander, primarily because of the accompanying cloud of insects that flew around his face. At first it had been bearable and he'd brushed them away without thinking about them, but for the past several minutes, it had been far worse. They were persistent, numerous, and refused to disperse no matter how enthusiastically he waved his arms. They were in his nose, his eyes, his ears, even his mouth, and he had begun to itch everywhere else in psychosomatic sympathy.

When he first spotted the tent's center pole through the trees, he stumbled forward a few steps to see more clearly, and only avoided falling into the stream by grabbing a nearby sapling. It bent under his weight as he scrambled for more secure footing. "Hey, everybody! I see something over here!"

He held his place until he had been joined by Sergeant Walters, a massively muscled man whose powerful shoulders brushed through the heavy vines as if they were cobwebs.

"What's the problem?" His voice rumbled irritably and he

began blinking as some of the insects found fresh prey.

Patrolman Krenkle pointed. "Looks like a tent to me."

Walters followed his line of sight then nodded and clapped an enormous hand on the other man's shoulder. "That's what it looks like. Good job." He turned and called back to the rest. "All right, people, there's a stream running through here. Everybody come forward slowly until you reach it and stop there, holding your positions. Watch closely for anything at all that might be relevant. No one crosses the stream until the detectives and the crime scene team gets here. Keep your eyes open and watch where you step."

Five minutes later, the campsite was officially a crime scene. When the technicians were done with their preliminary survey, they gestured to Walters, who came forward accompanied by Detectives Angela Harris and Vincent Marzocchi. They all glanced at the burned out campfire and neatly arranged tent without comment. Detective Harris was the first to actually look inside.

"Just a couple of sleeping bags. No sign of a struggle."

Two backpacks were hanging from a nearby tree, each tied shut.

Harris looked at them closely but didn't touch either one. "Sergeant, have your people search the surrounding area but keep them away from the campsite."

Walters nodded and issued terse instructions. Less than five minutes later there was another outcry and shortly after that the two detectives found themselves climbing a gentle slope to a wooded area where a pale blouse hung limply from a branch. One of the cadets was standing nearby.

"There's a bra over here. And there's a pair of jeans lying back a ways." The photographers were called while Harris and Marzocchi examined each of the discarded garments, not touching any of the evidence.

"No sign of blood," Marzocchi commented. "At least now we know where the girl's clothing ended up."

Harris shook her head. "Might belong to the other one." She crouched, picked up a stick and gently lifted the jeans away from the ground, revealing the toe of a sneaker. She let the jeans fall back.

"There's no obvious sign of a struggle. The clothes aren't torn."

"Doesn't mean anything," Marzocchi replied. "If they were

attacked, the guy might have had a gun or something. Forced them to strip."

Sergeant Walters had been crouching in the overgrowth where the two abandoned roads had intersected. He stood up suddenly and gestured for the detectives to join him. When they arrived, he pointed at a patch of disturbed ground at the edge of the stream. "What do you make of that?"

"Looks like someone dug something up," Marzocchi answered. "Might have been an animal."

Harris reached over and touched the raw wound in the earth. "Pretty recent. Do we have a picture of this?"

One of the photographers was called over and obediently snapped several pictures from different angles.

"Too small to be a body," Harris commented sarcastically.

"Buried treasure," suggested Marzocchi. "Who the hell knows?"

It was also Walters who found the chest, wedged behind two rocks a few meters away. "Look here! I think I've found what they dug up."

There was little doubt that this was the object that had been removed from the stream bank at the junction of the two dirt roads. It was the right size and general shape, and there were still chunks of mud adhering to it where the water had not yet had a chance to wash it clean. The lid was shut and Walters used a stick to pry it open, avoiding touching it with his hands, to reveal a dry and empty interior.

"What do you think it is?" Marzocchi sat down on a dry rock and began spraying himself with a fresh layer of insect repellent.

Harris shrugged. "We'd better take it with us just in case, but it looks like the girls or someone else dug it up, found out it was empty, and threw it away."

Walters shook his head. "If it was empty. Looks like they had to smash the lock open." The clasp was covered with bright scars where it had been struck repeatedly. "Do you suppose someone might have been hiding drugs or hot goods out here and the girls happened on them just as the wrong time?"

No one answered.

The search continued for the rest of the afternoon but with no further revelations. Back at the hospital, Rachel Darian had been interviewed once again, but she continued to insist that she had no recollection of anything from the time she had had crawled into her sleeping bag until she had found herself walking the breakdown lane in the early hours of Sunday morning. She remained confused and inattentive, and her mother had raised no objection when the hospital indicated it wished to keep the girl under observation for at least a day or two.

Skip Randolph and Judy Bowes were walking along the riverbank just above the point where the Upper Valley merged with the Providence River, slightly north of the border between Managansett and Providence. They'd been living together for two months in a small house they had rented nearby and still enjoyed exploring the stretch of woodland that extended between their home and the confluence of the two rivers. Skip was determined to reach the southernmost point of land on this side of the water before returning, but Judy had quietly glanced at her watch and realized they had spent more time walking than she had expected. She was still hoping to finish the latest Stephen King novel before calling it a day.

"It can't be much further," Skip assured her, sensing her impatience. "I can hear water on both sides now."

"Whatever you say, bwana," she replied. "All the trees look the same to us pack bearers."

The problem was that the area ahead had been heavily damaged by a hurricane the summer before, and it seemed as though at least half the trees had been uprooted. A web of vines had expanded enthusiastically over the downed titans, wrapping them in thick nets, and the result was a tangled, almost impenetrable mess. Skip was trying to keep the Upper Valley in sight to their right, but the soil along the bank had been undercut and that was where the trees had been the most vulnerable. Denuded crests half rose out of the water into which they had fallen, and the ground beneath their feet was torn, broken, and speckled with pools of standing water.

Despite his professed optimism, Skip was also having second thoughts. The terrain was much rougher than he had anticipated and at this point he would have been content with just a brief, distant glimpse of the junction, so that he could claim to have actually reached his goal. When he finally saw a reasonably clear defile leading directly to the water, he altered course thankfully.

"Why don't we rest a bit before starting back?" Skip pointed at a downed tree which was conveniently suspended at waist height. Judy knew him well enough to recognize that he was nearly as exhausted as was she; between the oppressive heat and the surprising level of difficulty they had encountered during the past half hour, they were both short of breath, their clothes sticky with perspiration, their arms smarting from countless tiny scratches and bites.

"I could go for that. Anything left to drink?"

Skip handed her the plastic bottle of fruit juice he'd been carrying. "You might as well finish it. That much less weight to carry back."

Judy was sitting on the tree, draining the last of the grapefruit juice, when Skip mounted the trunk and stood up, staring out toward the water. "What's that?"

"What's what?" She turned her head and squinted, but could see nothing.

"There's something caught out there." He took a tentative step forward, then another. The tree moved a fraction of an inch as he shifted his weight.

"Be careful," she said. "If you fall in, don't expect me to pull you out."

Skip dropped to his hands and knees, edging out over the water, in among the lower branches of what had once been a large and healthy tree. Curious herself, Judy rose to her feet and walked alongside the trunk, then ducked under it, advancing slowly toward the river's edge. "I don't see anything, Skip."

"Oh God," he said softly. "Judy, stay where you are. I think it's a body."

Judy laughed skeptically. "Come off it, Skip. You've been watching too many horror movies."

But from where he now stood, Skip could see the body of a young woman floating face down in the water, bumping slowly against a half submerged branch. He tried to convince himself it was just a manikin, but he knew that wasn't the case.

Judy had made her way closer to the water, but had to take so much care about where she stepped that she hadn't had a chance to actually look to see what had caught Skip's attention. She reached a patch of relative solid ground at last, and when she finally saw what was floating just beyond arm's length, she gasped. "Do you think she might still be alive?"

"No way. She's face down and she hasn't moved."

"Shouldn't...shouldn't we pull her out or something?" Her voice had grown so small she didn't recognize it.

Skip shook his head, then realized she couldn't see him from where she stood. "No, I don't think so. Look, we have to make sure it doesn't drift away before the police get here. I don't suppose you brought your cell phone?" She shook her head. He removed his belt and threaded the loose end through the buckle, making a loop. "I'm going to try to snag it and tie it to something." He couldn't think of the body as a "she"; that would imply personality. "As soon as I get that done, we have to get back to the house as quickly as possible and call the police."

"All right, but be careful."

Skip concentrated on keeping his balance, stretching his body full length along a branch just above the floating body. He dangled the looped belt and made several passes before it slipped over one foot. He pulled it up gently until he was certain the foot would not slip out, then made a knot around another branch to secure it in place. Carefully not to look down, he backed quickly away a safe distance and dropped to the ground.

Despite their fatigue, they made their way back in less time than it had taken them on the first half of the trip.

When the patrol car arrived at their house, they were escorted to the nearby riverbank where a police launch was already in sight. Once aboard, they stood together at the rail as the boat hugged the shore on its way down river, trying to identify their surroundings even though they were seeing everything from an entirely different perspective. After only one false alarm, Judy spotted a distinctive tree and a short time later the body of Teri Chin was officially recovered.

Judy turned away when they brought the limp form aboard, but Skip watched, fascinated. He had assumed she was a drowning victim, but when the police began lifting the body into the launch, he had a brief view of the dead girl's face and throat, and the sight was like a knife thrust into his body. He gagged and turned away, then leaned over the side of the launch and vomited violently.

Dan Scapelli was in his car when the report came over the police band. Unidentified female, age late teens or early twenties, apparent Asian background, body badly disfigured. He knew it had to be Teri Chin, but at the moment he was more interested in Rachel Darian's unexplained pregnancy.

Something had begun to stir at the back of his head, the sixth sense that had so often proven itself a reliable indicator of a profitable story hovering invisible but just within reach. All he had to do was reach out, grope in the darkness for a while, and grab it.

The Upper Valley River had deeply undercut its banks in several places, causing some of them to partially collapse, and where the old shore still existed, there were shallow caves and depressions into which daylight rarely if ever intruded. In one of these, several hundred meters from where Teri Chin's body had been discovered several hours earlier, the fall of night triggered sudden movement. A huddled, contorted shape slowly unwrapped overlong arms and legs, then half crawled, half slid sinuously toward the open. Although part of its body trailed through the slimy water, it remained dry, almost desiccated in fact. Outside its den, the creature swarmed up the bank and when it reached solid ground, slowly rose into an erect posture. From a distance, it resembled a rather tall man; from closer proximity, it was unmistakably something else entirely.

It began to move, following alongside the waterway south to the highway, never visibly troubled by the twisted terrain or any other physical barrier. It slipped under the overpass like a shadow, and reached the river junction just before midnight. From that position, a faint glow on the horizon marked the city of Providence, toward which the presence was being drawn as compulsively as a moth is drawn to a flame.

The woods receded steadily from that point forward, replaced by abandoned mill yards, storage facilities, parking lots, and railroad sidings. Many of these were fenced off to discourage intruders, but such barriers proved ineffective, as it advanced through, over, or under them. Once or twice, snarling dogs appeared in its path, but they backed off and disappeared quickly once they had caught its scent.

At two in the morning, it passed behind *Andy's Seaside*, a fish and chips shop perched on a slab of rock that jutted out into the river. *Andy's* had closed down an hour before, and the last of the staff had just driven away. The smell of fish and beer was strong in the air, as well as the odor of human sweat. It paused here for several minutes tasting the air but then, disappointed, moved on, its search continuing.

Fifteen minutes later, it stood under a pine tree in the grounds of *Green Pastures*, a small retirement home for the relatively affluent. Several clusters of attached apartments were scattered around a central administration building which housed the reception area, offices, a medical clinic, a small library, and an expensively furnished dining room.

The indistinct figure remained where it was for almost half an hour, its head slightly raised as though listening. When it finally resumed its steady movement, it crossed onto the property, passing close by the common building before leaving the grounds on the opposite side. Whatever it sought was not to be found here. It turned away from the river, entering a more developed part of the city. Silently, it swept past *Fletcher's Florist Shop*, a furniture store, and an abandoned gas station with all of its windows broken as it headed toward the commercial district. The night was aging quickly and it still had not found what it sought.

Downtown Providence had been rejuvenated in recent years. There were few empty shops and the influx of college students from the School of Design and Brown University had brought some semblance of nightlife back to streets that had been largely deserted for the previous decade. Old buildings had been torn down or refurbished and new ones built. The proliferation of malls and the flight to the suburbs had taken their toll, but the city seemed to be recovering at last. Only a few pockets of decay and depression persisted, isolated neighborhoods on the fringes of the redeveloped areas.

Bancroft Street was one of the worst of these, a row of dimly lit bars and decaying rooming houses which remained much as they had been for the past twenty years. Other priorities and greater opportunities had shielded the area from official attention so far, but it was only a matter of time until the last obstacle fell. The buildings on the next street over had already been razed to the ground, destined to be the site of a new underground parking garage designed to take the overflow from the better situated parking adjacent to the Providence Place Mall.

The main excavation and the first stages of construction were well underway, although problems with the financing had brought work to a stop with the ramps yet to be constructed. As it stood now, fenced but not guarded, the dimly lit recesses were ideal for casual business deals involving drugs or hand weapons. A handful of homeless people had staked out temporary accommodations where shallow cavities had been dug out in anticipation of columns and elevator shafts.

At four in the morning, the only person awake at the site was an elderly woman who sat in a dark recess with her back against a concrete buttress. She talked incessantly in a low monotone as she stared fixedly into a distance she alone could perceive. She never noticed when a darker shadow fell across the entrance to her cubicle, paused a second, sniffing the air to taste the flavor of the human sheltering inside, then moved determinedly on.

One level below, the intruder found what it had been looking for.

Billy DiChario was not strictly speaking homeless. He was fourteen years old and his parents lived in a well to do neighborhood in Cranston, where they fought constantly about finances, Billy's increasingly unsatisfactory school performance, the quality of Edith DiChario's housekeeping, their relations with their neighbors, William DiChario's ever lengthening "work" hours, and anything else that came to mind. His parents approached quarreling as though it was a skill that needed constant practice and he had to admit that they were good at it. Billy had run away from home six days earlier, having decided to "teach them a lesson", and probably would not have been surprised to learn that his disappearance had just provided another chance for his parents to fight.

Billy still had nearly fifty dollars of the money he had taken from his mother's purse before leaving, and had spent much of the evening smoking pot and contemplating a clandestine visit home while his parents were at work. His father always kept a few hundred dollars in a box in his closet "for emergencies". Billy figured this was an emergency. His stash was almost completely gone.

The candle he had lit before going to sleep had long since guttered out and the low, even sound of his breathing would have been nearly inaudible to human ears. But the presence that passed nearby had more than ordinary acuity, and it paused and turned its head toward the recess where the sound originated.

Billy DiChario was fortunate because he was still asleep when he was attacked. He woke briefly in the grasp of powerful arms that wrapped themselves around him but two points of piercing pain burned against the side of his neck and he instantly felt lightheaded, closed his eyes, and drifted back into unconsciousness.

CHAPTER THREE: MONDAY

Dan Scapelli spent a very frustrating afternoon and evening on Sunday. Every reporter in the state was trying to arrange an interview with Rachel Darian, or her mother, but neither was available, and no one associated with the case admitted knowing any more than had already been printed. The police admitted that Teri Chin's body had been recovered and identified, that foul play was suspected, and that an investigation was continuing. There was no evidence of sexual assault, no suspects, but a number of lines of inquiry were being pursued. The hospital was no more forthcoming, admitting only that the survivor was suffering from the shock of her ordeal, but was expected to make a full recovery. News of her pregnancy had slipped out, but the peculiar circumstances had not been revealed and Dan hoped that he was still the only journalist who had that angle.

On Monday morning, he tried to visit Mel Hollins but there was an unfamiliar guard on duty, who politely told him that he had been instructed not to admit anyone not employed by the hospital without permission in writing from the head of security. Thoughtfully, Dan retreated to the lobby, where he used a pay phone to call the laboratory. After a lengthy wait while the duty nurse located Hollins, Dan made arrangements to meet him for lunch at a diner two blocks away.

Thunderclouds rolled in at daybreak, filling the sky with dark masses that seemed poised to fall on the unwary. A distant, almost inaudible rumbling threatened a change of weather, but except for occasional light sprinkles, the rain shied away. A brisk wind had whipped the edges of the clouds into a tangled froth and there was an unseasonable chill in the air that drove people indoors.

Dan spent most of the morning at the Providence Library, where he'd been researching historic buildings for a series of short profiles he had been commissioned to write for the Southern New England Historical Society. Most of the documents he needed were non-circulating, and he made liberal use of the copy machine, although in some cases the materials were too faded to produce a legible facsimile. In those cases, he laboriously typed the relevant information into his laptop.

He became so engrossed that he lost track of time, and risked a speeding ticket rushing back through lunch hour traffic to the south side. As it happened, he needn't have bothered; Mel Hollins showed up a full twenty minutes late, and Dan was resignedly eating a corned beef sandwich when he finally arrived.

Mel Hollins had not come alone.

"Dan, this is Jenny Wells; she's a friend of mine, a transcriptionist. Jenny, this is Dan Scapelli."

Dan rose and shook hands solemnly with a woman he judged to be slightly older than Hollins. She was not unattractive, but her features were pinched together in a fashion that he found disconcerting. Her clothing was businesslike and neat, and while she seemed nervous, her voice was deep and under control.

"It's a pleasure to meet you, Mr. Scapelli. Mel speaks very highly of you."

Dan nodded. "We've managed to be of some help to each other from time to time. Please, sit down."

The three of them were seated and Dan flagged down the waiter, who listened without apparent interest as they placed their orders. Dan asked no questions, waiting for Hollins to explain.

"I hope you don't mind my bringing Jenny along, Dan, but I thought you might want to hear what she has to say."

"Not at all. I'd welcome illumination from any quarter at this point. No one seems to be talking to anyone about anything."

Jenny was noticeably uncomfortable. "There's one thing I have to know first, Mr. Scapelli."

"What's that?" The waiter delivered two cups of coffee and conversation stopped until he was gone.

She waited until the waiter was out of earshot. "I need to know that anything I tell you will, you know, be kept confidential. I mean, I'm not supposed to talk to anybody about what I hear. It's a breach of patient confidentiality."

Dan shifted uncomfortably. "Jenny, I don't want to get you into any trouble. You shouldn't say anything that makes you uncomfortable."

"It's just that I don't want my name to come into this. My job isn't all that great, but I really need the money right now." She looked at him expectantly.

"If what you tell me proves useful, I'd certainly share the

profit with anyone who helped me. And don't worry. I've never betrayed a source yet. Wild horses couldn't tear it out of me."

She glanced at Hollins who nodded. "Well, I guess I can trust you to do the right thing."

Their food arrived, a fruit salad for Jenny, a bacon, lettuce, and tomato sandwich for Mel. Dan waited until they had both had a chance to eat before trying to move the conversation forward

"So just what is it that you have for me today?"

Mel answered first. "Jenny here is a transcriptionist, works down in the morgue. You know, death certificates, autopsies and stuff."

Dan started. "The Darian girl hasn't died, has she?"

"No, no, she's fine. They've still got her in isolation, but that's to keep people away from her, not because of her condition."

"Then what..."

Jenny set down her fork and answered for herself. "They brought in the other girl, the friend, last night."

"I heard that, on the radio."

"Well, anyway, Dr. Whiteson did the autopsy first thing this morning, and the results were pretty strange."

"I gather she was stabbed to death." Dan had heard this from two separate reporters, both of whom had contacts within the police force.

Jenny nodded. "She was stabbed, all right, twice, both times in the throat. The weapon was triangular, half an inch in width, and both penetrations were approximately an inch and a half in depth. One wound severed the jugular." Her eyes were slightly distant and Dan realized she was recalling text from the autopsy report. "Although either wound would have been fatal, death would not have been instantaneous and the victim might have remained conscious and capable of resistance. There was considerable bruising and mild abrasion along the right side of the head and her right cheek was fractured. Additional trauma was limited to some small scratches which may have preceded the attack. There was considerable superficial damage to the face and throat inflicted post mortem, most likely incidental."

"Incidental?"

"Her body was, you know, partly eaten. Fish and birds and stuff. It was pretty minor damage; she hadn't been in the water very

long, but I guess it was pretty gross. I didn't actually see her myself."
She shivered dramatically, though perhaps artificially.

Dan interrupted before she could speak again. "This is all
very interesting, but what does it have to do with Rachel Darian. I
don't generally do crime stories, Jennie; there are plenty of other
reporters you could talk to, and I could give you a couple of names if
you want. It's the Darian girl's mysterious pregnancy that I'm
interested in."

Jenny looked confused, but Mel spoke up. "Hear her out,
Dan. I don't know if it's related or not, but whatever's going on has
some people really spooked."

When Dan nodded, Jenny continued, speaking more quickly
now. "Dr. Whiteson determined that the cause of death was blood
loss, but the amount she'd lost bothered him and he called in a
second doctor to confirm his observations."

She stopped talking and the silence grew prolonged.
"So?"

Mel finished the mouthful of sandwich he'd been working on
before answering. "The colleague he called in was Dr. Marin. Dr.
Marin is Rachel Darian's physician."

"So?" Dan repeated, beginning to wonder if he was wasting
his time.

"You remember I told you that the Darian girl had a lot of
superficial cuts and scratches but no serious wounds?"

Dan nodded.

"Well, among those were three lacerations of the abdomen,
each slightly over one inch in depth, evenly spaced, and triangular in
shape. Dr. Marin thought she might have fallen on some old farm
tool or something. He didn't think they were significant until he saw
similar wounds on the dead girl."

"Interesting, but I don't see that it tells us anything. Whoever
attacked the girls probably had some kind of weapon, maybe one of
those clawed things people use to work in gardens."

"There's one other thing." Jenny turned her head, as though
making certain they were not being overheard. "I was talking to one
of the nurses from the night shift this morning," she continued in a
low voice, barely above a whisper. "The Darian girl flatlined just
after midnight last night. She said all indications were complete
cardiac arrest, no pulse, no respiration, nothing. But by the time the

emergency response team arrived, everything was back to normal and she seemed fine except that her breathing was a little shallow and..."

"And...?" Dan prompted.

"And she was bleeding slightly in the abdomen, a few drops of blood from each of the three triangular wounds."

Dan picked up the tab for the three lunches and promised to let them know if their information proved useful. He was privately skeptical. It sounded like a coincidental equipment failure, a botched pregnancy test, possibly an inattentive nurse, and a highly imaginative and probably exaggerated story inspired at least in part by the secrecy imposed by the Providence police. Hospitals functioned as tiny, partially isolated societies, within which rumors mutated and spread with surprising ease and diversity. There were certainly some peculiar things going on, but Dan wasn't convinced there was a story waiting to be uncovered. He wasn't ready to drop the lead just yet, but it was growing increasingly unlikely that it would pan out.

On the other hand, he didn't have anything else more promising to pursue.

He returned to his apartment after lunch, downloaded his notes to the hard drive on his desktop, retyped them in greater detail while the material was fresh in his mind, and made himself a sandwich of slightly stale cold cuts and more than slightly wilted lettuce. When the sandwich was gone he saved his files, stepped into the corridor, and knocked, two times, followed by a short pause and a third. Kelly answered almost immediately.

"Hi, Dan. C'mon in. What's up?"

"The cost of bribery," he answered testily. "Do you know what lunch for three costs at Bernard's these days?"

Dan's apartment could never be described as neat or orderly, but Kelly's raised clutter to an entirely new level. She had covered most of the walls with corkboard, to which she attached clipped news stories, magazine articles, shopping lists long since obsolete, notes to herself, jokes she wanted to remember, phone numbers and addresses, and other bits of paper had been attached with pushpins, generally in so many overlapping layers that archaeologists might have found them fertile ground for exploration. Her furniture was functional rather than decorative and obviously inexpensive, plain lines, simple construction, and with most of the horizontal surfaces covered with books and magazines often piled precariously high. The second bedroom of her apartment was her reference library, freestanding bookshelves so close together there was barely room to move between them, with no space remaining on any of the shelves for more recently acquired volumes, which were piled on the window sill, in corners, or laid across the top bindings of the shelved books.

In one corner of the front room, Kelly's desk faced a prefabricated home entertainment center where her television and cd player were all arranged to be accessible while she worked at the computer. Two file cabinets stood to one side, with books and periodicals piled high on top and drawers filled with more clippings, pamphlets, and typescripts, all indexed in a computerized database. Her screen was currently filled with text and a fan of file folders was spread across the desktop.

"Working?"

"Was. What can I do you for today, sir?"

"Coffee?"

"You know where it is."

Indeed he did. Kelly kept a rather large pot brewing in the kitchen most of the time, and unlike Dan, she rarely let it sit around long enough to need rewarming. She was waiting for him when he returned to the front room, standing with one hip pressed against the corner of her desk.

"You know anything about virgin births?"

"Is this a trick question?"

"No, seriously. Other than the obvious instance, have you ever heard of anything like that?"

"You're serious, aren't you?" She reached down and picked up her own coffee.

"Very." He gave her a brief summary of what he had learned from Mel Hollins, knowing that he could trust her not to repeat it without his permission.

"You're kidding." He shook his head. "Then your friend got it wrong, or he's pulling your leg."

"I don't think so. Mel's not a social animal, but he takes his work very seriously and he's good at it. If he'd had a little more self confidence when he was younger, he might have ended up a doctor himself."

Kelly set down the cup, put the palms of her hands on the desktop behind her and stretched. Dan looked away, suddenly realizing that his eyes had strayed down from her face. He felt increasingly uncomfortable since realizing that he was beginning to feel physically attracted to Kelly. Dan had not led a chaste life, although he was currently uninvolved, but this was the first time the sexual impulse had showed up so late in an acquaintance and he wasn't sure how to react. His preoccupation caused him to miss the first few words of Kelly's answer.

"...at least not naturally," she was saying. "There's been a lot of artificial insemination, of course, and I suppose some of them could have been virgins in a technical sense. I've never looked into the subject. Why don't you try calling a gynecologist? Or I could talk to Dr. Brodsky next time I see her and ask her to suggest someone. I'll tell her you're writing a novel and need some background."

"Yeah, I suppose I could do that. The most likely explanation is that someone screwed up the original test and the girl's been pregnant all along, maybe without even knowing it. If Mel Hollins wasn't so obviously upset by the whole thing, I'd just shrug it off. But he's got an instinct for the unusual."

"You always were a sucker for the weird stuff. Didn't you do an article about vampires in Wickford?"

"Tiverton. And it was about vampire sightings, not vampires. Contagious hysteria."

"Right, and aren't you the author of 'Haunted Houses of Newport' and a series on regional superstitions?"

"You forgot the piece I did about clairvoyance. But in both cases I pointed out that most of the supposed manifestations could be explained quite easily without reference to the paranormal. Wishful thinking and overactive imaginations."

"I notice that the word 'most' appears in that sentence."

"The fact that we don't know of a rational explanation doesn't mean there isn't one. Some of the most notorious sightings took place so long ago that there's no way to investigate properly. I do try to keep an open mind though. There's a woman living right here in Providence who has an amazing record for accurate predictions. Too many to just be a string of coincidences, in my opinion, but even in her case, she has a convenient lapse in her talent whenever anyone tries to verify it scientifically."

"Is that Vera Maitlin?"

Dan nodded. "You've heard of her?"

"Her name came up while I was compiling crime statistics involving the elderly. She called the police a few times with tips that turned out to be surprisingly accurate."

"I remember that. She stopped calling when they brought her in for questioning a couple of times, but they decided she was harmless and her tips were just a coincidence."

Kelly folded her arms under her breasts. "Speaking of coincidences, did you hear the news story about *Green Pastures*?"

"The housing project? No, there wasn't anything on the radio just now. What's up?"

"They mentioned it on the television at noon. Three people died during the night, the only three patients in their infirmary."

"That does seem to stretch coincidence a bit far, but it's not completely beyond the realm of possibility. I'd guess they're going to find a common cause though."

"Their symptoms were apparently very different. All three died between two and four in the morning, a cerebral hemorrhage, a blood clot, and respiratory failure. None of them were supposed to be seriously ill or they would have been taken to a hospital."

"All right, it does sound odd. But there really are outlandish coincidences sometimes." He smiled. "Statistically improbable things are still possible, right?"

Kelly didn't take the bait. "Dan, the woman who died was Vera Maitlin."

That caught him by surprise. "Vera Maitlin is dead? Damn! Talk about spooky. But she must have been, what, in her seventies?"

Kelly shrugged. "How would I know? But she was living in a retirement home. And you're the one who interviewed her."

"Sort of. Most of the time it was over the phone or through correspondence, although I did meet her twice. She was a very private woman, secretive even. Either she was genuinely reluctant to discuss her alleged clairvoyance or one of the canniest manipulators I've ever met. I'll bet she was the cerebral hemorrhage."

"That's right. How did you guess?"

He chuckled. "Vera always said her head was filled to bursting with other people's thoughts and experiences. She'd suffered migraines since childhood. They told her she was delusional, treated her with drugs to suppress the visions she kept experiencing. She was well into her forties by the time people started taking her seriously, and when she retired ten years later, she had set aside enough money that she could live comfortably on the interest, even though she avoided publicity. I came across a reference to her when I was trying to sell a series about psychic powers, and found out she was living in Barrington. She was talking then about writing her memoirs, although as far as I know she never followed through. I heard she moved to Providence about a year after I last spoke to her, over on the east side somewhere, but I never had reason to look her up."

"What was that, five years ago?"

"Yeah, obviously she moved again. Either got lonely living with just a housekeeper for company or decided she needed to be closer to medical help. Didn't seem to do her much good, did it?"

"Maybe you can do an obituary for the *Journal*?"

He shook his head. "No, they'll have a staff writer do that. It might be good for an article though." He glanced at his watch. "I might just wander out there and see if I can find anyone who knew her. I'm not getting anywhere with the Darian story. Maybe if I don't think about it for a while, something brilliant will occur to my subconscious."

At Providence Hospital, Dr. Leonard Marin read the latest test results on Rachel Darian with bewilderment and displeasure. If he had not personally examined her, he would have been convinced that someone had falsified the report. He closed the file and sat back in his chair, massaging the lids of his eyes with his index fingers.

He should have been in a much better mood. The odd circumstances surrounding the girl's pregnancy were almost certainly going to make medical history and he was, after all, her primary physician. Not that the current situation could possibly last. Despite enviable professional credentials, Marin knew himself to be unimaginative, a plodder, competent enough dealing with the familiar but virtually incapable of responding to novel circumstances. The fact that Rachel Darian was both pregnant and a virgin fascinated but did not alarm him; the fact that in the last thirty-six hours her pregnancy had apparently advanced almost half a trimester did. During the same period, her blood count had plummeted and she had been given whole blood twice, although her vital signs had remained stable. None of the tests he had ordered had turned up anything else out of the ordinary, but that only made the situation worse. Like it or not, he knew he was out of his depth. It was too late to do anything further today but in the morning he intended to call for help. With luck, he would be a footnote in medical history.

His shift had ended, but Dr. Marin decided to visit the isolation ward on his way out. The police officer who had been stationed there had been removed earlier in the day, but now a security guard was sitting at the end of the hall, a white haired black man whom Marin knew only as Gus. He nodded solemnly on his way to room 313.

Rachel was still being held in isolation even though she was free of communicable diseases, simply because it was easier to keep outsiders away. Although the police still hoped to get a more coherent statement from her, they had lost their sense of urgency when a staff psychologist told them it might be weeks or even months before she would be able to consciously remember the circumstances of the attack, if she ever recovered those memories at all.

Rachel was sitting up in bed when Dr. Marin entered the room, hands crossed in her lap, eyes open and staring at the opposite wall. She was smiling to herself, cheeks flushed, breathing even.

"Rachel? How are we doing this evening?"

She turned her head slightly. "Dr. Marin. I'm sorry, I didn't hear you come in."

He crossed to the foot of the bed and made a show of looking at her chart, although his eyes never focused on the notations. "I understand you told the nurse you were experiencing some pain earlier today."

She gave a just perceptible shrug. "It's just, you know, my breasts are a little sore. I guess I have to expect that, being pregnant and all."

Rachel had indicated no surprise when informed she was pregnant, but had been unwilling or unable to identify the father. Nor had she reacted to her father's anger or her mother's tearful breakdown. Rachel's continuing detachment from the situation was just another of his concerns. She had also refused to submit to a sonogram.

"Well, it's a little early for that, don't you think?" He watched her face out of the corner of his eye, but there was no reaction. "Don't you think we should let the father know about this?"

"He knows."

"Perhaps if you told me his name?"

Rachel didn't rise to the bait. Instead, she slowly turned toward the window, her expression dreamy. "He came to see me last night, you know."

Marin's forehead furrowed. "Who came to see you, Rachel?"

"My baby's father. He stood right out there and waited until I invited him in, and then he kissed me right where, you know, where the baby is."

"Rachel, we're on the third floor. There's no place out there for anyone to stand."

"I know."

Marin felt himself shivering, blamed it on the air conditioning. "Rachel, have you remembered anything else about the night you were attacked?"

Every time this question had been asked in the past, Rachel had appeared both surprised and confused, and tonight was no exception. "Everyone keeps asking me that, Doctor, but I wasn't attacked. I told you, I just wandered away from the campsite and got lost."

No one had told Rachel about Teri Chin's death. "I imagine your friend Teri must have been quite worried about you wandering around in the dark."

For the first time since she had been admitted, Rachel's features twisted into an obvious and intense emotion. She put her arms down on the bed and leaned forward, staring directly at the doctor, her expression suddenly animated with rage. "That bitch is no friend of mine! She tried to steal him away from me!"

Startled by her intensity, Dr. Marin stepped back and remained silent while he recovered his composure. Rachel seemed locked in place, her face permanently twisted into a rictus of hate. Her expression was so intense that he couldn't meet her eyes, even when he stepped forward to gently take hold of her shoulders and ease her back against the pillows. "All right, all right, calm down,

Rachel."

Although she remained silent and didn't resist as he adjusted the bedding so that she was lying down rather than sitting, Rachel's eyes still glittered with animosity and her lips were pressed tightly together, but she didn't protest.

"I want you to get some sleep now, Rachel. You've been through a very stressful time and you need to give your body a chance to recover." She turned her head away but he felt as though her eyes were burning into him until long after he had retreated from her room.

On his way out, Dr. Marin prescribed a stronger sedative for Rachel Darian. Then he went home to take a milder one himself.

Dan Scapelli didn't have a whole lot of luck at *Green Pastures*. No one on the staff was talking, not to reporters, and certainly not to freelance writers. He tried to loiter near the service entrance to the administrative building but was chased off by security guards, rent-a-cops in fact, specially hired that same day. His luck was a little better in the parking lot, where he found three residents who were willing to talk about Vera Maitlin. A married couple described her as quietly friendly. "She'd always wish us a good morning and like that when we ran into her, but she didn't talk much. Kept to herself, mostly. Never invited anyone into her apartment that we know of." And a platinum haired woman walking a dog told him Vera spent a lot of time reading, "mostly trashy bestsellers". None of the people Dan talked to knew anything about her career as a clairvoyant, and the dog walker's expression had turned distinctly sour when he brought the subject up. "A lot of claptrap." None of the people he talked to remembered Vera having any visitors in all the time she had lived there, which was just under three years.

Reluctant to quit without having something concrete to show for the afternoon, Dan began visiting businesses nearby, hoping someone might remember her or provide a useful lead. He was convinced that if there was any such thing as a genuine clairvoyant, Vera Maitlin was that animal, and found it impossible to believe she had lived here for so long without some hint of her abilities getting out. Her gift, or curse, had been erratic and undependable, the flashes coming in small clusters separated by weeks, sometimes months, but when she was sure of one of her visions, they invariably proved accurate.

The cashier at *Andy's Seaside* was pleasant and talkative, and he recognized the photograph Dan had pulled from his files. "Sure, I remember her. Came in every Friday night and picked up her order. Can't remember ever seeing her actually eat here, though, but most of our customers on Fridays are take out."

"Did she come alone or with friends?"

"Alone, as far as I remember. Nice old lady, but she didn't say much. Always left a tip even though she took it away. I'm sorry to hear she died."

"Well, thanks. By the way, why 'Seaside'? That's a river out there."

The cashier laughed. "Andy, the owner, used to have a place down in Warwick, right on the water. The rent went up so he had to move, and he took the name with him."

Dan considered sampling *Andy*'s fare but remembered he had tentatively accepted Kelly's offer to come over for supper and decided otherwise. The following morning, he would be profoundly grateful that he had exercised that restraint.

He had no better luck elsewhere in the neighborhood. A dry cleaner acknowledged that Vera Maitlan was a regular customer, but couldn't remember ever speaking to her other than in the course of business. The pharmacy on the opposite corner had handled her prescriptions, but they were always ordered by and delivered to the clinic where she had died. She might well have patronized them for over the counter medicine and other merchandise, but no one present recognized her picture. The florist across the street was closed for the day. Dan saw two women talking animatedly in the green house, which was filled with drooping, sickly looking plants.

There were a couple of remaining leads he could follow up. Vera had a younger sister living in Keene, New Hampshire, and Dan had the name of her lawyer in his files. But that would have to wait for another day, if he bothered at all. His nose for the news was usually trustworthy, but lately it seemed to be leading him into a series of blind alleys.

Kelly Marsh had invited Dan over on impulse; she really

wasn't the domestic type, and while her apartment was moderately clean despite the clutter, she really didn't have a flair for or interest in formal entertaining. Her ambivalence about the developing familiarity of her relationship with Dan matched his own. She had just turned thirty-two a few weeks earlier and supposed that her aunts were all whispering about how she'd become an "old maid" despite several "wonderful opportunities" to land viable husbands. They would probably forgive her for dumping Ed Cogswell; she had, after all, caught him in bed with another woman. But she had already been tsk-tsked over for turning down Rick Olin's proposal and for breaking up with Scott Meninger before he'd even had a chance to become serious. Olin, brilliant attorney though he might be, had told Kelly in no uncertain terms what he considered the obligations and requirements of a proper lawyer's wife, and Scott Meninger, Quality Control Manager for Eblis Manufacturing, had blackened her eye and bruised two of her ribs before she shattered his knee cap with a well aimed kick. Officially, he'd fallen down the stairs on the last day of their relationship, a pretense she'd agreed to maintain because he simply hadn't been an important enough part of her life for her to care.

Kelly had dated infrequently since then, spent most of her time either at home or at the library. Over the previous few years she had developed an enviable list of clients, and until recently she'd had so many referrals that she had been able to pick and choose the most interesting projects.

She and Dan had passed each other in the corridor or on the stairs several times, but they hadn't spoken until one night when he had locked himself out of his apartment. She had saved the day by successfully popping his lock with a credit card, a trick she'd learned from her older brother, who had died of leukemia in his mid-twenties. Dan invited her in for a drink, they talked for a considerable time, and she had been impressed by his broad based, unfocused self education. On impulse, she'd asked him if he would be interested in helping out with some of the assignments she was considering declining. Dan was going through a very dry spell at the time and had jumped at the opportunity, never realizing how their relationship would change over the course of the next few months.

They were just good friends, she emphasized to herself, and this was nothing more than a casual get together. The small table in the kitchenette was one of the few areas she kept clear of her research materials, but she'd also taken a couple of hours out of her normal working schedule to clean up the worst of the clutter, and had even tidied the front room to something approximating respectability, running the vacuum cleaner, dusting off the most accessible surfaces. Dan wasn't a spotless housekeeper either, but somehow tonight seemed a bit more formal than their usual meals together, which generally consisted of beer and pizza, cold cuts, or take out Chinese.

Kelly had built up a well balanced investment portfolio over the course of the previous few years, and she reinvested the earning rather than draw it out. In another ten years, she expected to have a cushion large enough that she could continue to live in reasonable comfort even if she decided to stop working, and that promised security reconciled her to what she admitted was hardly the most stimulating or exciting style of life. The possibility of a more serious entanglement with Dan made her nervous. Olin, Cogswell, and Meninger had all been pleasant company at first. She wasn't sure that she wanted to be exposed to Dan's hidden, presumably darker side; she had come to value his friendship greatly. She would rather have a friend she trusted than a lover she doubted.

Dan showed up, uncharacteristically, right on time, half past six. Kelly set aside her work, and her misgivings, and answered the door cheerily.

"Jeez, on time even. I'm honored."

"Am I on time? Sorry, I thought I was supposed to be here half an hour ago. If I've upset your schedule, I could go away for a while."

"Only if you like your Stroganoff warmed over."

"Stroganoff? German takeout?"

Kelly put hands on hips and threw her head back haughtily. "I'll have you know, I cooked this myself. From scratch. Worked my fingers to the bone slaving over a hot stove. Come in so I can stop mixing metaphors and start mixing drinks. And close the door."

Dan, who had expected nothing fancier than burgers and beer, was disconcerted. "Sorry. Consider me suitably impressed. I thought you gave up cooking anything that wouldn't fit in a frying pan."

"I do make exceptions on special occasions. Mother Marsh

insisted I learn how to keep a man fat and happy."

"Is this a special occasion?"

She pushed out one cheek with her tongue and met his eyes steadily. "That remains to be seen."

Dinner turned out perfectly. They lingered over it for nearly two hours, until the meat was cold and the sauce congealed. The wine Dan had brought disappeared quickly, and Kelly managed to find a bottle of brandy she'd been given by a Brown University professor who considered her work more than satisfactory, and who perhaps had other than a business relationship in mind.

Dan, who found himself growing sleepy, requested coffee. All that remained were the dregs, so Kelly carefully washed them out and made a new pot. When it was ready, she filled two mugs and suggested they move to the more comfortable chairs in the front room.

As it happened, both chairs were piled high with books, but the couch was free and they cleared a space on the adjacent coffee table so that they could put down their steaming drinks.

"Any luck today, by the way?"

Dan shook his head. "Not a bit. Vera Maitlin apparently kept to herself, and if she was still experiencing clairvoyant episodes this past year or so, she didn't tell anyone about them. Or at least no one I could find who was willing to talk to me."

"Maybe she foresaw her own death."

Dan winced. "Vera was never particularly gregarious, and could be actively rude if she didn't like you. I think some of the people at the home were mildly frightened of her, although no one would say anything specific." He shrugged. "Unless she kept journals or something, we'll probably never know."

"Are you going to get in touch with her family?"

"I don't know. She has, or at least had, a sister. No other living relatives. I might drop her a line if I get a chance."

"Busy?"

He sighed. "No, quite the opposite, in fact. I've got a few proposals out, but all but one of them are long shots. I'm living on the fee I got for writing advertising copy last year."

"You could try writing short stories again. Or finish that novel you told me about."

"Not really a solution. Short stories don't pay more than

three, four hundred dollars, and the market has gotten much smaller lately."

"You sound discouraged."

"Maudlin, even. It's the booze. Vera Maitlin was a dead end. The Darian girl's story is going nowhere. All I have are incomplete stories from people who aren't even supposed to know what little they do." He let out an exaggerated sigh and rolled his eyes. "All the excitement has gone out of my life."

She moved closer to him, much closer, and her voice suddenly changed. "We might be able to do something about that."

And she was right.

The first food poisoning case was a teenaged boy whose parents didn't know about the order of fries he'd picked up in the middle of the afternoon. Coincidentally, the same doctor at the Evans Street Emergency Center treated Esther Waters half an hour later. Her husband began to display identical symptoms while sitting in the waiting room.

By nine o'clock, fifteen people had been admitted to Providence Hospital, six of them transferred from Evans Street. An hour later, the count was forty-eight, and one, a five year old, had died. By midnight, over two hundred people had sought medical care. The authorities quickly identified the common factor as *Andy's Seaside* and dispatched a patrol car to roust the owner, Andrew McClellan, from his bed.

CHAPTER FOUR: TUESDAY

At three o'clock Tuesday morning, Rachel Darian opened her eyes. The room was dark except for what little light penetrated the closed blinds on the windows. She let her eyes scan the room slowly, then sat up, reached over and removed the IV lead. It fell to the floor, already forgotten. Rachel stared at the small drop of blood that formed on her arm, then ducked her head and deftly licked it clean.

At the nurse's station not far away, a light began to blink. Helen Sandford, whose enthusiasm for nursing had begun to decline years earlier and who by now felt trapped in a job she hated, glanced up and made a low, annoyed sound. The Darian girl made her feel distinctly uneasy. It was not the mysterious pregnancy that bothered her. Helen refused to believe that the girl was still a virgin despite what the doctors whispered to each other; it wouldn't be the first time they had stuck stubbornly to a mistaken diagnosis rather than admit error.

Nevertheless, she felt uncomfortable in the teenager's presence. Rachel wasn't rude or uncooperative, but she stared at Helen when she was in the room, and her lips curled in a sly, secretive smile that made her hackles rise. Physically the girl seemed to be in excellent condition other than a mild, persistent anemia, although sometimes she tossed and turned in her sleep as though experiencing bad dreams. Most likely the girl had torn the leads out by accident in the throes of a nightmare. Reluctantly, Helen rose and walked quickly down the hall to investigate.

The bed was empty. This wasn't the first time Helen had discovered a missing patient during her shift. Her first impulse was to turn toward the bathroom door and that's the reason she had the briefest of warnings before a clenched fist struck the side of her head. There was a sharp crack as two of Rachel's fingers snapped under the force of the blow. Nurse Sandford stumbled away from the pain, staggered to the side of the bed, disoriented and barely able to stand. The second blow seemed to come from nowhere.

She stumbled backward, hit the edge of the bed and fell across it, stunned, not yet feeling any significant pain. She managed to raise her arms defensively just as Rachel threw herself at the older woman. For a second, they were locked in a silent struggle, Rachel baring her teeth as she pressed forward, Nurse Sandford trying to push her away. Years of training had inhibited her from doing anything that might hurt a patient, and when she finally realized that she was in serious trouble and tried to call for the security guard, she managed only a single syllable before Rachel twisted one arm free and swung her fist a third time. The blow landed right on the bridge of the nurse's nose and this time she felt the pain, for a split second at least, before she lost consciousness.

Rachel continued to pound the woman's face until it was swollen and smeared with blood. When her fury had abated, she crouched beside the motionless woman, bared her teeth and lowered her head to the nurse's throat. Mercifully, Helen never knew that she was dying, until she was already dead.

Helen was a couple of inches taller and twenty pounds heavier than Rachel, but her uniform fit reasonably well, certainly well enough to pass casual inspection. When Rachel left the room, she closed the door firmly, adjusted her cap, and walked past the nursing station to the elevator. The guard was at the far end of the corridor and when he glanced in her direction, she sketched a wave with her face averted and stepped through the sliding doors. Inside, her finger hesitated briefly over the lobby button, then dropped an inch further to press for the first sub-level.

A minute later, she left the elevator, turned right and passed a door marked "Medical Stores". A short distance further, she paused and tried the next set of doors, which led to the blood bank, but they were locked. Without changing expression, she turned and walked on, reached a stairwell, then climbed back up to the employee exit. A uniformed guard sat at a desk to one side, but he had fallen asleep, his head back, snoring loudly. Rachel hesitated, mesmerized by the pulsing of his exposed throat, but turned away reluctantly and slipped out through the door, closing it gently behind her as she did so.

Almost simultaneously, on the opposite side of the city, a tall, shadowy figure left its temporary lair in the partially constructed parking garage. Four bodies were concealed there now, tucked into a recess between one of the main supports and a horizontal cement rib. They were beginning to smell and although that didn't bother their killer, he knew from experience that this meant discovery might be imminent. It was time to find more a more secure location.

There were still at least two hours before dawn, that hateful time when the sky first began to fill with fire, the single element the vampire feared. It left the parking garage silently, seeming to drift across the outskirts of the city as though propelled by the night breeze, moving silently and unnoticed, avoiding the better lit areas. Eventually it reached the College Hill district, where Brown University and the School of Design intermingled their campuses. A bus tunnel cut directly through the highest of the hills, and the vampire instinctively moved toward it. Use of this poorly lighted accessway was restricted to buses which did not run at this time of night. Extensive maintenance work was underway and construction materials and equipment snuggled against the walls on either side.

The interior was inadequately lighted by a string of shielded bulbs, although the intruder did not require their assistance to evaluate its surroundings. A hundred paces into the tunnel, it paused at a maintenance door, snapping the lock with a single, deceptively mild tug. A moment later, the door was pulled shut from the inside.

In the smaller maintenance tunnels, in the pipelines, electric conduits, and other passageways that ran parallel to and below the main shaft, there was a sudden stirring. Dozens, then scores, finally hundreds of living creatures were roused from their torpor by the new arrival among them. Their first reaction was curiosity, then anger at this penetration into territory which they had occupied and made their own for countless generations. The bravest of these ventured forth to challenge the invader, and found themselves snatched up, dying almost instantly as sharp teeth penetrated their bodies and sucked them dry. The few who managed to avoid capture and get close enough to sink their own fangs into their foe quickly backed away, coughing out the bitterly dry flesh. Within seconds they felt their strength melt away as their guts clenched and they vomited explosively, dying just as surely as if their necks had been snapped.

The vast majority of the rats who survived those first few minutes fled in panic, erupting up through tunnels both natural and artificial. Hundreds of them poured out into nearby basements, other hundreds emerged into the sewer system or onto the streets above, exiting any way they could and heedless of what might await them outside. The only witness during that first mad rush was a lone motorist who swerved when his headlights picked out what he at first thought was a pack of small dogs.

Contrary to the legends, not even rats can tolerate a vampire.

Dan woke up in a bed that was not his own, and wasn't entirely certain how he had gotten there. This wasn't the first time he had found himself in this position, and in the past it had never proven to be a particularly welcome revelation. One of the reasons Dan preferred self employment was a deep rooted unwillingness to conform to the expectations of others. Although he had never ruled out the possibility of falling in love and getting married one day, he always thought of the possibility as being in the remote, uncertain future. Dan was not good at compromise, and a permanent relationship necessarily involved a lot of negotiating, for which he had little aptitude. Other freelancers fought for higher pay rates or other perks with editors, but Dan always accepted or rejected an assignment based on the first offer. He suspected this would not prove to be an effective posture in a close personal relationship, and had so far managed to avoid putting this theory to a test.

He was also disoriented. He did remember making love to Kelly the night before, on the floor in front of the couch. It had been a little clumsy, and they had both given in to storms of giggling from time to time, a combination of nerves and a bit too much to drink, but satisfying overall.

He sat up and stared around the room, blinking. He was in Kelly's bedroom. He was alone at the moment, but judging by the rumpled covers, Kelly had slept there as well. She'd obviously risen without disturbing him, although he was usually a light sleeper.

He shook his head, and immediately regretted it.

His clothes appeared to be missing and in the bright light of morning, particularly now that he was sober, Dan was less willing to parade around in the nude, no matter how intimate they had been the night before. He looked for a bathroom, hoping to find a towel, and then remembered that it, like the bedroom, opened directly off the short hall. Unless he was willing to try slipping into something of Kelly's -- and that kinky he was not -- he was just going to have to risk the chance of providing her with a peep show.

He swung his feet out of bed and stood up, at which point he noticed the blue terrycloth bathrobe sitting on a chest at the foot of the bed. Thankfully, he slipped into it and ventured forth.

Kelly was sitting at her computer, where she finished typing a few characters before turning toward him. She was wearing an identically cut peach colored bathrobe, sitting with her feet tucked up under her body.

"I thought you were an early riser."

Dan glanced up at the wall clock, noted that it was nearly half past ten, almost two hours later than normal for him. "I guess I needed a little more rest than usual."

"What's the matter, sport? Did I wear you out?"

"Maybe I'm just out of practice. Where's the...?"

"Coffee? In the pot, like always." She waited until he had poured himself a cup. "How's the head?"

"It's been better, but I'll live. Beer and wine are more my speed than brandy."

"Yeah, well I was saving that bottle for a special occasion."

"Was last night a special occasion?"

She tossed her head. "Yeah, you might call it that."

Dan glanced around curiously. "Didn't happen to see my clothes, did you? I seem to have misplaced them."

"Sure did. I hid them, as a matter of fact."

"Any reason in particular?"

"I figured you ought to take a shower first."

He nodded. "That thought had occurred to me, believe it or not. But this," he indicated the bathrobe, "really isn't proper dress even for the short dash over to my apartment."

Kelly unfolded her legs and stood up, and for the first time Dan noticed that her bathrobe was not fastened in front. "I kind of thought you might want to take one here."

And half an hour after that, they both took one.

Feeling quite pleased with himself and unusually domestic, Dan was making scrambled eggs in Kelly's kitchen while she returned to her work. The radio was playing, an oldies station Kelly listened to habitually. Dan was lost in his own thoughts, trying to concentrate on planning the day's work, but failing miserably. On the one hand, he was almost giddily happy about the sudden if not entirely unexpected turn of events, at the way the new intimacy had superimposed itself on their friendship without changing their easy acceptance of one another. But at the same time, he was nervous that they still might somehow spoil a relationship that he had come to value highly.

"Did you hear that?"

Dan turned from the stove, saw that Kelly had turned away from her computer to look at the television. "Did I hear what?"

"Some woman got attacked by rats in her basement on the East Side this morning, and two kids playing in an empty lot said they were chased by half a dozen of them." She shivered melodramatically. "I couldn't even stand the tame white ones in rat lab back when I was at school. Shifty little eyes watching you all the time."

"It's not likely they actually attack anyone unless they are surprised or cornered. Maybe the kids were throwing rocks or poking them with sticks."

"Rats, euuwww!" She gave a theatrical shudder. "When I was a kid, I baited hooks and poked at slugs and let spiders walk across my hands and stuff, but just the thought of a rat gives me the willies. My brother had gerbils for a while, and I couldn't even watch them without feeling queasy."

"So, the iron maiden has a soft spot after all. An unreasoning fear of rodents."

It wasn't quite as easy to dismiss the rat story an hour later. A mentally retarded homeless man was found slumped in an alley, bleeding from several small animal bites. Half a dozen people reported finding rats in their homes or seeing them outdoors, although the authorities stressed that many if not most of these might have been sightings of cats, squirrels, possum, and other misperceptions; the earlier stories had already led to a rash of spurious reports. Rat droppings had in fact been found in several instances, but police and animal control officers tried to reassure the public that it was not uncommon for small colonies of rats to be temporarily displaced by construction work, severe weather, or other changes in their environment. "Leave them alone and they'll leave you alone," said a public health official.

Then the assistant cook at a small diner spotted a rat in his kitchen. Armed with a meat cleaver, he chased it downstairs into the basement and succeeded in killing it, more through luck than skill. When he turned to go back upstairs, he saw at least three more scurrying up the steps, chased them out into the small dining area, much to the consternation of the owner and several customers, managed to kill one more near the cash register. All of the surviving rats escaped in the subsequent confusion. The local radio and television stations happily reported everything they heard, making little effort to separate truth from exaggeration. There hadn't been a decent news story for a week.

"Think there's an article in this somewhere?" Kelly asked as they heard yet another report on the radio.

"I don't know. It's certainly offbeat enough, and I'm getting nowhere fast with the Maitlin piece. Want to come along and see if we can find any of the rats to interview?"

"Very funny. No, I'll just slave away on this market study. Should I hold supper?" The question sounded casual, but Dan knew it was not.

"Sure. If I'm going to be late, I'll call you."

That morning was very different at the house shared by Skip Randolph and Judy Bowes. Skip had gone to bed early the night before, complaining of a headache and upset stomach. He became increasingly restless during the night, so much so that he disturbed Judy's sleep on two or three occasions. By the time the sun came up, she was feeling a bit ill herself, although she blamed that on lack of sleep.

Skip responded groggily when she shook his shoulder, but agreed to get up. He sat on the edge of the bed while she went to the bathroom and washed her face. Rather unbecoming, she told herself, staring into the mirror. Her eyes were bloodshot, skin dry, and complexion pale. She blinked at herself, wondering if they had both picked up some sort of bug.

Skip was lying down when she returned to the bedroom. "Do you mind calling in for me, Jude? I'm pretty dizzy. Don't think I should go into work today. You can take the car."

Normally Skip dropped her off on his own way in and while she was, in her opinion, a more prudent driver than he, she didn't feel up to driving herself this morning. "Maybe I'll call in and tell them I'll be late. I could really use another couple hours of sleep."

After fetching aspirin and a glass of grapefruit juice for Skip, Judy took the same cure herself, then drew a hot bath and settled in for a soak. When she emerged, she felt slightly better but still not well, and possibly even somewhat weaker. Skip seemed to have drifted off to sleep and she didn't want to wake him so she took her pillow and a comforter, called both their employers, then settled down onto the couch to finish her Stephen King novel.

She woke at mid-morning with the acute feeling that something was wrong. Her first thought was for Skip and she scrambled to her feet. Or at least, that's what she attempted to do. Her sense of balance was off and her legs couldn't support her weight. She staggered and her right knee buckled. Desperately she reached for the arm of the couch as she toppled, but she missed, and hit the hard wood floor with a crash.

As she lay there, trying to regain her composure, there was a pitiless throbbing just behind her forehead. She moaned and tried to roll onto her side, realizing as she did so that her clothes were soaked with perspiration and sticking to her skin. Obviously, she was sicker than she had thought, weak enough to require outside help. Concentrating, she pushed up to her hands and knees. As she did so, incredible pain shot through the muscles of her arms and legs and her stomach churned warningly. Judy froze, waiting for the nausea to recede, but immobility didn't help. A moment later she shuddered, her stomach convulsed, and bitter fluid rushed up through her throat. She struggled not to faint as painful convulsions quickly followed. The taste in her mouth was foul beyond belief, acidic, rotten, and she knew it was not an isolated spasm, that more discomfort was on its way.

"I must get to the phone," she thought, and actually started to rise to her feet. The movement made her head spin and the room seemed to disintegrate into a thousand points of light, each pursuing its own erratic orbit. Disoriented, she staggered and her knees folded under her, sending her topping forward. She was unconscious even before her chin struck the carpeting.

In the bedroom, Skip Randolph's fever had already crested, and his body was starting to cool down.

Toward room temperature.

Dan Scapelli suffered another frustrating afternoon. His efforts to interview witnesses and victims of the rat attacks were only slightly more successful than his earlier attempts to find someone who had shared Vera Maitlin's final years. The homeless man was hospitalized and mentally ill and unlikely to be of much help. The news story hadn't mentioned that he was also mute. The woman surprised by rats in her basement had been released, but no one was answering her doorbell, and the diner which had been overrun with rats was closed, for obvious reasons, and seemed to be deserted. The police couldn't or wouldn't provide any more detail than had been reported already, nor would they release the names of the children who had reportedly been attacked.

Dan parked on a back street convenient to the area most seriously affected and spent two hours walking the neighborhood. He found two separate women willing, in fact eager, to talk about the apparent plague of rats, but it was quickly obvious that neither of them knew anything factual.

He walked down Benefit Street, the site of the original Providence Settlement; many of the houses there bore historical society plaques. Most of the houses were in good repair preserved in as close to the original condition as was practical. The adjoining yards were small, sometimes heavily overgrown, and the entire area was a maze of footpaths, walkways, terraces, and small gardens. Dan knew there was little chance that he might actually see one of the mysteriously aggressive rats, but he kept his eyes open just in case. Legions of them could have been lying concealed within a few meters without his knowing it.

He persisted nonetheless, starting conversations with people he met, eavesdropping on others, hoping for a tip. Two couples sitting at a sidewalk table outside a coffee shop were discussing the incident at the rat infested restaurant, which the rumor mill had apparently embellished into an unprovoked attack by dozens of rats who had swarmed over people while they ate, biting several.

He stopped to offer an elderly man a light, but declined the offer of a cigarette in exchange. "I gave them up a year ago. I still carry the lighter from force of habit." They talked a bit longer and Dan explained why he was in the neighborhood. The other man laughed and shook his head.

"A lot of nonsense. I've lived here all my life and I've never seen a rat. People just need something to talk about."

Dan's personal theory was that the work on the bus tunnel had displaced a colony but he wouldn't have minded a more lurid explanation. As long as it was the truth.

With sore feet and nothing to show for it, Dan finally admitted defeat, at least for the time being, and returned to his parked car. He might have better luck if he spent the balance of the afternoon at the library, searching for any recent materials dealing with clairvoyance or Vera Maitlin. He had liked Vera; she'd spoken to him frankly and hadn't been offended by his initial skepticism. A real class act, he thought, regretting that he'd never thought to look her up again after he'd finished his article.

As he pulled away from the curb, Dan was unaware of the two sets of small eyes that watched from a shaded window across the street. The owners were away for the week, so no one was around to raise the alarm when several dozen frightened rats erupted from the sump housing in the basement, made their way up the steps to the open kitchen door, and invaded the pantry.

Dawn Reynolds made a quick pass through the kennel and adjoining area to make sure there was nothing amiss before dousing the light and returning to the front of Noah's Ark Pets and Supplies. She had only been trusted to close the store for the past three weeks and she was as proud of the new responsibility as she was happy with the ten percent pay raise that had accompanied it. Jacob Kaplan disconcerted her sometimes with his naive comments about her generation, but she had come to recognize that he was teasing her at times. She reminded her sometimes of her grandfather, who had died when she was eight.

It was just after ten o'clock. Dawn glanced out through the front window, watching for Denny Kirk, her current live-in boyfriend. But not for long, she told herself. She was already rehearsing what she hoped would be their final conversation. Although she hadn't minded when he moved into her apartment, had in fact suggested it herself, the relationship was not working out as she had hoped. Far from it. Denny had never quite grown up, and he expected Dawn to provide the same services as had his mother, as well as those she performed in bed. She was also tired of paying all of their bills.

To be fair, when he was working he contributed generously to the household budget, even when he was making considerably less than she did, which was usually the case. But he was as unreliable outside the job as on. He was supposed to be waiting at the curb by ten o'clock to take her home every night, and this was the second time this week that he'd been late.

"Come on!" She tapped restlessly at the glass with the tips of her fingers. "Where are you?"

Ordinarily, she would not have been as annoyed, but she hadn't slept well the night before and had been exhausted all day. For the past two hours, she'd been imagining how comfortable her bed would be when she lay down in it tonight, and at this point she was even ready to forego her normal late night meal.

Impatient, she stepped out onto the sidewalk, holding the door open behind her, glancing quickly in each direction. A taxi moved through the intersection to the right, and a bus approached from the left, its sign indicating "Off Duty". Dawn stamped her foot angrily and went back inside, then turned off all but the security light. She picked up her bag and hung it over her shoulder, then returned to the door, pressing her cheek against the cool glass as she stared out into the darkness.

It was still unpleasantly warm and humid despite the lateness of the hour. The fans were still turning but she'd turned off the air conditioner half an hour earlier. Dawn ran the back of her hand across her upper lip and it came away moist. She leaned forward, pushing the door slightly open again, and as she did so, someone who had approached without being seen reached up and grabbed the edge of the door, holding it in place when she stepped back instinctively.

"I'm sorry, sir, but we're closed." But he was past her in a second, less than that, and had already disappeared into the shadows of the store, so completely swallowed up that she wondered if she had imagined his existence.

In the back room, several of the puppies had begun barking.

"Hello?" She peered into the darkness, wondering if she should turn the lights back on. Had she really seen someone or had it been her imagination? She crossed to the light switches, but paused with her hand raised, trying to make up her mind. In that moment of indecision, there was movement, and an indistinct figure separated itself from the shadows.

His skin was dark, his hair cut close to the scalp. The eyes were clear and bright, shoulders wide, chin strong but very slightly misshapen. Some part of her mind told her that the man was remarkably, even hideously ugly, but at the same time she felt drawn to him, as though there was an inner beauty visible only to her inner eye. Despite the poor light, she could see him quite clearly, and his presence now seemed somehow completely proper. The fact that the store was closed no longer mattered. "Can I help you, sir?"

She dropped her hand from the untouched light switches and moved in his direction.

Dennis Kirk drove up ten minutes later, coming to such an abrupt stop that the tires and brakes both squealed in protest. He glanced nervously toward the door, anticipating either a frozen silence or an angry string of accusations, had already started working on a protective layer of fury of his own.

All but one of the interior lights had been turned off, which was unusual, and he wondered if Dawn had grown impatient and hailed a cab. He glanced at his watch. Fifteen minutes late. Surely she would have waited at least that long.

"Damn it, woman," he muttered, climbing out of the car. It wasn't his fault; he had left the employment agency in plenty of time to pick her up, but the traffic had been bad and he'd absentmindedly gone past the right exit from I-95, and by the time he got off and doubled back through several side streets, he knew he would never make it on time and that she was going to be pissed at him again. It wasn't fair. He had tried.

Denny knocked on the door, then leaned forward to peer inside. There was no movement except for the fluttering of birds in their cages against the far wall. He was about to turn away when his hand fell on the handle and instinctively he tried to open it.

The door wasn't locked.

Denny stuck his head inside. "Hey, Dawn! Are you in there?" There was no answer. "Shit!"

He started to let the door swing back shut when he heard something. It sounded very much like a woman's voice, low, almost inaudible.

"Dawn? Is that you? C'mon girl, don't play games with me. I know I'm late, but it wasn't my fault this time. Come on, I've got good news." He'd been hired by Eblis Manufacturing to work in their maintenance department, and the job was both full time and paid well.

The store was completely silent now; even the animals were hushed.

Denny pushed the door open and stepped inside. There was a security light in the front window, and another somewhere in the back, out of sight, but the rest of the front room was only intermittently illuminated.

The door closed behind him with a soft click.

Denny had grown up in one of the rougher sections of Boston, had run with Satan's Warriors for most of his teen years, and had seen his share of street fighting before moving to Providence. There was something about this situation that tickled his sense of self preservation and he unconsciously dropped into a low, wary crouch. Now that he was inside, he noticed a funny smell, an unpleasant sweetness that overwhelmed the inevitable odors of a pet store. Denny hadn't carried a knife for two years, but the fingers of his right hand were flexing as though to grasp an absent weapon.

He passed the first row of racks, laden with aquarium supplies, figurines of divers, boats, sunken cities, treasure chests, aerators, and a variety of fish food. The aisle beyond was empty. Next came dog and cat related products, leashes, collars, rubber toys, catnip, flea power, and a large selection of thin paperbacks with titles that were variations of *I Love My Transylvanian Toadhound.*

From somewhere close at hand came a soft sigh, and Denny opened his mouth to call out, then hesitated. Instead, he moved around the end of the next row with even greater care, shifting his feet slowly so they would make minimal sound.

At first, he couldn't make out the shape in the next aisle. Shapes, actually, There were two separate figures, close together, lying on the floor. The first was Dawn Reynolds, naked on her back with her arms above her head. The second appeared to be a man wearing dark clothing, who crouched low over her body. The man's skin at first appeared to be so black that it blended into his clothing, but he half turned and raised a single, pale white hand, glowing like a full moon, looking more like a spider or an octopus than a human hand. The figure rose and turned in a single fluid movement and Denny found himself staring into amber eyes so startling that it was another second or two before he noticed that the face was that of a rotting corpse wrapped in an ebony winding cloth.

"What the fuck?" He took a quick step backward, but it was

much too late. Fingers tangled in the front of his shirt and lifted him into the air. Old instincts took over and Denny struck out hit his attacker in the face, apparently without serious effect.

The headlights of a passing car briefly lit up the aisle and Denny saw the two protruding fangs quite clearly in the split second before darkness returned. "What are you, a fucking vampire?" He didn't believe it. He knew there were no such things as vampires.

He was wrong.

A few feet away, Dawn sat up, her head filled with a fog of disconnected thoughts and sensations. She recognized Denny, her current and soon to be ex-boyfriend, but couldn't understand why he would be fighting with the incredibly handsome man who had just come into her life. She longed for him to hold her in his arms, to bring her his special kind of love. Why wouldn't Denny just go away and let her be happy for once?

She struggled to her feet, just as Denny was thrown through the air to crash into a display rack of stuffed animals. The sudden violence broke through her torpor, at least partly, and she recoiled, frightened and confused. Her new lover looked different now, and she recoiled in sudden revulsion, then turned and ran to the front door. It didn't take long to draw the fallen man's blood, but by then Dawn was outside and had run somewhat unsteadily out into the street.

There wasn't much local traffic at that time of night, but one automobile at the wrong moment was one too many. A hand painted van decorated with ice capped mountains came rushing out of the night and its driver had barely time to try to avoid the running woman before the impact. The front fender struck her solidly and tossed her high into the air.

Dawn Reynolds died almost instantly after crashing head first through the plate glass windows of *Timoli's Deli*, a large sliver of glass having quite efficiently cut her throat. Her heart had already stopped beating by the time the van came to a complete stop. The being that had just been brought into existence within her womb a few minutes earlier continued to move for some time thereafter before it also became motionless, but the medics never noticed this activity, nor did they pay particular attention to the three triangular wounds in her abdomen. These would subsequently be discovered and remarked upon during the autopsy, but she was taken to City

Hospital and no one ever noticed the similarity to Rachel Darian's wounds.

Not that it would have made much difference.

On the other hand, Dennis Kirk's drained body went undiscovered until the following morning, when Jacob Kaplan came in to open his store and found the door unlocked.

Providence Hospital found itself in the throes of a major emergency. Things had started to go wrong just after nightfall and they had grown steadily worse since then. The first alarm was raised in the emergency room, when three victims of an automobile accident went into convulsions after being given blood transfusions. One died almost immediately, and the others were taken to intensive care.

Within the next hour, four more people had died in different parts of the hospital and another on the operating table during what should have been a routine appendectomy. By eight o'clock, all emergency patients were being redirected to other hospitals and no whole blood, plasma, or medication was being administered to anyone unless it was rushed in from another hospital. The entire blood supply in house had somehow become contaminated.

That wasn't even the worst of it. One of the deaths had been attributed to botulism and the CDC had been called.

This all followed the murder of Nurse Helen Sandford and the disappearance of a patient who might have been responsible. There was speculation about an organized conspiracy, possibly a terrorist attack, and the FBI had four agents in the complex.

As bad as things were, they were going to be a lot worse.

CHAPTER FIVE: WEDNESDAY

Dr. Emory Whiteson was not having a good time. He had completed his usual shift the day before but even though he'd spent a full eight hours asleep, he felt almost as tired as he had when he'd left the hospital. The disruption of his usual routine and the small army of investigators who had descended on the hospital probably contributed to his emotional state. The contaminated blood supply had been isolated but ineffective or spoiled medication was still showing up regularly in the hospital inventory, and he had been pulled from most of his regular duties to help determine which patients absolutely had to receive medication and where it could be found outside the complex. Already many patients had been transferred to other hospitals and health care facilities, and the administration was bringing in whole blood, plasma, and anything else it needed by courier on an as required basis. The Governor's office and the state Emergency Preparedness Agency had been notified and were provided what support they could, but no scenarios had been worked out in advance for this particular situation.

The hospital's new layer of precautions notwithstanding, the total number of patients believed to have died unnecessarily was now unofficially twenty-two, and several others remained in critical condition. There had been a rash of stress related accidents as well. One nurse had inadvertently switched medications between two patients, but it was clearly human error rather than a deliberate act. The murder of Helen Sandford and the disappearance of the patient who was apparently responsible was still reverberating within the institution as well, and some nurses refused to enter a patient's room, any patient's room, unless they were accompanied by another staff member.

Whiteson himself attended the nurse's autopsy. Although the woman was not a personal friend, he knew her by name and had worked with her from time to time. An unimaginative woman, in his judgment, who had lost her youthful enthusiasm for the job and settled into stolid acceptance. Childless and a widow, she'd been working night shifts for the past five years, had in fact volunteered for that duty, probably to take advantage of the shift bonus.

It was Whiteson's admittedly uninformed opinion that the

traumatic attack in the forest had unhinged the girl's mind, causing to her attempt to re-enact the crime in her hospital room. Or it might be that she had become unbalanced even earlier and that Rachel Darian had in fact murdered her friend and thrown the body into the river. Her own wounds might be self inflicted or the result of her struggle with her companion. That still left the question of the anomalous pregnancy, of course. A rational explanation would emerge there as well, he was certain.

What Whiteson knew of the circumstances of Helen Sandford's death puzzled him even further. Although she was a fairly muscular woman, she had been completely overpowered by her attacker, and there were no defensive wounds to speak of, no sign that she'd inflicted any damage of her own. There was, of course, a great deal of blood. Her throat had been torn open, the jugular severed, and the actual cause of death had been blood loss. The bed had been thoroughly soaked with it. There was no question about how most of the damage had been inflicted. There were bruises and incidental lacerations, but the serious wounds were quite unmistakable. The flesh had been torn by human teeth.

Whiteson had seen similar wounds once before, although the victim in that case, a ward nurse at a psychiatric hospital, had survived the assault by a mentally ill patient who had been judged hopelessly catatonic only a month prior to the attack. He had lapsed back into a comatose state minutes later, and to this day, no one really knew what had set him off.

Providence Hospital was, by and large, operating in a state of controlled, chaos. Barely controlled. The partial evacuation had been handled with reasonable efficiency, but in some cases it had been impossible to notify the families, who were now demanding to know why their loved ones had been moved without their permission. Others who had heard of the contamination problem were demanding to know why their wives or husbands or children or elderly relatives had not been moved. It was impossible to pass through the lobby without hearing someone shouting angrily.

Even in the midst of the ongoing crisis, the emergency room was doing an unusually heavy business. Whiteson had heard a radio report that two more restaurants had been closed because of cases of food poisoning. Many of their customers would be turning up as the news spread, actually sick or just convinced that they were.

Everyone in the city who had indigestion would be insisting upon being treated before the day was out, demanding that his or her stomach be pumped and the contents saved in anticipation of a lawsuit. Many of these people would not even have eaten at the affected restaurants.

A visibly disheveled orderly waved to him just as he was about to step into the staff lounge.

"Excuse me, sir, but Dr. Wolcroft asked me to keep an eye out for you. They're prepping a couple of DOA's for you downstairs. They want autopsies right away."

Whiteson frowned. "Now? With everything that's going on? The dead aren't in any hurry."

"I don't know about that, Doctor." The orderly shook his head. "I don't understand it either, if you don't mind my saying so, but there are a couple of police detectives with Dr. Wolcroft and they seem pretty determined. I had the impression they'd been arguing just before I arrived."

Urgent or not, Whiteson went into the staff lounge first in order to fortify himself with a fresh cup of coffee. It looked like this was going to be a very long day. I'm forty-eight years old, he told himself, and for the first time, I'm beginning to feel my age. Maybe it was time to consider going into private practice.

Ten minutes later, he was shaking hands with detectives Angela Harris and Vincent Marzocchi of the Providence Police Department. "Sit down for a moment, Emory."

Stan Wolcroft's office was large, by hospital standards, but just as aseptic and orderly as the best maintained ward. Wolcroft himself had just passed sixty and was already contemplating early retirement, a sentiment which had been growing steadily stronger during the past two days. He had never intended to be an administrator, but his life had fallen into that pattern almost by itself and he had resigned himself to it years before.

"We're holding a couple of DOA's for you, Emory. A woman struck by a van and a man whose body was just discovered an hour ago, although it appears from the preliminary report that he died sometime last evening. The coroner has asked that you expedite the examination."

Whiteson glanced at the police officers. "Am I supposed to be looking for something in particular?"

The woman, Harris, answered immediately. "We're not certain, Doctor. The woman was brought in late last night; she was struck by a moving vehicle and thrown through a plate glass window by the impact. She carried no identification so she was a Jane Doe until just an hour ago. At nine this morning, there was an emergency call from the owner of one of the stores in the same neighborhood, a pet shop. When he opened up this morning, he found the front door unlocked and a dead body, male, lying behind a counter. There were signs of a struggle."

"Coincidence?"

She shook her head. "We don't think so. His wallet and possessions hadn't been taken and we identified him as Dennis Kirk, who was known to be living with a young woman named Dawn Reynolds, who worked in the pet shop and who should have locked it up the night before. Her purse was still there and the picture on her license matched our Jane Doe. She has no family in the area but we had her boss come in to identify the body a short while ago."

Whiteson pursed his lips. "Sounds to me like a bungled robbery attempt. The girl ran out in the street and was run down. The van might even have been the getaway vehicle."

"That's a possibility," Harris admitted noncommittally. "But the driver did stop and call us, and waited around to make a statement when we arrived."

"So what do you expect me to find?"

"We'd prefer to let you draw your own conclusions, Doctor."

Whiteson sniffed, decided he was coming down with a summer cold. Just what he needed. "All right, I'll get right to it. How do I get in touch with you when I'm finished?"

Marzocchi crossed his legs and shifted his weight casually. "Oh, we'll wait for you."

"It might take some time," he cautioned them.

Harris nodded. "We're not in a hurry."

Jacob Kaplan spent most of the day in a complete daze. He'd been unpleasantly surprised to find the front door open when he'd arrived at the store that morning, and utterly shocked to stumble over Dennis Kirk's body lying amid the wreckage inside. He didn't know the man, never having met him, but when he noticed Dawn's shoulderbag sitting on a display rack near the door, he had expected to find her body as well. She was too conscientious to have gone off without locking up properly. A good girl. He'd been very fond of her.

The police had responded promptly to his call, asking him to wait outside while their technicians went over the premises. He had used the pay phone on the corner to try Dawn's apartment, but there had been no answer. Jacob's worst fear was confirmed a short while later when someone made the connection and asked him to come down to the hospital morgue to identify the body.

Although he had remained calm during his visit to the morgue, it had been a considerable ordeal. Jacob was no stranger to death; he had buried his wife and both of his sons, one of whom had committed suicide by throwing himself in front of a train following the breakup of his marriage. He'd fought in the Pacific during World War II, had lost several friends on Iwo Jima, and had witnessed a fatal shooting at a local bar less than a year earlier. None of these had had such a brutal impact on him as the sight of Dawn Reynolds, whose face had been so badly damaged that it was only with great difficulty that he was able to make a positive identification.

The store would remain closed all day, even if the police allowed him to open it, which seemed unlikely. The overturned racks and damaged stock would have to be taken care of, and he would need to replace Dawn quickly. He was too old to manage things by himself for any length of time. Weary and depressed, Jacob wanted nothing more than to go home, but he had responsibilities that could not be put off any longer. After a very frustrating wait on the telephone, a police dispatcher connected him with Detective Marzocchi, who was initially reluctant to allow him to re-enter the store.

"Listen, officer, I'd rather not go back there right now myself, but there are live animals inside, do you understand? Maybe they can go a day without food or having their cages cleaned, but in this heat, they must have fresh water."

Marzocchi hesitated but there was obviously no alternative. "Just please, sir, stay away from the areas that are taped off and don't disturb anything else unnecessarily until we tell you it's okay. One of the officers will have to accompany you."

"I understand perfectly, young man."

Officer Carnell was perfectly happy to wait just inside the

door while Jacob did what was necessary. The store seemed unusually quiet when he let himself in. The air conditioner was running on low in the background; he didn't remember turning it on but he might well have done so while waiting for the police to arrive. The atmosphere still smelled of blood. Most of the lights were off; their subliminal fluorescent hum was only noticeable when it was absent. The fish tanks against the side wall still burbled as the aerators chugged away. Jacob was halfway across the sales area before he realized that it was entirely too quiet.

The live pet area at the rear was completely silent. No barking, no rustling, no chirping birds. He was a few steps closer before he noticed the next anomaly. Nothing moved in the fish tanks except the rising bubbles of air. He looked more closely and saw that his entire stock of fish was floating forlornly.

Appalled more by the loss of life than by the financial loss, he rushed forward, carefully avoiding the area where Kirk's body had been discovered, and entered the rear half of the store, where rows of cages held puppies, kittens, a variety of birds, and a handful of snakes, salamanders, gerbils, guinea pigs, and turtles.

At first, he thought whatever had struck down the fish had killed everything else as well. The bird cages were filled with motionless bodies and the newly acquired Siamese kittens were sprawled inertly in their enclosure. But a snake uncoiled slowly as he walked past and at least one puppy listlessly raised its head. Those small signs of life cut through his shock and Jacob hastily crossed the room, used his master key to open the cage, and reached in to pet the six week old beagle, the only one of its litter that remained unsold.

The puppy flared its ears and soundlessly lunged forward, closing its jaws on two of Jacob's fingers. He cried out and drew back, but the puppy maintained its hold and was dragged out into the open. To either side, a handful of motionless puppies and kittens sudden burst into frenzied activity, pressing their muzzles against the glass walls, snarling and baring their teeth. More than half never stirred, however, and several of these lay in small pools of congealing blood. Jacob fought to free his hand and realized that his troubles had just gotten worse.

Dr. Whiteson considered the results of his examination of the two bodies more than slightly disturbing, although the two detectives listened to his summary with no visible indication that they were hearing anything unusual. It was only when he described the degree of blood lost by the male victim that there was any reaction.

"What you're saying is that Kirk was completely drained of blood, Doctor?" Harris appeared openly skeptical.

"The degree of exsanguination was quite marked, Detective Harris. The jugular was pierced twice and the body lay there for what, ten hours before it was reported? I would be surprised if he hadn't lost a great deal of blood. But no, although the blood loss was considerable, remarkably so in fact, it was not complete."

"But he lost at least a couple of quarts?" asked Harris.

"At least twice that, Detective."

Marzocchi stood up and started to walk around the room. "What would you say, Doctor Whiteson, if I told you there were only minor bloodstains at the site of the murder?"

"I'd say either someone cleaned up afterwards, or that he was killed at another location. We're talking about several quarts of blood, Detective."

"Under the circumstances, Doctor, neither of those scenarios seems likely." Harris was still seated, her hands clasped in her lap. "Is there any way in which the blood could have been removed from the body? Siphoned into a container, I mean. Something like that."

"Are you suggesting that the man's blood was carried off in some fashion? What on earth for?"

"Cults," suggested Marzocchi.

Whiteson made an impatient sound. "Well of course it is possible that some type of equipment could have been used to collect the blood. It would have taken quite a bit of time, though, and I can't imagine anyone calmly setting out to perform an operation like that with police hovering at an accident scene less than a block away."

"You might be surprised." It wasn't clear if Harris had meant her comment to be audible. She raised her voice. "The fact remains that something strange happened to Kirk's blood, Doctor."

"Maybe Dracula's back." Marzocchi meant his remark to be funny, but no one laughed.

There was an awkward silence before Harris picked up the conversation. "Would you say that the blood loss took place before or after death?"

"Before and after. I told you, it was the loss of blood that killed him. Except for the puncture wounds, the only non-superficial damage to the body consisted of two fractured ribs and a broken finger. Hardly fatal injuries."

"You're saying that he must have been bleeding for at least several minutes before he died."

Whiteson nodded. "At least, though presumably he was unconscious since there are no indications that he struggled or that he was physically restrained. Tied down, for example. He may well have been alive for quite a while after the wounds were inflicted. I couldn't tell you at this point, if ever, how long the process took. At least several minutes."

"That's as may be, but other than a few smears and spatters, and a slight stain on the victim's collar, there was no blood found at the scene. None at all."

"Then perhaps as I suggested he was killed elsewhere and moved after death."

Marzocchi turned around. "I suppose we can't rule that out, but it seems highly unlikely. There's sufficient physical and circumstantial evidence to indicate the attack took place in the pet shop where the body was discovered. And the owner tells us that the deceased often picked up the other victim after work, and the timing is right."

"I don't know what to suggest then." He paused and licked his lips. He'd been dreading what was about to come and had even been tempted to remain silent, but he knew it would come out eventually, and that it would only make matters worse if he waited. "The wounds may be significant for another reason."

Harris appeared attentive, but Marzocchi had turned away, seemingly lost in his own thoughts. "Significant how?" she prompted.

"The punctures were caused by a triangular weapon, possibly a garden tool. I've seen the same thing elsewhere recently, or something very similar. Are you familiar with the Chin girl's murder?"

Marzocchi spun on one heel. "Are you suggesting there could be a connection?"

Whiteson sighed, began massaging the bridge of his nose. "There's at least a similarity. Beyond that, I don't know. But the Chin girl also suffered dramatic blood loss, and the wounds on her throat were quite similar. Almost identical."

Marzocchi spread his hands and tilted his head back, staring at the ceiling. "We're back to a fucking vampire story again."

"There's more." Both detectives were silent, but it took a moment for Whiteson to organize his thoughts, to decide just how he wanted to phrase what he had to say. "The other young woman, Darian, the one who survived, also had similar wounds, although in her case they were superficial. Three shallow punctures located approximately equidistantly on her lower abdomen."

"That's very interesting, Doctor." Harris had a disconcerting stare..

Whiteson nodded. "Unfortunately, as I understand it, she claimed to have no knowledge of how she came by her injuries. You might talk to Dr. Marin about it; he was her doctor and would have more information."

"They haven't found her yet, have they?" asked Marzocchi.

"Not that I'm aware of."

"That's Scotson's case," Harris told her partner. "The Sandford murder."

"Christ, did she have triangular wounds as well?"

Whiteson shook his head, then drew a deep breath. They weren't going to want to hear this next part either. "No, she didn't, although her throat was pretty badly torn. But your accident victim has them too."

"Reynolds?" Startled, Harris betrayed more emotion than she had shown before. "But she was hit by a car and thrown through a window."

"Yes, she was. Certainly that was the cause of death. Her chest was crushed, both hips shattered, the heart and several other organs sustained severe damage. But I also found three distinct puncture wounds on her lower abdomen, which I measured carefully. They are exactly the same size and distance apart as those on the other cadavers." The silence that followed as oppressive.

The detectives took their leave a short while later, thanking Whiteson for his help, although Marzocchi clearly remained skeptical. Harris said little and seemed lost in thought.

Dr. Whiteson decided that he needed a cigarette badly and went out through the emergency room exit, passing an elderly man whose right hand was wrapped in blood stained white linen. It was Jacob Kaplan, now resigned to the fact that he had just been bitten by a rabid animal. He was crying silently, not because of the pain, but because he knew that every surviving animal in his store would have to be destroyed. Maybe it was time to listen to his sister and retire.

After leaving the hospital undetected, Rachel Darian had made her way parallel to the interstate south toward Narragansett Bay until she reached the mouth of a storm drain. Even though she was not a large girl, she experienced some difficulty as she crawled inside, squirming along its length until she reached a spot where the upper surface had cracked and partially collapsed. A portion of the earth above had fallen in, some but not all of which had been carried away by the intermittently swiftly flowing water. Straining, she pulled herself up into the resulting cavity, using her hands to hollow out an even larger space, so that she could stretch out on top of an undamaged portion of the storm drain, the untouched earth a solid roof just above, working entirely by touch in the darkness.

She remained relatively motionless throughout Tuesday and Wednesday night, drifting in and out of consciousness but not paying much attention to her surroundings even when she was awake. Her breasts as well as her abdomen continued to swell and the uniform she was wearing tightened until the seams burst. At just before mid-day on Wednesday, she removed both the blouse and the skirt and lay naked, the cool earth inches above her face.

By the time it began to grow dark a few hours later, her water had burst and contractions were well underway.

Dan and Kelly made love again on Tuesday evening, in Dan's apartment this time, and with considerably more deliberation. They opened another bottle of wine, but it was only half gone when they moved to the bedroom. Afterward, freshly showered and partially dressed, Kelly made them both grilled cheese sandwiches and managed to set off the smoke alarm, which wailed forlornly until Dan yanked out the batteries. They left the dirty dishes in the sink and went back to bed to satisfy a different hunger.

Once again, Kelly was up first in the morning, and Dan kissed her sleepily when she told him she was going back to her own apartment to get started on the day's work. An hour later, shaved, showered, and dressed, he stopped by to make dinner plans before driving back to *Green Pastures*, still hoping to find someone in authority who would talk to him about Vera Maitlin. As before, he received instead a brusque and practiced reply to the effect that they were not at liberty to divulge personal information about their clients, living or dead. Frustrated, Dan drove off, but not before noticing that *Andy's Seaside* had not yet reopened.

The rat story hadn't panned out either. There had been one more reported sighting; two Brown University students returning from a late party had spotted as many as half a dozen of the creatures raiding a dumpster behind one of the cafeterias, but no one else was attacked and city officials were dismissing the sequence of events as "atypical and insignificant", probably just vermin displaced by sewer work on the East Side. There was a new political scandal brewing in Cranston and none of the full time reporters were interested in what was at best a marginal summer story.

At noon, Dan called his own apartment from a pay booth and played back his phone messages, which included a request that he call Emil Torgov at his earliest possible convenience. Dan had worked for Emil before; he ran the city news bureau for the *Rhode Island Register*, one of the state's two major newspapers. Dan called Torgov and promptly found himself temporarily employed.

"Two months ago they made me reduce staff and now they can't understand why I haven't got all the bases covered," Emil complained. "I told those assholes they were cutting too goddamned deep, but did they listen? I mean, what do I know; I've only worked this job for what, twenty years? Anyway, half the city's falling apart and they want to know why I haven't counted all the loose bricks and suddenly money is no object." He paused, catching his breath. "Within limits, you realize. I've still got a budget here."

"Same deal as last time?"

"Sure, and maybe a bonus, depending on what you find."

"So what do you want from me, Emil? Rats? Providence Hospital? Food poisoning? The Linden-Lorber bankruptcy? Mayor Laughey's campaign law violations? What?"

"Rats? That's small stuff. I got a guy covering the hospital already. I got more people with the Mayor's staff and with the Governor, watching them point fingers at each other, and I got a stringer hanging around the police station. You heard about the nurse who got murdered, right?"

"I read the paper, Emil. The *Register* in fact, honest. Anything new on that?"

Pause. "Keep this to yourself, Scapelli, but one of the patients did it. And she's gone missing."

Dan's psychic radar twitched but he didn't say anything.

"We got another peculiar murder downtown, some black guy got offed in a goddamned pet store while his girlfriend was maybe accidentally being run down by a van a block away. I also got seven restaurants closed because of food contamination, and sixteen cases of rabies scattered through the city, and that rest home on the north side where three people died a couple days back lost four more last night."

Dan suddenly realized why the people at *Green Pastures* had seemed even more irritable than usual that morning.

"On top of that, we're getting calls that all the goddamned goldfish and canaries on the East Side are dying in their goddamned cages, and three florists claim someone polluted their goddamned water or something because all their stock died and wilted overnight. Should I go on?"

"I get the picture, Emil. So like I said, what do you want me to do?"

"Got a pencil? Ok, here's the names of the restaurants that got problems. Try them first; see if you can get anything from the owners, a common supplier or something. They're being pretty closemouthed but you've got charm, right? If that doesn't pan out, call me back and I'll give you the rabies story."

"Will do."

Dan spent the balance of the afternoon trying to arrange interviews with people who welcomed any kind of publicity except stories about food poisoning. "Look," one woman told him. "If there was a murder on the dance floor, a juicy sex scandal in the function rooms, a spy working undercover as a waiter, or even if some Mafia boss was seen eating in the place, I'd give you whatever you want. People would come just to say they were in the same place, you know what I mean? But this? All I can tell you is, we've met or exceeded every health and safety standard and we're convinced that the fault lies with one of our vendors. We're temporarily closed as a precaution for the safety of our customers and we'll reopen as soon as the source of the problem is identified. Otherwise, no comment."

Nor was the health department any more forthcoming. "We are not at liberty to release information about an ongoing investigation other than what was contained in the official statement issued last evening. At the present time, I am unable to tell you when we'll have more facts to release, but when we do, we will be happy to provide a copy of the text to all press representatives. Given the sensitive nature of the issue, I'm sure you can understand why we need to be cautious."

Dan called Emil and summarized what he had found out. It didn't take very long. "All right, c'mon in and write up what you've got. It's better than nothing, and at least I can point to it and say I did something. There've been a couple more rabies cases this past hour, and the entire stock of a pet store had to be put down, so maybe you can shake something loose there." He paused. "Damn! I just realized it's the same goddamned pet store where that guy got himself killed. They'll never open again, not in this city."

Dan tried to sound casual. "Want me to look into it?"

"Naw, I've got Pendleton on that one already. Might be a coincidence."

"Awful lot of coincidences lately."

"Yeah, too many."

"Might be a story in that."

Emil grunted. "I got too many stories already. You gonna make our deadline?"

Dan used one of the idle computers at the *Register* office to turn his notes into usable copy, as well as to produce an invoice for his services. Emil scanned the story and accepted it with a grunt, initialed the invoice and handed it back, then asked if Dan might be interested in further assignments.

"Sure."

"Check your phone messages then, if I don't catch you in. I can't promise a goddamned thing, but there's a funny smell in the air and I might be able to send some work your way."

Rachel Darian's moans were deep and constant but not loud enough to be heard outside the storm drain. Her body jerked with each powerful contraction, and they were coming at rapidly decreasing intervals. At times the pain was so intense that she beat at the packed earth above her head with clenched fists. Chunks of moist dirt broke loose and fell into her matted hair and her open mouth. Her pale skin was slick with sweat and she resembled an oversized maggot struggling through its metamorphosis into a fly.

At a few minutes after nine o'clock Wednesday evening, Rachel Darian gave birth. She was barely conscious at the time, her senses dulled by pain and fatigue, her mind so broken by her experience that she no longer thought of herself as an individual. The living thing that crawled out from between her thighs after biting through its own umbilical cord resembled neither of its parents.

It had four limbs, but they were neither arms nor legs but rather a compromise between the two, articulated almost identically, so that the body hung suspended like that of a crippled spider. Each digit was tipped with a thick nail that could almost have been a claw. Its tail was short and stubby and served no obvious purpose, but if it was vestigial it was still certainly more pronounced than a human coccyx. The head was mounted on a short, powerful neck, entirely hairless, the eyes lidded with thick nictitating membranes. Like its father, the nose had only a single nostril, but it was broad and flat, almost invisible in the wide, inhuman face. The lower jaw was massive, filled with short but very sharp teeth. Its entire body was completely with dark, overlapping scales and its overall appearance was more reptilian than mammalian.

The only thing Rachel remained aware of in the moments directly following the birth was the sudden easing of the terrible pain of the past twelve hours. The respite was brief. Her breasts had enlarged beyond her fondest dreams while she lay in the storm drain, the skin stretched so taut that it had become transparent. If she'd been able to see herself, she would have noticed a constant stirring behind that flimsy barrier, as tiny white worms no longer than a fingernail pushed their way through the yellowish fluid that contained them, boiling outward from within her body.

Rachel cried out as her child crawled up onto her thighs, then inched forward awkwardly, the tips of its nails digging into her flesh as it sought to nurse. She closed her eyes and arched her back, crying out when it lunged forward and began to suckle on her left breast. Needle sharp teeth pierced her flesh and hot, acrid fluid began to spurt through the ruptures. Mercifully she lost consciousness before the newborn creature, still unsated, turned to the other breast.

When she opened her eyes an hour later, Rachel was alone. More of the dirt ceiling had collapsed, and she had to struggle for several minutes before she broke free, and fell into the storm drain. She was weak, drained of energy, light headed, and the pain had returned, more generalized now, spread evenly from her knees up through her torso. Gore was smeared across her chest and stomach, and the smell of blood was mixed with something even less wholesome, the odor of festering wounds and rotted flesh. At the same time, she felt an overpowering hunger, or perhaps it was thirst; she had trouble differentiating between the two drives. She crawled along the storm drain until she reached the opening, then climbed outside and with great effort rose to her feet.

She stood without moving for several minutes, trying to gather what remained of her strength and reorient herself in the darkness. Shreds of her old personality had re-emerged, although they were so fragmented that she was incapable of speech and almost incapable of logical thought. All that mattered now was the craving, and finding the means to make it go away.

With considerable difficulty, she climbed up the embankment to the roadway, not far from an off ramp from the interstate. Two cars rushed past, their headlights spearing the night, but there was no indication that they had spotted the naked figure standing to one side. Rachel's body was so filthy and stained that she was barely visible in the darkness. She staggered across the highway in their wake, then descended the opposite embankment to a secondary road that wound away toward a brightly lit intersection lined with bars and grilles.

As she walked, Rachel's steps grew steadier, a sudden sense of purpose providing the impetus. In the distance, she saw two couples emerge from one of the bars, the taller of the women sporting a mane of artificially bright red hair. The foursome crossed the street and turned in her direction, talking animatedly among themselves. Rachel hesitated, then impulsively retreated into an unlit doorway, the entrance to a dry cleaning shop long since gone out of business.

The voices continued to grow louder and although she could no longer see the two couples, Rachel could tell they were quite close now. She had no plan, lacked the ability to contrive even a simple course of action, but instinct had taken over and she waited for her prey patiently, her fingers curling into claws.

It was the shorter of the two men who first caught sight of her out of the corner of one eye. He had turned his head and was opening his mouth to say something when she leaped for his throat.

He threw up his arm defensively. His companions were taken by such complete surprise that they stood frozen in place, unable to come to their friend's assistance. Rachel tore at his forearm with her nails, drawing blood before he could back away. The shock of pain was enough to overcome whatever scruples he might have had about striking a woman, and he responded with a clenched fist that glanced off the side of Rachel's cheek. She shrugged off the blow effortlessly, lurched forward and caught both of his forearms. With surprising ease, she pulled his arms down out of her way and leaned forward, her mouth open.

"What the fuck!" He tried to twist free, but one foot slipped on the broken sidewalk, and instead he fell onto his back. Rachel promptly threw herself on top of him, still trying to sink her teeth in his neck. One of the two women began screaming while the redhead looked as though she was going to faint. The second man finally recovered from his initial shock and grabbed her left arm, trying to pull her off his friend. Balked and enraged, Rachel reared up, bared her teeth at him, and that's when he first realized that she was nude, her body matted with filth and blood, her breasts torn open and hanging in ribbons down the front of her emaciated body. The realization stunned him long enough for her to make a fist and strike him directly in the groin. With a small sound of stunned surprise, he doubled over and collapsed to the pavement.

The other man took advantage of her momentary distraction to twist his body and kick himself free. He slid across the sidewalk on his backside, staring at his attacker with an expression of utter loathing. Rachel rose unsteadily to her feet, her face twisted into a mask of rage and desire.

More people were pouring out onto the street, drawn by the continuing screams. The redhead had recovered enough of her composure to rush over to a nearby car, and was now returning with a tire iron in one hand. Rachel ignored this threat, instead began to stagger toward her intended victim.

He tried to get up but she was on him before he could do so, her fingers digging into his shoulders as she forced him down onto the ground. Despite her deteriorating physical condition, there was still an incredible amount of strength in her muscles, and he could not break her grip as she lowered her head, mouth open to reveal a set of perfectly human but still dangerous teeth.

The tire iron smashed into the back of her head with stunning force. Rachel slumped forward and the man beneath her quickly rolled to one side, sliding free. She hadn't lost consciousness, but she was even more unsteady as she stood up and turned toward her new attacker. The redhead stood her ground, the tire iron at shoulder level, ready to strike again, but the fire that had sustained Rachel throughout the last few hours was already beginning to burn out. She bared her teeth once more, then turned and ran back toward the highway. No one followed her.

With increasing difficulty, Rachel retraced her steps, reached the mouth of the storm drain and crawled inside. The compulsion that had sustained her was nearly gone. Seconds after she had climbed back into the hollowed out earthen cave where her child had been born only an hour earlier, Rachel Darian lay back and closed her eyes.

She almost appeared to be at peace.

CHAPTER SIX: THURSDAY

Although they ate together Wednesday evening, Dan and Kelly were both preoccupied and decidedly not in a romantic mood. Kelly had just landed an interesting new assignment that would necessitate a visit to the John Oates Museum on the East Side, whose varied specialty collections included an enviable selection of works written during or about the early days of the Providence colony, including several hand written diaries. Dan, on the other hand, was trying to figure out how to further ingratiate himself with Emil at the *Register*. Although they embraced warmly after the dirty dishes were cleared away, Dan returned to his own apartment for the night.

Kelly left the building early the following morning while Dan was still in the shower. Although the library wasn't open until half past nine, she had a number of errands to run. Her aging Datsun was low on gas and she filled it up, wincing at the price posted on the pump, the first time she'd needed to do so in over a month, then stopped at the main post office to mail off several dozen solicitations for work she'd had printed a week earlier. When she reached the East Side, there was still half an hour to kill before the library opened, so she stopped for coffee and a donut at what was obviously a hangout for college students. Even then, she still had to wait briefly until the doors were officially opened.

The head librarian greeted Kelly warmly; she had visited on several occasions in the past, had once been a temporary employee helping catalog a large new collection they'd acquired. Although she rarely published anything under her own name, Kelly was well known among insiders as a minor authority on certain aspects of New England colonial history.

"Haven't seen you in a while, Kelly."

"I go where the job takes me, Stan." Stanley Johnson had been running the Oates Library for almost twenty years. "Hasn't been much call for your particular area of specialization lately. Most of my recent work has been market analysis, political research, and pop culture."

Johnson grimaced, furrowed eyebrows underlining an otherwise totally hairless skull. "You're wasting your talents, you know."

"So you keep telling me," she laughed.

"There's a position opening up here in a few months," he continued seriously. "Martha Wellesley is taking early retirement. I could almost guarantee you the position if you want it."

Kelly sighed. "I'd be climbing the walls within six months, Stan. You know that. Sure, I get some pretty boring assignments freelancing, but they never last very long and there's always something new coming up. Besides, what does it pay?"

He pursed his lips and mentioned a number.

She nodded. "Right, and Martha works what, a minimum of fifty hours per week?"

Johnson sighed. "You know I'd offer more if I could. Our budget seems to get tighter every year. The endowment keeps shrinking and fresh donations are smaller and harder to attract. We had to put new humidity control equipment in the sub-basement this year, and when they installed it, we found a number of faults in the foundation that will have to be taken care of sooner or later. We've got a leak in the roof, fortunately over one of the offices rather than the stacks, our telephone system is so old God could have called in the Ten Commandments, and we have four recently acquired collections in storage off the premises because we don't have the money to catalog them or the space to house them."

Kelly had heard a similar story last year and, although she was sympathetic, she didn't want to spend her day listening to Stan Johnson's problems.

"I need access to some of the restricted collections today."

Johnson shrugged at the change of subject. "Can't convince you, I gather. So it goes. Morgan's guarding the gates to the lower levels today; I'll tell him you're authorized, though I suspect you'd charm yourself past him anyway." He picked up the intercom. "And don't be such a stranger."

Kelly had a list of sources she wanted to consult, some of which were in the main stacks. She spent the morning skimming through histories, journals, and facsimile editions, ate a light lunch at a nearby coffee shop, though not the one she usually patronized. *Sandy's Sandwiches* had a notice on the front door advising the public that it had been closed by order of the Board of Health.

She had filled several dozen pages with notes by mid-afternoon, and had used all of her loose change making photocopies of selected documents. After a brief break during which she took a brisk walk around the block to clear her head, she returned and made her way to the rear of the ground floor, where a waist high wall barred access to the rear stairwell.

"Anybody home?"

An impressively overweight man in his late fifties emerged from a small office, blinked once, then broke into a broad smile. "Miss Marsh! We haven't seen you around here for ages."

"It's been awhile, Morgan. I hope you haven't rearranged things downstairs."

"Not me. But I think you'll find things stirred around a bit. We've had construction, you know." He pressed the buzzer that released the security gate and Kelly stepped through, letting it swing back into place behind her. "The basement lights are already on. Will you be using the sub-level?"

Kelly glanced at the sheet of paper on which she'd written the shelf locations of the items she wanted to examine. "I think so, depending on how much I have time to look at today. Dr. Johnson tells me you've had some work done down there as well."

Morgan frowned, his multiple chins creasing. "They made an awful mess. We had cloths thrown over everything, of course, and the more delicate items were locked away until they were done, but the dust got in everywhere. It should be all right now, though, but you'll have to turn on the lights on your way down. We keep them off most of the time to save electricity."

Kelly searched her memory. "The box at the top of the stairs?"

"That's right. Switches one to four. They're marked."

"I'll make out all right."

Kelly spent better than two hours in the first basement level, which held many of the actual physical records of the early townships in the southern half of the state. By the time she had finished, only three items remained on her list, all of which were in the sub-basement.

A modern door closed off the lowest level of the Oates Library, in which were kept the most fragile documents, maps, town charters, deeds of ownership, personal diaries and correspondence. She found the switch box and turned on the lights, which buzzed loudly as the fluorescents came to life, fragmenting but not eliminating the shadows.

Kelly started down the stairs.

Emil was even grumpier today than he'd been the day before. Word had leaked that many of the patients at Providence Hospital had contracted cholera or botulism, diseases supposedly known and controlled. Although most of the staff remained close mouthed, those who were willing to talk contradicted each other so regularly that it was impossible to get a clear picture of what was going on. The Center for Disease Control had sent an investigating team, but they were even less forthcoming, and the Governor's office was putting pressure on the media to keep a clamp on things to avoid causing "unnecessary alarm".

Dan spent most of the morning following up on the restaurant closings, which had now reached a total of twelve. Except for *Andy's Seaside*, they were all clustered in the College Hill area. Those of their competitors who remained open were reporting a decline rather than an increase in business. People apparently weren't willing to chance eating out on the East Side just now. Shortly before noon, Dan managed to corner an inspector for the Department of Health, who admitted that it was "quite a mess" before refusing to comment any further.

Dan tried to call several people he'd used as sources in the past, assuming that at least one of them might be willing to exchange a tip for a free lunch, but those he could reach were defensive and noncommittal, including the secretary he knew from Health and Human Services, the office manager at City Hall, and the Assistant Director of Security for the state legislature. Someone had put a very tight lid on things and people were afraid to talk.

A very harried Emil accepted what little information he could provide, approved his invoice, but could promise nothing further. "If you wanna look into any of this on your own and hit gold, we'll work something out. Right now, I've got nothing definite for you."

Discouraged, Dan called to see if Kelly had come home earlier than expected but her answering machine picked up. He replaced the receiver without leaving a message, then walked distractedly through downtown Providence. The city looked the same as it always did, but entirely different as well. There were fewer people on the sidewalks, and they moved quickly, alone or in small groups, staring almost warily at everyone they passed. The buildings and streets themselves seemed dirtier than usual, the gutters filled with windblown litter, the storefronts untidy. The sky had clouded over, although rain was not forecast, and although it remained hot, there was an unpleasantly cool, damp breeze. Almost slimy.

He suddenly felt an irresistible desire for human company and turned into the first open diner he reached, a narrow and not particularly clean looking coffee shop. The waitress who set his order on the counter wasn't particularly friendly, but at least she wore the sketch of a smile. The food, which he hadn't really wanted, was quite good, but he was so lost in his thoughts that the taste barely registered.

At the opposite end of the counter, a short haired woman in her late thirties sat slumped forward, leaning on her elbows, staring into the dregs of a cup of black coffee. Angela Harris had been a detective for the past four years, for most of which time she had been partnered with Vincent Marzocchi, not the worst she could have drawn, but not the best either. Marzocchi worked hard, but lacked initiative and imagination. He had worked out a system during his investigations and refused to vary from it even when it was obvious that a different approach would have helped. For his part, he'd been less than thrilled at drawing a woman for a partner, but had since recognized her talent and, although technically he was senior, he'd gotten into the habit of deferring to her if she took the lead.

Despite the many petty annoyances she experienced because she was a woman, Harris was essentially satisfied with her chosen career. There were frustrations and reversals, particularly because she hated to give up an unsolved case, and the department often lacked the resources to give every murder or robbery the kind of attention they received in television crime shows. She had trouble letting go of the cases where she'd failed. The money could also have been better, of course, and the hours were brutal, particularly this past week.

The murder of Dennis Kirk and the presumably related death of Dawn Reynolds were theoretically their primary assignments at the moment, but the situation at headquarters was growing chaotic. Lieutenant Mancini was out with food poisoning, Captain Pirelli hadn't returned to duty since his boating accident, and two other detectives were on protracted medical leave. Apparently at least one of the members of the search party had been carrying some sort of bug, because four of the cadets and three officers had fallen ill; Sergeant Krenkle had been hospitalized.

Of course, everything else started to go to hell at the same time. A full scale investigation was underway to determine whether the contaminated drugs at Providence Hospital were the result of negligence or of deliberate action, possibly terrorists. Homeland Security and the FBI were taking point on that one, at least theoretically, but they required a liaison and were empowered to draw upon local resources. Similarly, several of the restaurants whose customers had fallen ill insisted that their food supply had been deliberate contaminated and were demanding a more active investigation, although no one could suggest a credible suspect. Then there was the usual crop of burglaries, drug related violence, and a handful of nutty cases like last night's report that a naked woman had assaulted and badly injured a man in front of a bar.

She glanced at her watch. Marzocchi was supposed to be meeting her here before they left for their follow up interview with Jacob Kaplan, who was confined while undergoing treatment for rabies and nervous exhaustion. He was already five minutes late. Harris sighed, signaled for a fresh cup of coffee.

She had lived in Providence all her life. Unlike most of her high school classmates, she never intended to move away as soon as possible. She'd gotten her degree from Providence College, all three of her apartments had been inside the city limits, and she never even considered applying for a position with another police force. The rejuvenation of the downtown over the course of the last several years had made her proud of where she lived, and even the unsavory characters she had to deal with on a daily basis were unable to dampen her enthusiasm. The recent rash of crime was wearing, but she'd seen things get very busy before without letting it affect her mood. What bothered and discouraged her now was the way the entire city seemed to have slipped into an emotional decline. You could see it in people's faces, in their eyes. They were frightened, confused, and distrustful.

There had been no room in the newspapers these past few days for the less dramatic crimes, but assaults, burglaries, and DUIs had become so numerous during the last few days, it was almost as if they were being coordinated. Young hoodlums didn't even wait for darkness before pulling out a handgun in a convenience store. There had been a rash of hit and run accidents, at least a dozen bar fights just the previous evening, and an avalanche of calls about incidents of domestic violence or suspicious prowlers. There had also been a rash of reports of rabid dogs and other animals, and although most of these proved to be false alarms, some had been authentic, enough of them to keep the stress level high. "The whole damned city is going to hell," she muttered.

The waitress, who'd been refilling her cup, blinked. "What was that, ma'am?"

Harris shook her head. "Nothing. Thanks."

Even the coffee tasted off, not just bitter the way she liked it, but sour too, as though there was something funny in the water.

Kelly dropped her notebook in one of the small study carrels just inside the doorway. A few meters away stood the door to the vault, the climate controlled room where the more fragile and priceless of the library's stock was kept. It was closed, probably locked, at the moment, but she didn't need access to anything there. Off to her right, a section of shelving had been removed to lay bare one of the exterior walls. There was a walk space between it and the side of the vault, currently pitch dark although she could see where temporary lighting had been strung inside.

Despite the fluorescents mounted on the ceiling, the sub-basement was gloomy and ill-lit. The shelving units here were close together, filled nearly to capacity, and shadows overlapped one another on every side. Kelly consulted her notes for the shelf codes and retrieved the documents she wished to consult, then sat down at the relatively well illuminated carrel to complete her research. The last of these, a personal journal written in delicate longhand by an early 19th Century merchant, was so interesting that she became caught up in it, continued to read long after she'd finished taking notes.

She didn't look up until she was distracted by the sound of a small thud somewhere in the sub-basement.

Kelly looked up from the journal, puzzled rather than alarmed, waiting for the sound to repeat. After a few seconds, she heard what sounded like the rustle of cloth, but it lasted for only a second or two and she couldn't positively identify it or locate the source. She closed the journal and set it down on the desk, then rose to her feet.

There was another thump, this one louder, as though a book had fallen from a shelf.

Kelly was quite certain that she was alone and that what she had heard had been exactly what it seemed, perhaps an improperly shelved volume finally succumbing to the effect of countless tiny vibrations until it overbalanced and slid down to lie flat on its shelf. Curious, she walked to the side of the vault, turning her head as she tried to recall from which direction the sound had originated.

She was half determined to forget the whole thing when it happened again, another distinct thud, softer but quite specific. Her curiosity fully aroused, she moved forward, then turned to walk along the side of the vault, scanning one row of shelves after another as she did so. She had almost reached the rear wall of the sub-basement when she detected movement.

It was just a flicker, a hair below eye level, behind a double row of leather bound journals. Kelly grew much more cautious, suspecting that a bat or a rat had somehow gotten in, perhaps through one of the holes the construction crew had dug into the cement walls to run power lines from the upper floors. With the rash of recent rat sightings still fresh in her memory, she wasn't about to charge in recklessly, but she still wanted to know what she was dealing with before reporting it to the staff upstairs.

She was pretty sure the sound had come from the very last free standing row of shelves at the far end of the room. Kelly looked around for something to use as a weapon if the need arose, finally picked up a small wooden stool and held it pressed against her chest. Moving very cautiously, she edged her way along until she could turn and stare down into the dimness.

Two slim, oversized volumes were lying on the floor; three shelves up, three more were lying flat but skewed so that they extended precipitously out beyond the edge of the shelf. Somewhat relieved, Kelly closed the distance quickly and reached out with her left hand to push the dangerously balanced volumes back into place.

Something small and dark burst from cover behind a row of books, raced along the shelf for a meter or so, then froze, hissing warningly. Kelly only needed one quick look at that long, tapering tail to know she had indeed discovered a rat. Still holding the stool, she began to back away. This was the library's problem, after all; let them call the exterminators.

When she felt the wall of the vault at her back, she relaxed slightly. Her research was finished, so she could simply gather up her material and leave, letting Stan or one of the other staff members know what she had discovered. It was later than she thought, she realized, glancing at her watch, almost seven o'clock. In fact, Dan was probably wondering what had happened to her. They had tentatively planned to eat at her place this evening. Neither of them had any intention of dining out until the rash of food poisoning was over.

But when Kelly turned toward the exit, she discovered that she had attracted more company. Two rats stood on the floor less than three meters away, blocking her escape route, and both clearly were aware of her presence. Their heads were turned in her direction as their tails moved slowly back and forth over the rough, cement floor. A split second after she saw them, she caught movement out of the corner of her eye, saw a furtive shape moving on one of the shelves further along and above her head. Another emerged from hiding in the far corner, leaping from one shelf to another, and the sound of more tiny running feet came from somewhere out of her line of sight.

With both hands tightly clenching the legs of the stool, she extended it away from her body. "Shoo!" She felt foolish as soon as she spoke, but neither of the rats confronting her seemed impressed; they continued to watch her with steady, unfrightened eyes.

The stool had a comfortingly solid feel; its top was a thick circle of real wood, the legs inset and braced with crosspieces. Kelly waved it warningly as she advanced, hoping and expecting that the rats would abandon the field of battle. Unfortunately, they seemed to be behaving very atypically. Both of her original adversaries raised their heads warily at her approach, but neither gave any ground, and they were joined now by a third, who watched Kelly cautiously but with no evidence of alarm. There was more scurrying in the shadows and Kelly glanced nervously around, but quickly brought her eyes back to the more immediate danger. She didn't want to think about how many of them might be gathering just out of sight.

"Back off fellows, I'm warning you." Kelly found her own

voice reassuring. One rat rose onto its back legs, and for a split second bared its teeth menacingly. There was a subtle change in the posture of the other two, but it was the first and largest of the three that suddenly sprinted toward her.

Kelly gasped, but instinctively raised her makeshift weapon and brought it down with all the strength she could muster. The edge of the seat slammed into the center of its back, pinning it to the floor. Kelly pushed down to hold it there as it scrabbled desperately, glaring up at her. As soon as she was sure it could not get free, she lifted her eyes to check on the other two. One had run off somewhere out of sight and the other had not moved, but two more were calmly walking out from behind the corner of the vault and turning in her direction.

She knew she couldn't remain crouched as she was, so she stood up abruptly, raising the stool for another blow. It was unnecessary; the rat's back was broken. It began to crawl toward her, pulling with its forelegs while the back ones moved spastically and to no purpose, its teeth bared. There was a smear of blood under its body.

There was a burning sensation in the back of her throat, but Kelly choked down the bile and moved forward, avoiding the disabled rat and waving the stool at the others. The three visible ones all retreated beyond her reach, although none of them showed any sign of panic. Her notebooks were of no importance any longer; she simply wanted to reach the stairs unmolested and escape.

Halfway there, she looked to her right. At least half a dozen pairs of eyes were staring at her from scattered locations in the stacks and she could hear more of them moving in the gloom. There were five on the floor in front of her now, two more having arrived while she was looking elsewhere. Presumably the new construction had given them access to the basement. They couldn't have been here for long, or evidence of their presence would have shown up earlier.

Kelly feinted several times with the stool as she moved toward the stairs. Sometimes they retreated a few paces, more often they stared at her curiously but with no evident alarm. She was at a loss to understand why they were behaving so aggressively.

A few steps short of the staircase, Kelly thought she'd gotten past them all. Just as she was about to throw away the stool and run up to the next level, a small dark shape leaped from the top shelf of the closest bookcase. Kelly caught the movement out of the corner of one eye, flinched away, raising the stool and swinging it wildly. There was a jarring impact and she almost lost her grip, but the rat's leap was deflected and it struck the floor and skidded away.

She didn't wait to see what would happen next. She dropped the stool, turned and started to climb, pulling herself up with the handrail, not looking back to see if she was being followed.

Dozens of tiny claws moved in the murkiness below.

Evan Graham searched the shadows, hoping to find a new face. He'd already visited most of the more likely locations, several pickup bars, Sturtevant Street, the *Sundowner Club*, but all he'd seen was the usual mix of prostitutes, both professional and amateur, some of them dope addicts as well. Evan was a regular customer, so regular in fact that he knew many of the women he encountered by name as well as by sight, or at least the names they used when they were working. His sexual adventures were rarely imaginative, but occasionally he decided to find a new partner, and his hunting ground had been extended to include the entire city of Providence and most of the surrounding area, at least those neighborhoods where some kind of nightlife existed.

Tonight he was particularly restless. He'd been approached by several of his former "dates", but he hadn't been interested in a repeat performance with any of them. Tonight he craved novelty. It had been a hell of a day; the market had taken an unexpected downward plunge that had cost him, on paper at least, nearly a quarter of a million dollars. The fact that this left him with a balance not quite ten times that amount did little to sweeten his sour mood; Evan's investments had grown steadily since he had resigned from a brokerage house ten years earlier, a few days shy of his twenty fifth birthday. A combination of skill, luck, insider information, and a hefty amount of investment capital willed to him when his parents died had made Evan Graham one of the richest men in the state, a fact that he carefully concealed from his neighbors and acquaintances. Evan had no friends.

He drove past the Marriott and turned toward the East Side. There was a darkly lit club up near the Brown University campus where he'd picked up a coed from time to time in the past. Evan was normally wary of rank amateurs; they were too unpredictable. On one occasion, he'd been forced to prevent a liberal arts major from slashing her wrists in the bathroom at his apartment, and a self proclaimed anarchist had tried to roll him when they'd taken a motel room together. In general they wanted to talk too much, and demanded more in bed than the basic style he preferred. Sometimes both at the same time.

At the summit of College Hill, he started watching for a parking space, finally pulled in to the curb in front of a large brick building currently undergoing a facelift. Two blocks down he entered the club, which was unusually empty, even for a Thursday night. There were a few couples sitting at scattered tables in the gloom, another pair dancing to the music from a digital jukebox, a handful of people sitting at the bar. Evan crossed the room, avoided taking a seat, and ordered a beer while surreptitiously checking out the clientele.

There were three women who appeared to be unaccompanied, one a perennial drinker he'd seen before, a painfully unattractive young woman who glared whenever anyone brushed against her but who never seemed to speak except when ordering a drink. Of the two remaining, one was a doper, pretty in a vapid sort of way. Evan had picked her up on two previous occasions, during one of which she'd fallen asleep in his bedroom and ended up spending the night, much to his annoyance. Tonight she appeared too stoned even to recognize her surroundings. The remaining woman was a stranger to him, mildly attractive, and he was considering an approach when a burly young man with curly hair emerged from the men's room and crossed to her side. They were obviously together.

Evan took his time over the beer, watching to see if anyone else would show up, but when he had finished, the clientele remained unchanged and he left a generous tip and walked outside.

Despite the heat of the day, the night was chill and wet, clammy in fact, but it seemed appropriate to his mood. There were a few more places he might be able to score, but the thought of chasing around further that evening depressed him and he slowly began to resign himself to an evening of chastity. Patches of fog were moving in from the river, looking almost artificial as they gobbled up the landscape.

Evan decided to take the long way back to his car. Walking

was no substitute for sex, but it would help to settle his nerves. Picking a direction almost at random, he started off into the darkness.

Ten minutes later, he came to an abrupt stop, inexplicably convinced that he was no longer alone. He stood on a well maintained sidewalk at the corner of two residential streets, the houses largely hidden in the thickening fog. Cars had been passing him with some regularity despite the lateness of the hour and it was a fairly public place, but he still felt unsettled. He'd been mugged twice in his life, once in Boston, once in New York City, but even though he had always considered Providence a far safer city, he was well aware of the fact that such things could happen anywhere, at any time.

There were no pedestrians in sight at the moment. He listened intently, but all he could hear was the whispering of leaves brushing against each other, the distant sound of traffic, a radio playing inside one of the houses. He read the street signs, mentally reviewed a map of the East Side as he plotted the most direct route back to his parked car. His desire to walk alone in the darkness was now satisfied. Once he had oriented himself, he turned left and set off quickly but without panic.

And almost immediately spotted the woman who was standing silently under the arch of a gate, watching him.

The gate was wrought iron, hung between two concrete pillars, recessed half a meter from the sidewalk. The watcher, who appeared to be in her early twenties, was standing there in the shadows, motionless, wearing a strangely cut jet black dress that was almost a sarong and which clung tightly to her body from ankle to throat to wrist. If it had been a heavier material, it would have been stiflingly hot, but it was clearly flimsy, perhaps silk, and it was a perfect match to her long fall of black hair. The light from a nearby street lamp fell between two branches of a tree and across her face, and her pale white skin was a sharp contrast to the clothing, accented in turn by a bright purplish red slash of lips. Her features were vaguely oriental, he thought, perhaps Pakistani or even Egyptian. And then he realized that he'd stopped short directly in front of her.

"Sorry," he said gruffly. "I didn't mean to stare. You caught me by surprise."

She stepped, or rather glided, forward so that the spill of light widened to include her breasts and shoulders. Evan licked his lips unconsciously, felt his sexual desire resurgent. His previous uneasiness had been completely forgotten.

"Uhhh, you really shouldn't be out here alone this late at night, miss. There's been some trouble in the area lately." Which was true; there had been a rash of minor assaults and even a few rapes.

The woman continued to watch him silently, lowered her head for a moment, then raised it after what was quite clearly a frank appraisal. Evan felt his self confidence return. "If you'd like, I'd be happy to walk you to wherever you're going. My name's Evan, Evan Graham." He was mildly surprised to discover that he'd used his real name; to most of the women he'd dealt with professionally, he was known as Kevin Carlisle. He reached forward to shake hands.

The woman recoiled just perceptibly, then raised her hand to her lips, shook her head clearly and negatively. Evan blinked, confused for a second, then realized the woman was indicating she was mute. That took him by surprise, and it might even have put him off under other circumstances. But this one was a real looker, and when he stopped to think about it, a woman who couldn't speak struck him as embodying the best of all possible worlds, particularly when the woman looked like this, and clearly acted as though she were interested.

Ten minutes later, she was sitting beside him as he pulled away from the curb and started toward his house, just over a mile away.

Evan took considerable pride in his home. It was small, brick fronted, set toward the rear of a half acre lot not far from Swan Point Cemetery at the north end of Blackstone Boulevard. He'd done most of the landscaping himself, which included fairly elaborate gardens and meticulously pruned shrubbery, quince, mock orange, forsythia, lilacs, and mountain laurel. The garage door opened when he tapped the remote and was already closing as they stepped out of the car. He managed to brush his hand against the woman's fingers as he unlocked the door to the house proper, recoiled from the lack of warmth he felt there.

"We'd better get you inside where it's warm. You've picked up quite a chill." She gave him an enigmatic look, then waited until he'd stepped through the doorway and turned on the lights. "Come on in," he said cheerily. "You don't have to wait for a formal

102

invitation." At this last, she smiled warmly and, he thought, rather lewdly, her face promising the rewards that her tightly wrapped body were already advertising.

She entered the house.

Evan offered her a drink, which she declined with a small but distinct movement of her head. He was a bit spooked by her silence, but titillated at the same time. She was an undeniably attractive woman, and the urge to get her to the bedroom grew so powerful he felt a physical pain between his legs.

As if she had read his mind, or more likely his body language, the mysterious woman slowly looked around, then walked through the living room, unerringly locating the master bedroom. Evan took a moment to drop his wallet and Rolex into a lockbox disguised as a dictionary before following.

"I don't suppose there's any way you can tell me your name?" But the words were barely out of his mouth before she had wrapped two surprisingly strong arms around his shoulders and covered his mouth with her own. Somehow she had managed to shed her clothing during the few seconds she'd been out of sight, and the brief glance he'd been afforded of her body exceeded his most optimistic estimation. Her aggressiveness surprised him, but not necessarily unpleasantly. Under normal circumstances, he preferred to initiate the action, but occasionally he chose a different role. He wrapped his own arms around the small of her back, noticed again how chilled her flesh had become in the night air, dismissed the thought as she maneuvered him over to the bed.

He fell backwards and she followed him down, her tongue exploring the inside of his mouth. This wasn't a new experience for him, but something felt odd, as though her tongue was not quite the right shape, and he wondered if it might be deformed, if that might be the reason she had been deprived of the power of speech. But rational thought was fleeing fast now as he drank in the sensation of her presence, the press of her body against his own, not heavy exactly but firm and powerful. He felt her hand at his pants, opening the belt and the fly, and arched his back so that she could ease them down over his hips. It never occurred to him to wonder how she could have gotten a hand free, since both of her arms were still wrapped around his upper torso.

If he'd had the opportunity to look into the mirror at the end of the room and see the reflection of what he really embraced rather than the projected image overlaying the reality, Evan would have realized the seriousness of his error sooner.

   She lowered her body over his erection and it was a cold fire of ecstasy burning through his loins. At the same time he felt his mouth starting to go numb as her tongue darted about, the sensation almost like novocaine, except that it was a delightfully peaceful numbness that spread up into his brain, lulling him into a detached state of near orgasm. Evan closed his eyes and moaned, head back, his arms releasing their grip and he lay limply on the bed. He never even noticed when she slowly drew back, withdrawing her tongue, rising from his body, carefully sliding back past his still rampant penis. As she did so, the illusion slowly faded, and if he'd looked toward her, he would have seen a face pockmarked by running sores, a face that was neither male nor female nor in fact human at all. The deformed head darted forward and down, driving three fangs deep into the flesh just above his testicles.

   Evan's body convulsed, no longer able to distinguish between pleasure and pain, and there was a futile spray of his own semen, the last orgasm he would ever experience. But not even that release could waken him from the trance into which he'd fallen, and when the other figure had finished its task and withdrawn from the house, Evan Graham remained lost in another world, whose only feature was a burning, destructive pleasure.

CHAPTER SEVEN: FRIDAY

Dan and Kelly slept together Thursday night, in her apartment, but they didn't made love. He'd arrived to find her still shaking with reaction from her encounter in the library sub-basement, and although she related the entire sequence of events in a steady voice and with no hint of hysteria, he knew her well enough by now to realize how shaken she was. Talking about it seemed to calm her down, and when she finally began to act more normally, he told her about his own relatively uneventful day, hoping to take her mind off her experience. Although she seemed more relaxed, he could tell that she was still stressed because she twice allowed a cup of coffee to grow cold without finishing it. Until now, he'd never known her to let one sit long enough to stop steaming.

They eventually moved to her bedroom where she asked to be held for awhile and they subsequently fell asleep wrapped in each other's arms. When he opened his eyes the following morning, she had managed to quietly extricate herself and was, as usual, up and about while he was still slumbering away.

"How do you manage to survive with so little sleep?" He stumbled out into the living room to find her typing away at her keyboard. "You couldn't have been out more than, what, six hours?"

She turned to answer him without removing her hands from the keys. "Most people sleep a third of their lives away; I'm trying to cut it to a quarter. I figure I pick up about forty days per year. That's like adding seven or eight years to a normal lifespan." She grinned at him before turning back to her work. "You, on the other hand, seem more likely to lose twenty days or so."

"Sleep is my reward for working hard when I'm awake."

"Not much of a prize if you're not conscious to enjoy it."

He crossed to her side, and ran the fingers of his right hand through her hair. "I can think of a better one."

This time she stopped typing and turned to face him, the grin more mischievous. "What have you done lately to deserve such a prize?"

"I think I've been a good boy."

"Maybe we should find out just how good."

An hour later, they were sitting at the kitchen table, drinking coffee, listening to the radio. "I don't know, Kelly. Maybe we should get out of town for a few days."

"You think it's that bad?"

Dan shrugged. "You heard the radio. Hospitals and emergency rooms overwhelmed with people carrying contagious diseases, rabid animals running loose, three fatal shootings last night alone. There's already been a run on the grocery stores; I tried to pick up a few things on the way home last night and even the pet aisle was half empty."

Kelly stared down into her cup. "To say nothing of rats in the basements. Yeah, something's going on all right. What's happening, Dan? Why all of this at once? There's got to be some connection."

Dan was massaging his unshaven chin. "Damned if I know. I talked to Mel Hollins yesterday and he says some of the doctors are talking deliberate sabotage. The CDC has a crowd here already and more are coming. Half the people I've talked to think some terrorist group is responsible and the rest are convinced some secret government germ warfare project is responsible. The Governor is considering declaring a state of emergency, the National Guard is on alert and Emil at the *Reporter* tells me FEMA has sent a small advanced team. But most of my usual sources aren't talking, not even off the record. It's creepy."

Kelly was thoughtful for several seconds, but at least she shook her head. "I don't know, Dan. I don't like the idea of being driven out of my home." She made an expansive gesture with her hands. "I mean, I know it's not much and it's a mess most of the time, but this is me, almost as much as my body is. I'm for sticking it out, at least until things get a lot worse than they are already."

"I guess I feel the same way. All right, but we eat canned food and stay out of dark basements."

"What about the water?" She pointed at his coffee cup. "Maybe that's how the germs or whatever are spreading."

"Hmmm, good thought. I'll pick up some bottled water for drinking while I'm out today, just in case."

"Where are you going?"

" Hollins tells me there's something fishy going on with a couple of bodies that were just autopsied. No one's talking about that either and even Mel doesn't know the details, but he did get me the names of the police officers assigned to the case. The detectives don't usually want to talk to reporters but I might try running them down. There are still a couple of restaurant people I haven't spoken to yet, but I don't think they're likely to know any more than the others."

"Do you suppose it really is some kind of terrorist attack?"

"I suppose it's possible. But why Providence, for God's sake?

"Why not, if it's just a test for something bigger??"

"I have no idea. Listen, I need to get shaved and dressed and on the road." He stood up. "You're staying home today, aren't you?"

Kelly nodded. "I might pick up a few groceries down the street, but I've got plenty of work to keep me busy here." In the front room, the notebooks that Stan Johnson had recovered from the sub-basement sat on her desk beside the computer. "Plague or no plague, I still have to pay the bills, and this project is on a tight schedule."

"Okay, look, I'll call around noon and let you know what's going on." He walked around the room divider and crossed to the door as Kelly rose and half followed him, leaning on the counter top with folded arms.

"Hey, Scapelli!" She called softly and, when he turned to look back, "Watch yourself out there."

Dan was only half shaven when his telephone rang. He set down the safety razor and left the bathroom, foam still covering one cheek and his jaw.

"Yes," he held the phone an inch away from his mouth.

"Dan, is that you?"

"Yes it is, Mel. What's up?"

"They just brought in another body. I haven't seen it, but I guess it's pretty messed up. Even the paramedics looked pretty rocky and they're used to some pretty bad shit."

"Another plague victim?"

"I don't know. I hear it washed out of a sewer or a water main or something and some passing motorist spotted it."

"Sounds like a homeless person, Mel. Sad, but there's a lot of bad things happening lately. What's so special?"

"It wasn't a he, Dan. It was a young girl."

"Rape victim?"

"I told you, I don't know. But Dr. Marin was on duty when she came in and he recognized the body. It's Rachel Darian, the patient who disappeared the night the Sandford woman was killed."

Dan's free hand rose to massage his chin, even though it was still half covered with shaving cream. "All right, Mel, I'll come down as soon as I can. I'll probably have trouble getting past security, though. The guards have been a little edgy about letting me in lately."

"Doyle's on duty. I'll talk to him."

"Okay, thanks a lot."

Evan Graham's house was silent and dark when the sun came up, and it remained silent all of that day. Graham's car was parked in the garage, his big screen television and high performance stereo system were powered down, and no one used the shower, stove, exercise machine, sauna, microwave, or computer. If anyone had listened in, the only sounds they would have heard would have been the settling of the building, the on and off cycling of the thermostatically controlled central air conditioning, the occasional clicking of the refrigerator, and the faintest whisper of human breathing from the bedroom.

Graham lay virtually motionless all day, eyes closed, chest rising and falling ever so gently, nude and semi-conscious, lost in a dreamlike state that suppressed personality and emotion. He had become virtually a prisoner in his own body, his will partitioned off in one small corner of his mind. Evan himself was the only thing that changed during the course of the day. His abdomen was already slightly swollen when the sun came up, a mound of skin stretched taut except where it was puckered up around three small, triangular wounds. The swelling grew progressively larger and had reached the size of an apple by noon time. His internal organs were pushed away into a new configuration within his body, making room for what was growing there, a transformation for which his body was not well suited. But it would suffice.

Although the guard at the staff entrance looked harried and irritable, he nodded when Dan told him he had dropped by to see Mel Hollins. "I know you're okay, Mr. Scapelli," his voice was hoarse, "but there are a lot of outside people, government people, in the building. It'd be best if you stayed out of their way, if you know what I mean."

Dan did indeed and promised to be careful.

Ten minutes later, a very drawn looking Mel was ushering him into a storage room filled with enigmatic equipment arranged neatly in rows and on shelves, most of it covered with translucent plastic.

"This place is going crazy again today," Mel advised him. "Now we have contractors poking into the corners. They're planning to install a whole new security system, pass cards, more cameras, the whole works."

"Doesn't surprise me. Are they still thinking sabotage?"

"Yeah. The contamination was in too many different places to be an accident. We had bad medication everywhere, most of it still sealed. Almost the entire blood supply was affected, whole, plasma, the works. And not all the blood came from a single source, and none of the other hospitals supplied experienced any problem." He shook his head. "Anyway, they've got full time guards posted everywhere and it's no secret they're doing background checks on everyone who's working here, and probably the patients as well."

Dan glanced around. "Would you feel more comfortable if we talked outside the hospital? I don't want to get you into any trouble, Mel."

"No, that's all right. I don't like going outside much lately. Too many things can happen to you, if you know what I mean. At least in here, I know where to find a doctor if I need one."

"I don't suppose there's any way I could see the body?"

The other man looked horrified. "No way. I had trouble getting into the morgue myself, and I was supposed to be there."

"But you've seen the body?"

Mel nodded. "I wish I hadn't though. I don't know what killed her, but some kind of animal must've gone after the body. Her abdomen was ripped open and the...baby...was gone, placenta and all. Plenty of internal damage. Her breasts were missing too, and there were teeth and claw marks from her shoulders to her waist. Rats, maybe, or even dogs. Probably ate the parts that were missing."

Mel was visibly shaken and Dan decided maybe it was just as well that he couldn't see the body himself. "Do they have an official cause of death yet?"

"No, not yet. Two uniformed cops were with the paramedics when they brought her in, but a few minutes later, the detectives showed up with lots of questions no one could answer. They're trying to schedule an autopsy for later today but," he shrugged, "things are pretty busy here and the patients who're still alive are getting priority."

"So the girl is dead, the virgin pregnancy has come to an end, and the nurse's murder will probably never be solved. I don't suppose you got the names of the two detectives?"

"One of them's Harris, the woman. I never heard the guy's name. But there's more."

Dan raised one eyebrow. "More?"

Mel licked his lips. "Look, Dan, this could cost me my job but I owe you big time for helping out my sister."

"You don't owe me anything for that, Mel. Your sister is a class act; she just wobbled a bit there under pressure, and I was glad to be able to help out. Whatever passes between you and me is business, pure and simple, and I pay for value received."

"Yeah, well, I don't know that I even want to get paid for this one." He licked his lips again and glanced around nervously. "I'm not so sure I even want to know about it."

"About what?" Dan prompted when Mel seemed to have drifted off into his own thoughts.

"Sorry, I'm just tired." He pinched the bridge of his nose. "Dr. Marin came into the staff lounge after the police were gone. I was the only one there and when I saw his hands were shaking so bad that he spilled his coffee, I asked if he was all right. Marin's not the friendliest guy on the staff, but he's a rock, you know? Never gets upset, never flustered. When he works in the ER, you'd think he was tending a garden or something. Anyway, he looks at me and shakes his head and starts telling me about the conversation he had with the detectives. I was kind of surprised because he's never done that before but it was like he had to talk about it or he'd burst."

"So what'd he say?" asked Dan after Hollins lapsed into another silence.

"Marin says the police let slip that the body showed up not far from where a naked woman attacked some people, then ran off. One of them had a sketch of the attacker and wanted to compare it to the body, so Marin brought them down to see the body. Their theory is that the Darian girl went crazy, found herself a place to hide during the day, and went looking for something to eat at night. But she was too weak by then to do much and she crawled into that storm drain and died, hopefully before the rats and dogs got to her."

Dan nodded. "Sounds plausible to me. It still doesn't explain the pregnancy or what drove her crazy in the first place, but that's not their problem."

"No, but Marin had already done a preliminary examination of the body. He says the damage was even worse than it looked, and it looked pretty bad. All of the internal organs in her lower torso are damaged, most of the lower intestine is gone, and her breasts look like they were torn right off. There's no way she could've been walking around with injuries like that. The shock and blood loss would've killed her in minutes, if not seconds."

Dan shook his head. "You're assuming all of the wounds were inflicted at the same time. Probably most of the damage was done after she showed up at the nightclub, not before."

Hollins shook his head. "Marin says otherwise. The witnesses all describe the woman that attacked them as skinny, flat bellied. So the baby was already gone by then, and most of the internal ruptures and tears were older than those on the womb."

Dan was silent for a few seconds. "And you're saying that she couldn't have been walking around in that condition."

"That's right."

"Marin might be mistaken."

"Maybe." Hollins didn't sound convinced. He shook his head. "That's probably what the police think. And he didn't tell him his other conclusion, because he knew they'd laugh at him. He said that based on the tissue degeneration and other evidence, he concluded that Rachel Darian has been dead since some time Tuesday night."

Frowning, Dan filled in the timeline in his head. "That's the night she disappeared from the hospital, isn't it?"

"Got it in one. And that means...?"

"That means there's no way she could have attacked anyone on Wednesday night. Either Marin's wrong, or despite the identification, there was another naked woman running around Providence."

"Another naked woman with her breasts torn off who just happens to fit the same description?"

"Well, then, Marin's wrong. It wouldn't be the first time a doctor made a mistake, and you said he was under a great deal of pressure."

Mel nodded. "Maybe you're right; maybe Marin's not as smart as his reputation says he is. But I know him, Dan, and I talked to him, and he is one scared man."

Kelly worked without a break until noontime, at which point she rose and stretched while trying to decide what to have for lunch. Despite Dan's admonition to stick to canned food, she poked through the freezer and found a package of tiny frozen shrimp, which she then mixed with a pre-packaged spicy rice concoction and heated on the stove. She poured herself a tall glass of pink grapefruit juice and sipped some of it while she was waiting for her lunch to be ready.

The view from her kitchen window was not an enviable one. This side of the apartment building faced a residential area dominated by two and three story houses with virtually no yards, many of them lacking even a driveway. It was neither the richest nor the poorest part of the city, and while many of the early warning signs of decay were visible at ground level, from this height she couldn't really see the cracking paint, crumbling facades, missing shingles, untended gardens, cracked window panes, or the trash that had begun to accumulate in neglected corners of the property. There was no pride of community here; most of the residents were either young and considered this a temporary situation, or retired and living on a fixed income. Only a few residents actually owned their homes; most had been divided up into tiny apartments.

Traffic was unusually light today, and there were few pedestrians in sight. Those whom she could see walked alone, and quickly, as though they were only outside by necessity and wished to be done with their business as quickly as possible. There were no children playing in the abandoned lot that served as the neighborhood's "park". The sun was intensely bright overhead, the humidity was comparatively low, and it should have been one of the most pleasant days of the summer. Kelly stood in her window for a long time, wondering where everybody was, finally roused from her reverie by the PING of the stove clock telling her that lunch was ready.

When Dan called a few minutes later to tell her he was going to try to arrange an interview with a Detective Angela Harris of the Providence Police, Kelly felt an almost overpowering urge to ask him to come back to the apartment, to tell him that she didn't want to be alone, that she had sensed an enormous yawning emptiness that frightened her. It was as if a great ball of actual, physical nothingness had opened up nearby, a black hole sucking all of the life and vitality from everything around it.

But she didn't say anything. She wished him luck and invited him to supper, then returned to her computer and the notes she still needed to transcribe. But she stared at the screen for almost half an hour before finally moving her fingers to the keyboard.

Dan tried unsuccessfully to arrange an interview with someone who might be able to expand on Mel Hollins' story. Detective Angela Harris refused to speak to him even over the telephone. His inside sources at the police department either knew nothing about the case that wasn't already public knowledge, or weren't willing to talk about it. There wasn't even an official press release because the case was "still under preliminary investigation". Nor was anyone at the hospital more forthcoming. Armed with a description of Dr. Marin, he tried to catch the man on his way home, only to discover that he'd already missed him. No, they could not release the doctor's home address or phone number and, as Dan subsequently learned, the latter was unlisted. He thought about trying to see Rachel Darian's parents but, upon reflection, decided that was a variety of ghoulish journalism in which he had no desire to participate. Frustrated, he accepted that it was time to start home.

Despite its many recent problems, Providence Hospital remained unnaturally busy even after the fall of darkness. As ebony shadows crept across the parking area and grounds, pedestrian traffic thinned out and moved more quickly. Departing and arriving staff and visitors were not inclined to socialize in or on the way to and from the parking lots. Halogen lights flooded the area, of course, but even though the sky was clear and there wasn't the slightest trace of fog, the illumination seemed weak, almost as if it was being filtered.

Something moved among the shadows at the edge of the main staff lot. If anyone had chanced to glance that way, they might have thought a stray dog was lurking there. Certainly the shape was not large enough to be an adult human being, and what would a child be doing lurking in the grounds? It seemed to glide rather than walk as it moved from the shelter of one parked car to the next, avoiding the brightest areas, eventually slipping through a double railed steel fence and darting toward the cluttered enclosure that surrounded the receiving docks. There were two small outbuildings here, one in which the groundskeepers stored their mowers and other maintenance equipment, the other providing access to a tunnel through which the main power and water lines led into the hospital proper. It was to this building that the shape moved, hesitating a moment at the locked door. There was a brief shriek of tortured metal and the entrance was open. Once inside, the intruder pushed the door back into place and climbed down a ladder into the main underground service tunnel. It never hesitated and chose the most direct route to the destination it had in mind.

Patrolman Lawrence Capobianco threw in his hand. "That's the third time you've had gin on the fourth draw. You're the goddamned luckiest man I've ever played with."

Milton "Nudge" Nighbert, the morgue attendant, collected the cards and began shuffling, his eyes twinkling as he watched Capobianco tally up the score. "You know what they say. Lucky at cards, unlucky at love."

The policeman glanced at the tally sheet and winced as he realized his opponent was only fifty points shy of beating him for the third consecutive set. "Well then you must still be a virgin."

Nighbert laughed. "Well, I've been divorced three times, if that means anything." He began to deal the next hand.

"You must have played cards with your ex-wives until they had to either divorce you or kill you. I've only known you since yesterday and the thought had already occurred to me."

After setting the deck to one side and turning over the top card, Nighbert gestured with one thumb toward the door to the hospital morgue. "Actually, they just got upset 'cause I was always bringing work home from the office."

Capobianco grimaced. "How can you joke that way? They're goddamned stiffs. Gives me the creeps even with a door between us." He passed over the up-card, drew from the deck, and immediately discarded the one he'd selected. Nighbert swept it up almost before it had come to rest.

"I ain't got no complaints. The patients here are quiet, don't ask for much attention. I used to work in the violent ward at a psychiatric hospital. That place gave me the creeps. Some of 'em have such a powerful set of delusions, they almost seem to make sense. Makes you start wondering about yourself, you know what I mean?"

"At least they're all in one piece there, more or less."

"The bodies maybe. The brains? That's a whole 'nother story. And some of 'em, well, they do things to themselves that I don't like remembering."

Capobianco drew a third ace, rearranged his hand, and on the next play picked up Nighbert's discard, which filled in a four card straight flush. He had an unmelded pair of fives and an unrelated nine remaining in his hand. All things considered, guarding the morgue tonight wasn't the worst duty he could have pulled. There'd been a startling increase in the number of violent crimes in the city this week, and he'd been called in to stop two bar fights and a domestic quarrel since Tuesday, his two least favorite situations. And lately, people just didn't seem to care about the uniform, or getting arrested or anything. They seemed mad at everybody. Creepy and dull though this assignment might be, he found the quiet monotony almost soothing.

"What's the deal anyway?" Nighbert asked casually. "How come they got you guarding a morgue?"

"Beats me." He played a card. "Requested by Detective Marzocchi is all I know. Maybe he thinks someone's planning to steal the corpses."

Nighbert grunted. "We sure got plenty to spare lately. Anymore and we're going to have to start doubling up, two to a gurney."

"Better be careful then. You don't want them fooling around when you're not looking. End up with lots of little baby corpses and then you'll be even more crowded."

Two rounds passed uneventfully and Capobianco picked the top card off the deck. It was a five. He had just begun to smile and pull his final discard out of his hand when there was a metallic impact from somewhere inside the morgue.

"What the fuck was that?"

Nighbert's relaxed expression had vanished and he was already rising to his feet. "Something must have fallen over." But he didn't sound certain.

Capobianco rose as well. "Sounds like someone's in there."

Nighbert shook his head. "No other way in but through here, not even a window, and you were with me when I checked the place out. There's nowhere to hide."

The patrolman looked uncertain. "Maybe one of the, you know, corpses wasn't really dead. Just in a coma, like."

"You watch too many of the wrong kind of movies." But Nighbert's expression remained serious and he had already removed his keys from their place on his belt. "Let's check it out."

"All right." Instinctively, Capobianco reached down and unsnapped his holster, but he made no effort to draw his weapon. What was he going to do? Shoot a corpse?

Nighbert unlocked the door and the two men cautiously entered.

The outer room was a small office and holding area, where the incoming and outgoing bodies were logged into a computerized database as well a redundant manual card system. Other than a desk and a filing cabinet, the room was bare and nothing was out of place. On the opposite wall, another door led to the holding area.

Here the men found themselves surrounded by gurneys, all of them bearing shrouded bodies. Capobianco felt a sudden chill that was not entirely the temperature as he entered this room, which normally held only those awaiting autopsy or transfer. Another locked door led to the freezer room, where longer term occupants were placed in individual drawers and preserved more or less indefinitely. The morgue had been unusually crowded for the last several days; not only was it filled to capacity, but several cadavers had already been transferred to other facilities.

"I don't see anything," Capobianco whispered.

Nighbert was more perceptive, however. He moved to the far corner of the room, picked up a metal grille and pointed to an exposed cooling vent above his head. "Looks like this came loose." He shook his head. "Maintenance went over this room just last month. I guess somebody must not have screwed it back on tightly enough. We get a lot of vibration in the system sometimes."

The other man felt some relief but remained very ill at ease. "Sounds good to me. Let's get out of here."

But at that precise moment, the sheet covering the corpse nearest to Capobianco rustled, then fell over the side of the gurney as a dark form emerged from beneath it. The policeman's eyes had time to widen and the corners of his lips twitched, but he had no chance to draw his weapon before something heavy and even colder than the surrounding air struck him squarely in the temple. He flew backward off his feet, slammed into the adjacent gurney, then slid limply to the floor, unconscious and unaware.

Nighbert had more time to realize his danger, although he squandered several seconds staring at what had emerged from its hiding place. The creature looked vaguely like a deformed child, perhaps a meter tall, standing erect on two legs. The stubby tail it had sported when it was born in the culvert had disappeared, the snout was shorter and less reptilian, and the scales had begun to lose their sharp definition, but if Rachel Darian had been alive to see, she would certainly have recognized her only child.

With one arm raised protectively in front of his face, Nighbert took two quick steps toward the door before the creature attacked.

Nudge Nighbert was not a weak man. Although he'd recently passed his fortieth birthday, he had stayed in shape. His two hundred and forty pounds were evenly distributed thanks to a strict regimen at a local gymnasium and a metabolism that seemed predisposed to build muscle instead of fat. So when he felt his upper arms grasped, he instinctively spread them apart despite considerable resistance, twisted and broke free. It was only then that he had time to look closely at the heavily lidded eyes, the muscular, elongated jaw and the hairless skull. Overcome with revulsion, he swung a fist and the back of his right hand thudded against the side of the creature's head.

There was a sharp hiss as it jerked away from the blow, but the malevolent glare of the amber eyes never dimmed. It struck back immediately, a sweeping blow that came up from the hip. Taloned fingers plunged deep into Nighbert's abdomen, ripping up through intestines, the wall of his stomach, rupturing the spleen and pancreas. The morgue attendant was slammed back against the wall, eyes already glazing with the shock of impending death, and the feeble arm motions he made to ward off his attacker were brushed aside easily as it pressed closer and lowered its jaws toward the man's throat.

Several minutes later, Nighbert's rapidly cooling body lay in a surprisingly small pool of his own blood. Officer Capobianco was still alive but unconscious, unaware that the door to the freezer room had just been opened.

The creature went unerringly to the proper drawer and after fumbling with the handle for a few seconds, pulled it forward. Rachel Darian's body was covered with a sheet, which it tossed aside carelessly, staring down with unblinking eyes at the unmoving corpse of its mother. Most of the visible damage had been inflicted during its own initial feeding frenzy, but there were other wounds, the marks of scavengers. Her breast bone was exposed in one spot and her left arm had been gnawed through at the elbow. One ear and both eyes were missing and there were minor wounds all down the left side.

The intruder nuzzled her hip with the tip of its snout, trying to provoke some reaction, and the sound it uttered might almost have been a whimper. Frustrated, it prodded the inert body with its talons, piercing the flesh at shoulder and thigh. When there was still no response, it drew back slightly and became motionless, as though considering the situation. The three triangular wounds were no longer visible on her abdomen; there was too much damage for them to have survived intact. With no visible cue, Rachel's inhuman child positioned itself exactly as had its sire less than a week earlier and extruded three stubby triangular fangs.

They penetrated dead flesh.

Its first instinct was to draw her substance into its own body, but young and unformed as it was, the creature knew there was no sustenance to be found here. Responding to some instinctive knowledge that resided in the individual cells of its body, it reversed the process, sending a fluid which could not be called blood from within itself into the corpse of its mother. The process took only a few seconds, after which it raised its brutish head and watched silently.

And then Rachel Darian stirred, raised her ruined arms to the sides of the drawer, and sat up. Her eyes were open, their normal brown sharpened to a dull amber. She seemed aware of her surroundings, but her movement was awkward, like a puppet whose strings were tangled.

There was no true intelligence behind her eyes, no pulse in her veins, no heartbeat, no independent volition. But when the creature turned to go, she climbed out of the drawer and followed it into the outer room. Patrolman Capobianco had begun to stir, groaning softly, not completely conscious but gradually gathering his wits. He never saw the pale, staggering figure that walked almost blindly out of the freezer room, because by the time she reached him, his throat had already been torn out.

The cooling shaft wasn't really big enough for Rachel, although she wasn't a large girl even when alive and had shed much of her weight during her stay in the hospital and afterwards. As she struggled to follow her offspring on its circuitous escape route, chunks of flesh were torn off by protruding bolts and other sharp edges.

But she never noticed.

Two miles away, Evan Graham's body stirred slightly, shifting to adjust to the changing configuration of its lower abdomen. The bulge was gigantic now, and the skin had long since begun to tear along the sides of his hips. Pressure had cut the circulation to his penis and testicles, which had already begun to wither and die. The flow of blood into his legs was affected to a lesser extent, and if he had somehow been restored to consciousness he would have found himself unable to rise.

Earlier that day, the letter carrier who delivered his mail noted that the batch she'd dropped off the previous day was still in the box and she crammed the newer mail in with some effort. Graham had a box big enough to accommodate the *Wall Street Journal* and his many magazine subscriptions, but only if he emptied it daily. An hour later, his paperboy dropped off both the *Register* and the *Journal*, placing them on top of the ones already lying on the doorstep, and wondered briefly if Mr. Graham had gone off somewhere without notifying him to suspend delivery. But he didn't worry about it for very long.

CHAPTER EIGHT: SATURDAY

Dan decided to spend Saturday morning straightening up his apartment. He was an admittedly careless housekeeper, although the disarray was more clutter than dirt, and he did keep the kitchen and bathroom comparatively clean and organized. Kelly had been in his place several times and had never made him feel self conscious about the way he lived, in part because her own rooms were similarly chaotic. Dan estimated she had close to ten thousand books crammed into four rooms and a half bath, along with hundreds of magazines, abstracts, folders of correspondence, and other material related to her work. Their apartments were nearly identical in layout, although his was in a corner and hers was not. Kelly also had two storage lockers elsewhere in the city, "for the overflow", and Dan had begun to entertain the possibility of renting one himself, if only to relieve the pressure of "stuff" on his living space.

He was trying to decide whether or not to rearrange his own, comparatively small library when the doorbell rang. It couldn't be Kelly; she always knocked. It had been a long time since anyone else had come calling.

The man standing outside was tall, thin, with dark ebony skin and short hair twisted into tight curls pressed close against his head. He was wearing an expensive business suit but his shirt was open, no tie, the expression of his face controlled but suggesting impatience.

"Mr. Scapelli?"

Dan nodded. "That's right."

His visitor smiled and extended his hand. "I'm Roger Miles; I live down on the first floor."

Dan shook hands. "I'm Dan. Nice to meet you. Would you like to come inside?"

Miles shook his head. "Maybe some other time. I'm on my way out, just stopped to pick up a few things from the apartment." His smile vanished. "I've been out on Cape Cod, missed all of the unpleasantness this week and, frankly, I don't have any intention of bringing my wife and son back until this mess gets straightened out."

"I can't say that I blame you. Is there something I can do for you?"

"Actually, no, I just wanted to bring you these." He raised his left hand which, Dan now noticed, held several pieces of mail. "These were mixed in with mine. The mailman must have put them in the wrong box. I thought I'd better drop them by in case any of it's important."

Dan accepted four envelopes, one of which was his electric bill. "Oh, thanks. I appreciate your taking the trouble."

"No problem at all. I'll see you around."

"Yeah, right." Dan nodded enthusiastically, but Miles had already turned away and was heading for the elevators.

He closed the door and turned toward his desk, shuffling through the mail. In addition to the electric bill, there was an advertisement from a local travel agency, a small and long overdue royalty check for one of his short stories, and what appeared to be a personal letter. When he saw the return address on this last, he tossed the rest of the mail onto his desk, unopened and forgotten.

It was from Vera Maitlin.

Dan stood holding it in his hand for several seconds. Judging by the postmark, it had been mailed the day before Vera Maitlin died, and the incredible coincidence involved was unsettling. He walked out into the kitchen, dropped the envelope on the table, and poured himself a fresh cup of coffee. Only after he'd taken his first sip did he sit down and rip open the flap. There was a single sheet of understated stationery inside.

Vera Maitlin's handwriting was elegant and graceful, and the letter itself was quite short.

"Dear Mr. Scapelli," he read. "Some years ago, you did me the kindness of attempting to describe my abilities in objective and unmelodramatic terms. Although I don't think I ever completely convinced you, I felt confident that your mind remained open throughout, a gift which I hope has not deserted you. My clairvoyant episodes have always been so erratic and unclear that confirmation has been problematical at best, and the specific one which has led to my writing this letter is no less so despite its unusual intensity."

Dan paused, remembering the half dozen cases he had investigated in detail. Although Vera Maitlin's predictions had been accurate, they might have been the result of shrewd guesses and coincidence, and possibly some clandestine research. She had accurately predicted the day the Redman boy's body would be found and had even described its condition with reasonable accuracy, but her claim that the fire at the Armory was arson had never been confirmed, even though she provided the "guilty" party's last name and a partial address. Although he had never felt that she had proved her case, Vera seemed to believe in her own ability. If she was a fraud she had fooled herself as well.

"I have for some time now sensed a great evil approaching, something incredibly old and powerful. As you may remember, I have always believed my abilities to be entirely physical in nature. I am not and never have been a superstitious person. But in this case, I feel that what we have to fear is not now and never has been a human being. I should not have said 'we' in that last sentence, as it has become evident to me that my time has come at last, and perhaps that is best. My body has begun to fail rapidly this past year and I can no longer count upon it not to betray me. Nor can I be too specific in my warning, except to say that you are personally in grave danger. You must find a woman named Harris or Harrison; I have no idea who this person is or where she may be. When you find her, tell her that Timmy Blake wants her to give you the Prison Chest; it's a weapon that may save you. That's all I saw, Mr. Scapelli, that and the figure which I have inscribed below. God keep you well."

She had very conspicuously capitalized the "Prison Chest".

The letter was signed with a flourish. Below her signature, Vera Maitlin had drawn an elaborate stylized letter "W", with wings on its two upright arms. It didn't strike the faintest chord in Dan's memory.

Dan's innate skepticism told him that Vera Maitlin might have grown senile in her final days, but the name Harris was a disturbing coincidence. He'd been trying to reach detective Angela Harris for the past two days, after all. Vera had died well before the Rachel Darian case and the disturbances at the hospital. She couldn't have plucked the name out of a news story.

Something very peculiar indeed was going on.

Uncharacteristically, Dan had failed to turn on the radio, and the quiet was suddenly unnerving. He reached over and tapped the power button and the nasal voice of an announcer for the local all-news station immediately filled the kitchen.

Dan was pouring another cup of coffee when he first heard about the two new killings at Providence Hospital.

The announcer provided very few details and the moment the story ended he was on the telephone, trying to reach Mel Hollins. The hospital switchboard was busy and his hold turned to a busy signal after five minutes; the pattern repeated itself when he tried a second time. He disconnected, then tried to reach his contact inside the police department. The same thing happened there, and he slammed the receiver down in disgust.

The death count in the Providence area passed two hundred that morning, although almost half of these had yet to be discovered by the authorities. The stories about contaminated medications had made people reluctant to bring sick relatives to any medical facility in the area, despite frequent public reassurances that the danger had been abated. A nearly palpable cloak of distrust and fear had settled over the city. Outbound traffic was much heavier than that inbound, and many of those cars held families and luggage. Several small businesses had closed down indefinitely.

Nor did the official death tally include the bodies crammed into the recesses of the underground parking lot, or the growing number accumulating in the service tunnels beneath College Hill, none of which had been discovered as yet. Crimes of violence had increased dramatically, shootings, stabbings, bar fights, domestic quarrels, street crime, all were at record levels. Some of the violence erupted spontaneously. A priest broke an altar boy's jaw when he dropped a chalice following a wedding mass. While attempting to intercede in a loud family quarrel, a seasoned patrolman struck the woman of the household three times before being restrained by his partner. A fourteen year old girl pushed her best friend in front of a passing car during an argument over a movie they'd just seen. A seventeen year old babysitter suffocated the infant under her care and then hanged herself in the bathroom. The mayor's secretary committed suicide leaving a note that said she'd seen the devil himself walking the streets of Providence. She was one of fifteen successful suicides that day.

There were other signs as well. Although there had been no new cases of food poisoning for over twenty four hours, most of the restaurants in the city had voluntarily chosen to close until the source of the infection was discovered. There had been a run on the grocery stores, whose shelves were now mostly bare, at least of canned and packaged goods. Nightclubs continued to do a good business and, in fact, some of the restaurants reopened their bars, after posting notices indicating they would not be serving food. The police were overwhelmed and had been supplemented in some cases with national guardsmen. There were as yet no restrictions on travel into or out of Providence, but the CDC and city officials were already at work on a quarantine plan, if it became necessary.

The state police had also raised their profile, although this inevitably led to increased tension with the city police, including a standoff between two contingents of officers at the site of a break-in during which weapons were actually drawn. There were rumors of a heated exchange between the Mayor and the Governor, and confirmation that both had sent their families off on extended vacations outside the city.

The CDC was not the only federal agency involved. The local FBI office had been unusually active, and a stringer for the *Journal* had recognized Scott Pointer, who served as a liaison between the CIA and the National Security Council, and who was a specialist on terrorism working for Homeland Security. There was a contingent from FEMA staying at the Marriott. CNN had set up a temporary office in the Richmond Park complex and the other networks all had camera crews based in the Biltmore. The Vice-President had made a passing remark about the "unusual outbreak" in Providence, but hadn't appeared to consider it a serious issue, certainly no reason to alter his opposition to the jobs plan currently under consideration by Congress.

The undifferentiated anxiety that gripped the city was formless, but people spoke openly of their feeling that some terrible disaster was about to break over them, and some even suggested that unseen forces were arrayed in an evil conspiracy against the city.

Detective Angela Harris was not immune to the contagious gloom. She struggled constantly to hold back depression and frustration. Everything seemed to be climbing up onto her back at the same time. She suspected there might be a connection between the Darian case and the deaths of Dennis Kirk and Dawn Reynolds, but the latter had been assigned to Tarmont and Wallecher. Two more detectives were out for medical reasons, and two others just hadn't come to work that morning.

Harris didn't think much of most of those who still came to work. She doubted Tarmont could solve a jigsaw puzzle, let alone a murder, and while Wallecher was intelligent and had an enviable service record, he was less than a year from retirement and had already begun to lose interest. Harris rather liked Wallecher; he was one of the few old timers who hadavoided making her life miserable when she made detective, but she didn't expect him to go out of his way to be helpful.

Her working hypothesis was that the Darian girl had experienced some kind of breakdown, killed the nurse, then wandered around randomly until she'd been attacked by animals. She'd said as much to Dr. Marin and he'd nodded rather abstractedly, not contradicting her. Nevertheless, she had the distinct impression that the physician was holding something back. Although she'd tried to press him, he had just shaken off her efforts, insisting that he was overtired and preoccupied. Her sixth sense told her that he knew or suspected something that didn't fit the pattern, but she couldn't think of a way to draw him out. Predictably, Marzocchi wanted to close the case and move on, but Harris was unwilling to sign off on it just yet, much to his annoyance.

"Why can't you ever just leave things alone?" he complained. "Why don't you just accept the easy answers and go with them?"

She hadn't dignified that with a reply. And there was still the question of Teri Chin's death. Had Rachel's insanity started earlier? Had she killed her friend in some fit of rage and then remained quiescent until something set her off again? And could she really somehow have summoned the strength to kill Dennis Kirk? Harris had more questions than answers.

Wallecher had let her look through his notes on the Kirk case, but they hadn't helped much. No fingerprints, no blood except for the victim's, no witnesses, no motive, no physical evidence of any consequence. Tarmont believed that Kirk had come to pick up his girl and the two of them had been surprised by one or more crazies, perhaps intending to rob the store. Kirk had been killed in the subsequent struggle, during which the Reynolds girl escaped, only to be struck by a passing van. The driver was almost certainly not involved. The fact that nothing was missing from the pet store implied that the attacker or attackers had panicked and disappeared in the confusion, although there hadn't been much to steal in the first place. Tarmont shrugged off the unusual wounds and loss of blood, but Wallecher admitted privately that it was all "very strange".

She couldn't stop thinking about Dr. Marin's strange behavior. It was possible to construct scenarios that tied everything together. The Darian girl had witnessed the murder of her friend that night, had escaped a similar fate but with had suffered some kind of mental breakdown. Later she confused the unfortunate nurse with her attacker and reacted violently, escaping despite her disorientation. Tarmont's reconstruction of the Kirk case might be accurate. The only question remaining was Darian's inexplicable pregnancy, but that wasn't her problem.

It could all be made to fit but Harris wasn't buying. Darian was a near model student. She had an excellent record in school and was popular with everyone they'd interviewed, the cheerleader type. There was nothing to suggest that she was mentally capable of such violence. She might have been able to take the nurse by surprise and overpower her, but the savagery of the attack was disturbing.

She closed the file and pushed it angrily away, sitting back in her seat and staring up at the ceiling of the small office she shared with Marzocchi, who was at that moment laboriously typing up the report on the Nielson stabbing, a straightforward case with plenty of witnesses, a good suspect in custody, an incoherent but legal confession, and no loose ends. They should all be so easy.

She stood abruptly, pushing her chair back. Marzocchi glanced away from his typing. "What's up, Ange?"

"Just need a break. I'll be back." She wanted to get out in the open air, away from Marzocchi's hesitant tapping, the constant ringing of the telephones, the nicotine stink that pervaded the entire building despite the smoking ban. She waved greetings to a few people she knew as she descended to the ground floor, then left the building, wandering down past the city library, with no real goal in mind. Traffic was light, mostly delivery vehicles, a handful of cabs and private automobiles. A bus turned the corner, most of the windows empty, and roared away toward the south side.

She glanced at her watch; it was well after noon and she hadn't eaten lunch, unless the six cups of coffee she'd consumed so far counted as a meal. Harris had wondered in the past if she had made the wrong career choice, but never as actively as she was doing now. Although she dropped out of college during her junior year, it was because of a lack of interest rather than bad grades. By then he was already disenchanted with her history major, and put off by the academic atmosphere in general. There had been a steady guy back then, but even at the time she had known that a future with Carter Blake was not what she was looking for, and there hadn't been anything approaching that degree of intimacy in her life since she broke up with him.

Harris shook her head. This type of retroactive introspection was unlike her. She lived for the present and the future, rarely brooded over mistakes made along the way, missed opportunities, oversights, bad judgments. "It doesn't do any good to feel regrets," she had once told a friend. "It's what you from this point forward that counts."

Harris scanned the buildings on either side of the street. Today, somehow, they seemed dirty and dingy, the graffiti more pronounced and offensive, each crack in the glass storefronts larger, the stock displayed cheaply made and pointless. The gutters were choked with discarded cigarette wrappers, paper coffee cups, and fast food wrappers and the pavement was cracked and crumbling. She grimaced and moved her foot away from a used condom, then fumbled in her pocket, found and lit herself a cigarette.

She was drawing the smoke into her lungs when a hand touched her shoulder.

Kelly tried to concentrate on her work, but she kept fidgeting and getting up from the computer. Often she walked out to the kitchen, where the letter from Vera Maitlin lay on the table. Dan had stopped by to show it to her on his way out that morning, and even though she remained as skeptical as ever about the woman's alleged clairvoyant abilities, the coincidence of the letter's arrival disturbed her. There was something else that also bothered her. Neither she nor Dan had been able to identify the stylized "W", but where Dan confessed himself at a complete loss, Kelly had the distinct impression that she should know what it was, that its secret lay hidden somewhere in the masses of unrelated data she had stored in her mind. It was this that kept interrupting her typing, leading her back to stare at the folded sheet of paper.

Angela Harris drew back instinctively, as though she feared

attack.

"Excuse me, aren't you Detective Harris?"

The man who stood beside her was two or three inches taller than she, and good looking in a vague sort of way. He was well dressed, obviously not looking for a handout, and his face seemed open and friendly.

"Who wants to know?"

"My name's Dan Scapelli." He offered his hand, which she shook briefly, without committing herself. "Look, I'm sorry to approach you on the street like this, but I've called and left messages several times. I noticed you coming out of the station and you fit the description I was given, so I just had to take a chance."

"Scapelli?" The name was familiar and in a second, she identified it. "You're a reporter, right?" Her expression changed from neutral to annoyed; she didn't care for the press.

"Freelance writer, actually, though I do string for the papers occasionally."

"Mr. Scapelli, I don't grant private interviews, and they're against policy in any case. If you'd like to be notified of the time and place of any news briefings..."

Dan raised a hand to cut off the flow of words. "Please, Detective Harris. This doesn't have anything to do with police business. Or maybe it does. I really don't know. But it's not for a news story. I need your help for...personal reasons."

Harris paused. He didn't look like a nut, and he certainly sounded earnest enough. But she didn't have time for distractions right now. "I really need to get back to work, Mr. Scapelli. Is this something that can wait?"

He shook his head. "I don't know; I don't think so. Do you...did you know a woman named Vera Maitlin?"

Harris blinked rapidly, searching her memory. "I don't think so. Should I?"

Dan sighed. "I don't know the answer to that question." He shifted his weight from one foot to the other. "Could we go someplace and talk?"

"I'm on duty, sir." True, but an excuse rather than a reason.

"All right, listen. Vera Maitlin was a clairvoyant. You know, she could sense things about which she had no personal experience. Nothing very spectacular, I'm afraid, but she had a remarkable record locating lost items, made a few surprising predictions. That sort of thing."

Her face twisted. "I'm quite sure I didn't know the woman, then. No offense, but I've never been much interested in that sort of nonsense."

"Yeah, well I'm pretty much of a skeptic myself, but she was a nice woman, and she believed in her own abilities. I wrote a couple of articles about her a few years back." He noticed that the detective was growing increasingly restive. "Anyway, Vera Maitlin wrote me a letter shortly before she died and told me that it was very important that I talk to you."

"She named me specifically?"

"That's right," he nodded, stretching a point. "She wanted me to ask you about some box, 'the prison chest' is what she wrote."

Harris shook her head. "I'm afraid she's sent you on a wild goose chase then, Mr. Scapelli. I don't know anything about a prison chest or clairvoyant messages. My name is a matter of public record; she could have picked it up from a newspaper story or off the television, or just called the station and asked for the name of a homicide detective." She dropped her cigarette to the sidewalk and ground it out with her heel. "Perhaps you should ask her to be more specific."

"I'm afraid that's not possible. As I said, she died a few days ago."

"That's right. I'm sorry," she answered neutrally. "If there's nothing else..."

She was already turning to leave when Dan tried one more time. "She said to mention Timmy Blake."

Harris stopped in mid-step, the words an almost physical blow. "Timmy," she said softly, so softly that Dan didn't hear the word, although he could tell that the name had shaken her. "How did you know about Timmy?" She asked the question without turning in his direction, her voice level but throbbing with emotion.

"I didn't, Detective Harris. Vera Maitlin did."

She stood motionless for so long, Dan feared she had forgotten him. When she finally turned, her complexion was pale and her eyes were glittering. "All right, let's go some place and talk."

They found a booth in a coffee shop a block away – the only one in the downtown that seemed to be open - and by the time their order arrived, they were on a first name basis. Harris seemed reluctant to discuss Vera Maitlin or Timmy Blake at first but she was clearly agitated. "Do you have the letter with you?"

Dan shook his head. "Sorry, no, I left it with a friend. To be completely honest, I don't understand what's going on here."

"Nor do I. But there isn't a living human being who could have known about Timmy Blake, no one at all."

"Did you know him? Is he someone from your past."

She shook her head and looked down into her cup, staring into lost memories. "He's from my past, all right, but I never knew him. No one knew him. He was my son, or he would have been."

Dan sensed a deep emotional undercurrent in her words, and decided not to speak, to let Harris sort things out in her own way.

"During my junior year at college, I got pregnant. The father was a friend, but not a close one; we slept together a few times but marriage was never really in the cards although I fantasized about it a few times. I didn't want to get involved in a long term relationship, and I don't think the idea had ever even occurred to Carter. That's Carter Blake, the man I was seeing. But when it happened, I realized that I wanted very much to have the baby. I never told him about it; we broke up more or less by mutual agreement a short time later. After I finished the term, I dropped out of school, moved back to the city, but three weeks later, I spontaneously aborted." There was a catch in her voice and she broke off, covering her emotion by raising the cup to her lips and pretending to drink.

"Right from the day I found out I was pregnant, I knew somehow that it would be a boy." She looked up and met Dan's eyes. "Silly, I suppose, to believe such a thing. I was living alone, my parents had both died but they left me a pretty good sized inheritance, enough to pay for college if I wanted and then some, so I figured I could have the baby and then decide whether or not to go back to school. But things didn't work out, obviously."

She set the cup down and lit herself another cigarette. "His name would have been Timmy; I'd decided that early, but I never told anyone, not even my doctor. And the father's name was Blake so I thought of him that way, even though I suppose if things hadn't gone wrong, he'd have been a Harris."

Nodding, Dan played with his own cup but left it on the saucer. "Then if we discount the possibility that against all odds

Vera Maitlin made an incredibly accurate guess, then we have to accept that she was an authentic clairvoyant."

"So it would seem." Harris did not seem comfortable reaching that conclusion.

"If that's true, then we have to assume that the rest of her vision, or whatever one calls it, was accurate as well. So what could this prison chest she mentioned possibly be?"

Harris shrugged. "Beats me. Or wait a minute." She frowned. "There's a box down in the evidence room that might be the one she's talking about. We're not even sure if it's material to the case, but with a murder and possible assault involved..." she shrugged. "Anyway, it's an old wooden box with metal straps and lots of symbols and things carved in the sides. Is that what you're looking for?"

"Could be, I suppose. I'm as much in the dark as you are. A murder, you said?"

"Yeah, one teenaged girl killed, the other was found suffering from deep shock. We never did..."

Dan sat erect. "Wait a minute. Are you talking about the Darian girl?"

Harris nodded. "That's the one."

"Look, something weird's going on here. The reason I was trying to get in touch with you even before I received this letter was because I was trying to develop a story there."

"The official line is going to be that the case is solved. The Darian girl went nuts as a result of the attack, killed the nurse and ran off, then died of her injuries."

"Did you know she was pregnant?"

"Yes, I've spoken to her doctor."

"Did you also know she was a virgin?"

Harris stared at him. "Come again?"

Dan drew a deep breath and began telling her everything he had learned from Mel Hollins.

The vampire abandoned its lair beneath College Hill shortly after darkness fell that evening. Although there was no indication that its presence there was suspected, it had grown increasingly disturbed by the activities of those who moved by day. Exterminators had been setting traps in the upper levels, gradually making their way deeper into the maze of tunnels, and maintenance people were sealing doors and blocking off unused areas. Thousands of years of experience told the creature that it was unwise to stay in any one place for too long. It had been captured once already because it had lingered when it should have fled.

Under cover of darkness, it moved soundlessly through the streets, avoiding those few areas where there was still significant human activity, heading south toward the head of Narragansett Bay. Beyond the interstate highway, a cluster of darkened buildings crowded one upon the other, some still tenanted, but manufacturing space was now given over to storage, factories transformed into warehouses.

The largest of these was also the most poorly maintained. Its doors and windows had been boarded over, but several of these barriers had been removed by homeless people seeking shelter. Portions of the roof had collapsed, allowing in enough rain to hasten the collapse and several of the floors were now so untrustworthy that even the most desperate avoided them.

The vampire hesitated only a moment before exploring the interior and choosing a place where it could shelter from the painful touch of the risen sun. Satisfied, it left the same way it had come, turning its eye toward more populated neighborhoods and set out to hunt for tonight's meal.

Faded, almost obliterated by wind and rain, the name of the original company housed here was emblazoned across one wall -- Wexler's Wood Products. The first letter of "Wexler" was drawn three times as large as the rest of the name, painted in a different color, and embellished with ornate curls and sprays. A wing extended outward from each of its upright arms.

It was identical to the sketch at the bottom of Vera Maitlin's last letter.

On the opposite side of the city, in the basement of a small house whose elderly occupants lay butchered in their beds, Rachel Darian clasped her child tight against her ruined breasts. She lay propped against a wall, eyes open and fixed. Her body continued to function after a fashion, sustained by whatever life force had been passed on to her by the child, but Rachel's mind had long since departed.

The vampire's child had continued to change and had by now shed most of its reptilian appearance. The scales were completely gone, although the skin remained dry and rough. Its three, triangular fangs had become more prominent, particularly as the muzzle had foreshortened and altered its shape to accommodate them. It bad gained weight but its musculature and posture were less brutish, Cro-Magnon rather than Neanderthal. Rather than talons, its fingers and toes now ended with thick nails and there was a very light fuzz visible across the top of its misshapen skull. The sexual organs had grown larger but no less deformed and the eyes were still lidded. Although it was not mature, its strength and endurance had already become formidable.

Frustrated by its inability to suckle, the creature growled menacingly and ran its nails down Rachel's torso. The skin parted but there was no blood, no pain, no physical reaction at all, no change of expression. The child stood up abruptly and Rachel, or rather the husk that had once been Rachel, fell slowly over onto its side.

The smell of blood from upstairs was stronger than ever. The child raised its head, sniffing, and headed for the stairs.

CHAPTER NINE: SUNDAY

Evan Graham lay in virtually the same position as when he had first been attacked. Although not conscious, he was not completely unaware. A desperate kernel of personality recognized that something horrible and indescribable was happening. His abdomen bulged enormously, the skin stretched so taut that it had split in a series of parallel lines between navel and hips. The flesh had taken on a strange sheen, yellow white, and there was movement as well, irregular, unpredictable, often spasmodic, the skin rippling erratically as something shifted and turned and grew beneath the surface.

An hour before dawn on Sunday morning, this agitation became more frequent, regular, and violent. Fortunately, the partitioning of his mind insulated Evan Graham from most of the pain; unfortunately, it did not insulate him from it all.

The convulsions grew in strength with each passing minute. Graham's spine would arc, raising his buttocks from the bed for a few seconds before dropping back. Secondary tremors ran through the muscles of his thighs and calves; his legs jerked in tiny, spastic jumps as nerve endings fired and misfired, carrying frantic but erratic messages from the brain. He made almost no noise, his breathing was raspy and there were occasional faint gasps but no outcry. This continued for more than fifteen minutes after which there was a particularly violent convulsion, marking the final stage of his ordeal. Graham's weight was supported by his heels and the back of his head as he thrust his abdomen toward the ceiling, arms trailing limply to either side. There was a sudden sharp crack as his spine snapped under the strain, but his body remained rigidly locked in place as the skin bulged, then split wide with a spray of red that dappled the ceiling, walls, and surrounding furniture. With a small sigh, Graham's shattered body fell back onto the bed.

What emerged from the wreckage could almost have been a twin to the thing that had spawned from Rachel Darian's body, that same reptilian form reproduced on a slightly smaller scale. As it emerged from its parent's body, the creature differed otherwise only in that it displayed small but anachronistically mammalian breasts and between its legs, rather than the malformed male sexual organs, a thin crevice lined with two rows of tiny teeth.

It crawled forward over the suddenly relaxed body that had nurtured it, dry lips moving across the chest beneath which Graham's heart continued to beat, though with increasing irregularity, attempting to suckle at one of the dysfunctional nipples. There was no sustenance to be found there and, frustrated, it moved angrily to the other, leaving a trail of blood where it had lacerated the fragile flesh. Seconds later it raised its head, eyes glaring balefully as it stared into the face of the man whose body had been used to give it life, a body already failing. Evan Graham was near death now, his blood soaked the mattress and springs, his heart vainly attempted to continue functioning despite the massive damage.

Suddenly enraged, the child thing began striking out with all four limbs, tearing gashes in Graham's sides, laying bare his ribs. His consciousness and life fled quickly after that, but the tiny maelstrom of destruction continued to flail at the corpse for almost half an hour, and when it finally crawled from the bed, what remained behind bore little resemblance to a human being.

No evil magic would ever be sufficient to reanimate this body.

Evan Graham's "daughter" instinctively made its way to the window, but there was already a faint glow on the far horizon, harbinger of the morning sun. Hissing angrily, it turned away, walking erect by balancing unsteadily on its back legs with its body hunched forward, knuckles almost touching the floor.

It only took a few minutes to find the basement door, and shortly after that, it was tucked away beneath an overturned wheelbarrow, curled up and sleeping peacefully, its hunger ignored but not forgotten.

"This is getting very weird, Dan. I'm not sure I like it." Kelly pushed her cup back and forth across the surface of Dan's kitchen table. "I know you find spooks and stuff fascinating, but I feel more comfortable with nuts and bolts, you know?"

They'd slept together the previous night, in his apartment this time, and even made love, but it had been an act of mutual reassurance rather than passion.

"Is this any weirder than ancient plagues reappearing in a modern city, or rats suddenly attacking people in their homes and in libraries, or hospitals whose supplies are suddenly and mysteriously killing the people they're supposed to help? Let's face it, Kelly, the whole city's been relocated to the Twilight Zone."

"It's just such a mess." Her eyes moved restlessly around the room as she struggled to find the right words to express her feelings. "Everything so far has been a physical manifestation, and even if some of it has been pretty strange, there are probably going to be rational explanations eventually. A letter from a dead woman with mysterious information that she plucked out of the air..." She paused to draw a deep breath. "I'm not easy with this at all, Dan. It's too much like...voodoo or something."

Dan suppressed a nervous laugh, afraid it might offend her. Despite his own open mindedness on the subject of clairvoyance, he shared her uneasiness. "There might be a physical explanation for that as well, you know. Telepathy has been an unpopular but not totally discredited scientific theory for years."

"This is more than just telepathy. She not only knew something that this Harris woman had never told anyone, she also saw something coming, something dangerous and evil and apparently not human. Mind reading I can accept as a possibility; evil monsters are another thing entirely."

They had gone to bed early last night so hadn't heard about the riot until they turned on the morning news. A bar fight on the south side of the city had erupted into the street and spread to several adjacent clubs and bars before ending, as much through exhaustion as the efforts of the outnumbered police. There had been over fifty arrests, three deaths, and scores of injuries, including two police officers. Three automobiles and one building had been set on fire. A gang of teenagers had gone on a spree of arson on the west side at almost the same time, torching two empty buildings and three tenanted multi-family homes, along with an abandoned gas station and a block of small shops. Firefighting crews had been pelted with stones when they arrived to douse the flames, and were held at bay for several minutes while a National Guard unit was deployed to chase off the stone throwers.

"What time is she supposed to be here?"

Dan glanced at his watch. It was nine o'clock. "Any time now."

As though summoned by their words, Detective Angela

Harris rang the buzzer at that very moment.

Dan let her in, introduced her to Kelly, and poured a third cup of coffee.

Harris seemed ill at ease and came right to the point. "I have to tell you, when I woke up this morning I almost decided that we were both crazy."

"We probably are," he responded.

She lifted a small briefcase onto the table and unsnapped it. "For the record, I'm showing you these because you might be in a position to provide information relevant to an ongoing investigation." She extracted a file folder and placed it on the table, then closed the briefcase and set it aside. "I did two of each surface. Some of the symbols are worn and I don't know if they're legible."

Dan opened the folder, which contained photographs of the sides, top, and bottom of the chest currently held in the evidence room at the police department. He recognized a few of the symbols, an ankh, a reversed swastika, a cross, but they seemed random.

Kelly took the top picture and stared at it thoughtfully. "Some of that looks like Latin, but I don't recognize the words. And some of it is Greek, I think. Deciphering ancient languages was never one of my strong points."

Dan flipped through the rest, most of which seemed reasonably distinct. "There's certainly a variety here."

Harris crossed her arms and sat back in her chair. "The whole thing is covered with them. In a couple of places, they overlap each other and one set of lines seems to have been inscribed between older, faded markings. You say you know someone who might be able to translate?"

"I don't, but she does." Dan nodded toward Kelly, who nodded.

"I've done scut work for a lot of the faculty at Brown University. Two of them specialize in ancient history, and one is an expert on Near Eastern languages. He helped translate the Dead Sea Scrolls and did a lot of field work with Sumerian relics. I wish I could say I learned something transcribing his material, but it was too obscure for me."

"What do you hope to find out?"

"I don't know." Dan massaged his forehead as he struggled to answer the question. "Either this is all an incredibly complex string of coincidences, or Vera Maitlin had a glimpse of what was about to happen in this city and, apparently, learned that this box was somehow important in determining the outcome. Unless she misunderstood her...vision, whatever it is. One of the reasons she was never accepted was that she often misinterpreted what she saw. After the fact, it was usually obvious, but it doesn't take a clairvoyant to have hindsight. Even if we accept her warning at face value, we don't have any idea how to proceed. Maybe, if we can find out what these inscriptions mean, we'll have a better idea what's going on."

"I hope you're right. The situation is getting worse, not better. Have you heard about the curfew?"

Dan and Kelly looked at each other. "What curfew?" she asked.

"It'll be on the news shortly if it hasn't been already. The Governor and Mayor issued a joint statement a little while ago. No one is to be out on the streets of Providence after eight o'clock under penalty of arrest unless they have a written pass from the police department or the Mayor's office. There are going to be other emergency regulations shortly. Officially, we're not supposed to know, but the Mayor isn't making a move without discussing things with his new advisor, a pin striped suit type with a Washington accent."

"What provoked that?"

"There are still rumors that terrorists are behind everything and the rioting last night scared people. It could easily have been even worse. Anger blows over fast; fear tends to fester and erupt again. There are going to be travel restrictions too."

"What kind of travel restrictions?"

Harris made a point of deliberately picking up her coffee and draining half the cup before continuing. "The interstates will remain open through the city, but there will be checkpoints on all the on and off ramps. Most retail businesses are being quietly asked to shut down temporarily except for grocery stores, pharmacies, etc. They're going to let the bars stay open until curfew because they're afraid of the reaction otherwise, but everything they can do to cut down on public gatherings will be done. No one who appears to be sick will be allowed to leave."

Kelly made a disbelieving sound. "I can't believe people will stand for that."

"They won't have any choice," Harris answered. "The truth is that new cases of disease -- cholera, diphtheria, even small pox -- are showing up in alarming numbers. Unofficially, there are two hundred dead and ten times that many seriously ill. The National Guard took over the YMCA and the Convention Center this morning to use as emergency wards. My guess is that for every case they know about it, there's another lying sick in bed at home, waiting to die and too afraid to ask for help."

Dan looked at Kelly. "Maybe it's time we left the city. While we still can."

Harris made a noncommittal sound. "If you're going to go, do it soon. I talked to a friend of mine down in Warwick and she says helicopters full of troops were landing at the airport all night. It's probably only a matter of days, maybe hours, before they declare martial law."

Harris had one more thing to tell them before she left. "I tried to call Dr. Marin this morning, to ask him a few more questions about the Darian girl. I wasn't able to speak to him. It seems he had a stroke last night and hasn't regained consciousness."

After she was gone, Dan slipped the photographs into a file folder and retrieved his car keys. "Are you coming with me?"

Kelly shook her head. "No, I don't think so. I've still got some work to do and I worry less if I stay busy. Professor Concord probably won't be able to tell you anything right away, you know."

"Yeah, but I'm hoping he'll at least be able to give me a general idea what they are, something I can work on while he's doing his thing."

"Dan, you'll be careful won't you?"

He grinned. "Sure, always. What's the matter? I thought you didn't believe in the supernatural?"

"There are plenty of natural dangers out there. And I'm not sure what I believe in right now. In fact," she hesitated, "come with me a second."

"What...?" But Kelly was already on her way out of the apartment and he hastened to follow her, locking the door as he did so. He found her sorting through the contents of a large cardboard box half buried in one corner of her bedroom.

"Here it is!" She stood up, brandishing a small, metallic

cross.

"You're full of surprises, aren't you? I didn't know you were religious."

"Lapsed Catholic," she confessed cheerfully. "Scandalized my aunts, as a matter of fact." She held out the cross. "Here, take it. Wear it around your neck or carry it in your pocket or something."

"Good luck charm?"

"Something like that. It was personally blessed by a Cardinal, or so my Aunt Meredith told me. It's been in my family for generations, since before they came over from Europe."

"Marsh doesn't sound very Catholic."

"My grandmother was a Famigliano, from Milano, and my mother was a Riley."

"Sounds like an explosive combination to me."

"Volatility is my middle name."

Dan accepted the cross warily. "I don't think I should take this, Kelly. I'd feel terrible if anything happened to it."

"Not as bad as I'd feel if anything happened to you." Her face had become serious.

"If things are that risky, maybe you should keep it for yourself."

She shook her head. "Vera Maitlin's letter said you were in danger, not me."

"Vera Maitlin's visions were always partial and unclear. It sounds to me like everyone in Providence is in danger."

"I'll be careful." She leaned forward and kissed him. "Watch yourself."

It wasn't a long ride to the building where Professor Henry Concord had his office. Dan sat in the outer room for five minutes, pretending to browse through a magazine devoted to translations of inscriptions on village wells. When Concord appeared he rose quickly, and found himself shaking hands enthusiastically.

"Good morning, Mr. Scapelli. A pleasure to meet you. Miss Marsh said that I could repay an old favor by helping you with a translation of some sort?"

Concord was a mildly obese man, short and balding, his hair two white wings swept back over his ears. He wore a tweed suit that was more than slightly out of style and a bow tie that looked like it was hand tied. His expression was good natured but Dan sensed a very faint impatience, more in the man's tone and stance than in his words.

"I hate to bother you like this, Professor Concord, but there's a possibility that these inscriptions might have some bearing on a case currently under investigation by the local police."

Concord raised an eyebrow. "Are you working for the police, young man?"

"With them, in a sense at least. I know one of the detectives assigned to the case, and since they're running rather shorthanded at the moment, I thought I should help out if I could." Which wasn't exactly a lie but certainly was a misleading oversimplification.

"Very well. I take it you have a copy with you?"

Dan raised the folder from his side and Concord accepted it. "Is there a number where I can reach you later today perhaps, or should I call Miss Marsh?"

"It's probably easiest if you call her. But I was rather hoping you could look at them now..."

Concord frowned. "Mr. Scapelli, even if I can identify this language quickly, a translation may take quite some time."

"I realize that, Professor, but if you could just tell me your first impressions, it might help me to develop further lines of inquiry."

The older man's shoulders rose and fell. "All right, come into the office for a minute. The lighting out here is atrocious."

Dan sat in a rickety wicker chair as Concord opened the folder and began leafing through the pictures, pausing for a moment or two over each sheet. When he had reached the bottom of the pile, he dropped them to the desk, tilted his chair back, and removed his glasses, staring off into space for so long that Dan wondered if he had forgotten he had a visitor. At last, he replaced his glasses and cleared his throat.

"You did say that all these pictures are of a single object, didn't you?"

"Yes, sir. A wooden box with metal straps, apparently buried up on the northern side of the city. Quite old, I believe."

"Old indeed, assuming the inscriptions are the originals. Is there any chance that I might be allowed to examine the artifact itself?"

"I'm not really certain. It's currently in police custody, but I suppose something might be arranged."

"I think that would be wise. Has it been opened?"

"It's open and empty, is my understanding. You realize, I haven't actually seen it myself."

"Empty, of course." Concord pushed the rubbings so that they were spread in a fan across his desk. "There are at least two dozen different written languages represented here, ranging from Sumerian to Latin. Some of it is Asian, some Arabic, some European, some I can't identify without further study. It would be useful to know if they are an accumulation of entries or whether they were all carved at more or less the same time."

Dan shrugged. "Detective Harris said that some parts showed signs of heavy wear and others were relatively untouched. That would seem to indicate they are of different ages."

"Not necessarily. It will take some time, perhaps several days, to translate all of this, or at least as much of it as I am able to decipher."

"Is there anything you can tell me at all?"

"Oh, certainly. There are several fragments which are quite legible and recognizable. Here, for example, is the Sumerian symbol for...call it a demon." He shuffled the papers. "Here's a fragment of quite clear Latin, which refers to someone with two children, 'a daughter born of man and a son born of woman', whatever that might mean. And somewhere," he started to sort through the papers, then stopped. "One line identifies the box as a burial urn or casket."

Dan stirred restlessly. "Is there any reference to a plague, or disease?"

Concord glanced up in surprise. "Yes, as a matter of fact there is." He selected another page. "This glyph refers to 'the father of all pestilence' and there was a reference elsewhere to the 'Reaper of Souls'."

"Anything else?"

Concord moistened his lips with his tongue. "I would not be happy to discover that this was all an elaborate practical joke perpetrated by my colleagues, Mr. Scapelli."

"I assure you, sir, that this is no joke, at least not that I'm aware of."

"I don't mean to doubt your word, but this," and he held up

one of the sheets and pointed to a set of very distinct characters, "is very ancient Greek and it identifies the owner of this artifact, one Pyandor."

He paused, as though expecting some reaction, but the name meant nothing to Dan. "I don't understand the significance. I'm afraid my background in ancient history is pretty spotty."

"Then how is your background in fairy tales, Mr. Scapelli?" When Dan still looked confused, he relented. "It appears that what the author of this inscription would have us believe is that what we're dealing with here is Pyandor's, or perhaps I should say, Pandora's Box."

Kelly spent the day trying to finish two large projects she'd promised to turn in on Monday, including the one whose research had resulted in her encounter with the rats. She was only able to concentrate sporadically and had to force herself back to the job at hand. The radio played constantly in the background, and she paused to listen to every news broadcast. For some reason, the stories seemed less violent and chaotic today, and by noon she was convinced that the news was deliberately being toned down.

As expected, the curfew had been announced "to prevent a recurrence of last night's unfortunate incident". There had also been a bland statement that all travel into or out of the city was being closely monitored to prevent the spread of disease. The National Guard had been called up to "assist". Earlier speculation that bacteriological warfare was involved, either intentional or accidental, were now officially discounted, but no new explanation was offered.

She finished one project but instead of starting the next, she stood up and retrieved Vera Maitlin's letter instead. The stylized "W" still seemed familiar to her, but she couldn't place it. Preoccupied, she wandered into the front room and crossed to a wall filled with bookshelves, scanning the bindings until she found the one she wanted, a history of early industrialization in New England. She carried the book and the letter over to the couch and sat, opened it in her lap, and began paging through the illustrations.

On page 147, in the chapter dealing with the textile industry, she found an inset photograph of a large factory building located on the Providence waterfront. The first letter in its name was an identically formed "W", complete with wings.

Rachel Darian's body lay motionless as it had since her son had left her; her heart didn't beat and she wasn't breathing, but she was still not entirely dead. She had felt her child's presence all day, but with the fall of darkness it had abandoned her, and now she was alone. Or almost.

The rats were drawn by the smell of the blood and they found what remained of the elderly couple first. Within minutes the two bodies were covered with a furry mass that tore flesh from bone. There was very little blood; most of that had been taken the night before. There were too many rats for the feast, and the weak and the latecomers found themselves excluded, some nipping at the tails and legs of their fellows, the more enterprising setting out to explore further.

Eventually they found Rachel.

She made no effort to resist when the first bit into the cold flesh of her left calf, displayed no discomfort when sharp teeth began to flay the flesh from the bones of her arms, sides, hips, wherever they could reach. Word of this new banquet spread quickly, almost telepathically, and they came in ever greater numbers, until she too was covered by frantic vermin.

Whatever consciousness had animated her body during the past twenty four hours remained for only a little while longer, but it made no protest, provided no resistance, as she became inanimate for the very last time.

Dan spent most of the day trying to find someone who would speak to him. After considerable argument, he convinced the Mayor's office to confirm his temporary employment with the *Register*, and a taciturn clerk grudgingly provided him with a valid permit to remain outdoors after curfew. This effort consumed a large chunk of the afternoon, and Dan was impatient and irritable when he called Kelly to find out if Professor Concord had been in touch. He had not.

"On the other hand, I found out something myself."

"Oh? Anything of use?"

"Maybe, maybe not."

He waited. "All right, I give up. What is it?"

"I think I've identified the fancy letter at the bottom of Vera Maitlin's letter."

"And...?"

"And," she said heavily, allowing some sarcasm to show, "I have a book here that shows a picture of it."

"All right, if I get a minute this afternoon, I'll stop by, otherwise you can show me tonight."

Kelly frowned, disappointed that he didn't sound more enthusiastic. "Don't make a special trip," she said shortly.

But Dan was already trying to figure out the best way to bypass the new security regulations at Providence Hospital and was only barely paying attention. "See you tonight but don't worry if I'm late." And he hung up.

Kelly went back to her typing, mildly miffed and more than a bit disappointed, particularly since she felt quite proud of herself for having traced that errant memory back to its source. To soothe her hurt feelings, she threw herself so deeply into her work that she finished the second project without taking a break, working right through what would normally have been her supper time, not even noticing when seven o'clock passed, and then eight.

At a few minutes before nine, she saved the last of the files and turned off her computer, then gasped as she realized how late it was. Dan had told her not to worry, and she told herself that he was well able to take care of himself. But her hands were shaking so she poured herself a brandy and sat down to wait for him. Fifteen minutes later, she had closed her eyes and her breathing was level and regular.

When Dan showed up an hour later, letting himself in with the spare key she'd given him, he found Kelly lying curled up with her face pressed into the cushions. He thought about gently waking her, but he was exhausted himself, and decided not to. After covering her carefully with a blanket from the bedroom, he turned off all but the kitchen light and quietly let himself out of the apartment, returning to his own bedroom for the night.

From its lair in the abandoned factory, the vampire emerged under cover of darkness, drawn once more by the lure of fresh blood. The previous evening, two homeless men had died just a few blocks away, and their drained bodies had been thrown into Narragansett

Bay. One would be pulled from the water by dock workers on Monday morning; the other would not be found at all.

Tonight it would choose a different hunting ground in the outskirts of Brown University. There it concealed itself in a dumpster half hidden under a cluster of Japanese maple trees, watching with unblinking eyes as small groups and individuals hurried past, hastening to complete whatever errands were necessary before the curfew went into effect. Although the campus had tried to insulate itself from what was happening around it, many students had withdrawn from the term, or from Brown entirely. The vampire could taste the fear in the air. Most of those who had not fled would have preferred to do so.

Patiently, it waited as the volume of traffic grew more intermittent. There was still some vehicular traffic, mostly police cars and National Guard jeeps, occasional ambulances and even a few private automobiles driven by people with a legitimate reason to be abroad, or the temerity to disregard the curfew. Many buildings, particularly the dormitories, remained brightly illuminated; most people had gotten into the habit of leaving lights on even in the rooms they were not currently occupying, and a surprising number avoided sleeping in the dark. If asked, they would probably not have been able to explain the sudden desire to banish the night, but neither would they have been sufficiently embarrassed to turn the lights off.

The vampire had not moved for over an hour, but now it turned its head, the single nostril flexing slightly as it caught the scent of potential prey. With eyes that easily pierced the darkness, it searched the shadows and detected a hint of movement, then smiled in satisfaction as two figures emerged from behind a privet hedge half a block away.

Sean Walton and Cherie Cullen hadn't really planned to be out past curfew, it had just sort of happened. They had been taking advantage of a sheltered spot they'd discovered in the wooded hillside that faced the downtown, completely concealed from passersby thanks to a heavy growth of mock orange and forsythia, and had unwisely fallen asleep in the weakening sunlight of early evening after an enthusiastic bout of rather uninventive sex.

"We're going to be in big trouble, Sean," she whispered tensely as they inched their way along the privet hedge. "Somebody's going to see us."

"Just keep your voice down and we'll be all right. Look, there's your dorm right over there." Indeed, loud music poured out through windows open to the cooler night air.

They froze as headlights stabbed in their direction from an intersection several blocks away, but the oncoming vehicle turned a moment later, heading downtown. "Come on. Now." Sean waved Cherie forward energetically. "Let's run for it while we have the chance."

Because he was looking back to see whether or not she was doing as he had suggested, Sean never saw the tall, dark figure which seemed to materialize in front of him. His eyes were turning back in that direction when it raised an arm and clawed fingers ripped three deep gouges across his throat.

Cherie blinked uncomprehendingly, and even when she realized that Sean had just been attacked, she didn't immediately recognize the danger to herself. The dark, indistinct figure glided toward her. Terrified, she turned and ran, reacting so quickly that she surprised her attacker. The vampire hissed angrily and started after her.

Cherie ran across the front lawn of a small house and around the side of the building. There were no lights on, no sign that anyone was home, but she ran up onto the porch, pounding at the door with clenched fists. She tried to call out but all that emerged was a thin croak. Just behind her, the steps creaked and she spun around, lost her footing and fell against the porch railing.

Something hard dug into her side. Cherie's fingers closed around a wooden shaft, and she grasped it desperately. It was a garden rake, tipped with a metal head, the spikes sharp and clean. She raised it and swung at the advancing figure, brought the spikes down directly toward its chest with all the force she could muster.

There was an impact, not solid exactly, more as though she had struck a rotting pumpkin. Her attacker hissed angrily and the shaft was jerked forward, out of her hands. Cherie looked around for an escape route, but the vampire moved before she could make a decision, grabbing the front of her blouse and lifting her into the air.

She had time to just begin a scream for help before she was thrown from the porch. She soared over the railing, smashed through the shrubbery, and landed heavily in the gravel driveway. The vampire angrily pulled the rake from its chest, tossed it aside, and vaulted the rail. Enraged by her attack, it made certain she could see its true face quite clearly before it ripped open the front of her blouse and plunged triangular fangs into her throat. Her final attempt to scream was a gargled gasp.

By the time it was able to return to Sean's body, he was completely unconscious and much of his blood had already spilled onto the sidewalk. It crouched over his motionless body and consumed what remained.

Tonight, it made no effort to conceal the bodies of its victims. It had felt the life of its second child, and while neither son nor daughter had matured to the point where they were yet tolerable company, it would only be a matter of a few days before they would be fit to join him in the destruction of the city that surrounded them.

CHAPTER TEN: MONDAY

By Monday morning, Providence was visibly a city under siege. No one knew how many had already died. Officials were tight lipped and steps had been taken to disperse the bodies to disguise their number, but this effort seemed to have had no measurable effect on public confidence. Many more were seriously ill and temporary treatment centers were straining to accommodate the constant influx of new patients.

Despite the curfew, there had been considerable violence Sunday night. A riot in the Federal Hill area had moved downtown, leaving smashed windows and several fires in their wake. Similar incidents had occurred on a smaller scale throughout the night. More fires had been set on the east side, and there had been at least a score of shootings and stabbings scattered across the city. One man had deliberately run down a neighbor with his car, then backed up over the man's prostrate body. A twenty year old coed had been discovered on the Brown campus with her throat slashed, only a short distance from her dead boyfriend. There had been some looting, primarily smaller shops, and a large group had broken down the doors to a discount store and made off with a considerable quantity of goods before police could respond. Dr. Edward Marin's wife was fatally shot when two men broke into his house, believing it to be empty. As if in sympathy, Marin himself died less than an hour later in the intensive care ward.

It was impossible to investigate any of these crimes in the detail they deserved. Detectives took down statements from witnesses where they were available and technicians searched the immediate areas for physical evidence in the more serious cases, but there was no time to pursue leads, run background checks, question suspects, or even type up preliminary reports. Harris and Marzocchi started with an early morning shooting incident, then were rushed to the home of Edward Pianelli, who had strangled his wife over the breakfast table. No sooner had they finished their preliminary work than they were called to a convenience store just off Elmwood Avenue. The store manager was in critical condition and not expected to survive the three bullet wounds in her chest. The cash register was empty. They had barely had time to look around when they were called to the waterfront, where another body had been found floating under a pier, the fifth in two days.

Elsewhere, the country read its morning papers with concern or morbid curiosity or active distaste, or watched the inconclusive and carefully edited coverage on cable news. Various internet sites blamed the government for not doing enough. Other site claimed the government was deliberately exposing people to bacteriological agents and psychological warfare as some sort of test. Although the authorities reassured people that the rash of illness and related violence was confined to a relatively small area, hundreds of people across the country were showing up in emergency rooms claiming to have contracted one mortal illness or another. The White House issued a statement to the effect that the outbreak was under control, that travel restrictions in the area were temporary and purely precautionary, and that the situation in Providence was expected to return to normal within a few days.

But confidence in the veracity of the current administration was at an all time low.

Dan had been up until well after midnight, collating his notes, typing up a brief story for the *Register*, skimming through some reference books he'd withdrawn from the library just before it had closed "for the duration of the emergency". When Kelly knocked on his door at half past eight, there was no answer, so she used a credit card to pop the lock. He was sleeping peacefully, so she decided to leave him undisturbed and talk to him later, after she had delivered the two projects she'd completed the night before.

An hour later, he read the note she had taped to the bathroom mirror and shook his head. He didn't like the idea of her going out of the building alone, even during the daylight. Things were just too unsettled.

His phone rang a few minutes later, and for a change it was good news. The executor of Vera Maitlin's estate was Tim Cook, a lawyer whom he had met socially and he had called to ask permission to examine her papers, hinting that it might be possible to rework them into a publishable manuscript. It was Cook's secretary, telling him that she'd spoken to the manager of the retirement home and that he was free to make his preliminary appraisal at any time. "Actually, I believe Miss Maitlin's will names you as custodian of her journals."

Kelly hadn't returned, so he answered her note with one of his own and left it taped to the screen of her computer. After locking both apartments, he descended to the garage and drove to the north side.

Half an hour later, Kelly returned, found Dan's note, and sighed grumpily. She still hadn't had the chance to tell him about her discovery and she had a feeling that it was important. Restless, she made a peremptory effort to work on some long term assignments she'd relegated to the back burner, but kept returning to the book and the photograph she'd found. It was one of several factories sited close together, but the caption simply repeated the name of the firm, which was self evident, but without mentioning the address. There wasn't much visible in the background, but it was clearly situated close to Narragansett Bay. A lot of new construction had taken place in that area, the interstate highway system, a new hotel, attempts to gentrify several blocks and convert others to park and other recreational space.

It was quite possible that the building in question no longer existed, or that it had been altered dramatically so that it was no longer recognizable. On the other hand, there were still several crumbling factories just beyond India Point. Kelly had never actually been in the area, but she could see them from the highway when she took the interstate.

Kelly felt increasingly restless and frustrated, and was unable to maintain her interest in the survey of failed legislation in New England state assemblies that was the next project on her list. By noon she had already consumed as much coffee as she usually drank in an entire day, and she pointedly washed but did not refill the pot. She was eating leftover chicken warmed in the microwave when she finally decided to drive down to the waterfront and see if she could locate the building herself.

The telephone rang as she was halfway to the door. It was Henry Concord, his voice filled with such uncharacteristic animation that Kelly didn't recognize him at first.

"Dan's not here at the moment, Professor. I'm not sure when he's going to be back."

"Oh, I see." Pause. "It is imperative that I speak to him at the earliest possible opportunity. Frankly, Miss March, I suspect that this is some sort of hoax, though I'll concede that your friend is not a party to it, but even if that's the case, it's still fascinating. Do you know anything about the origin of the photographs he brought me?"

Kelly frowned. "Only that they were taken from some kind of box that turned up during a police investigation." She decided not to mention Vera Maitlin's clairvoyant warning.

"Ah, yes. He did say it was in their custody. Do you know who the actual owner might be? Or where it was found?"

Kelly shook her head, then realized the gesture was pointless. "I'm not sure anyone owns it. It was found in a wooded area on the north side of the city, abandoned and buried."

"Well, then, I'll have to see if I can convince the university to attempt to claim it. Preferably with a minimum of fuss. If it is in fact a forgery, it would not do to suggest even by implication that we had been fooled."

"Have you been able to translate the inscriptions then?"

"Some of them, yes; others, not yet; a few, perhaps never. On the other hand, most of them are repetitious, variations of the same phrases. Magical wards against evil, that kind of thing. Invocations of fire as the breath of the gods. Many warnings against opening the box, 'wherein lies the demon' or some such."

"Warnings?"

"Yes, of the most dire variety. The box was meant to imprison a kind of evil spirit, an immortal force of evil that could be confined but never destroyed. Probably some poor unfortunate madman, if there really was a body inside at some point. I can't judge the size from what I have. More likely it was some other object, a symbolic representation. That kind of substitution is quite common, you know."

"An evil spirit, you said?"

"Something along those lines. We found an Arabic reference to an afrit, for example, a djinn, a Sumerian glyph probably referring to a demon, and another reference in fairly modern German, a single word in fact."

"What word is that?"

"Nosferatu. The walking dead, my dear. Vampires."

Kelly left a note for Dan summarizing her conversation with Concord. She neglected to mention her own plans for the afternoon except to say she had some errands to run. Before leaving, she checked to be sure the can of mace and the police whistle were both in her shoulder bag.

The city looked as though it was under siege. There was traffic, both vehicular and pedestrian, and many stores and businesses she saw appeared to be open, but very few had customers. Police and guard patrols were everywhere but they looked almost as harried and frightened as the civilians around them. The drive took much longer than usual despite the small amount of traffic. On one occasion she was held up while an ambulance was loaded with two stretchers carried out of an alley; she could not determine whether the victims were alive or dead. Later she had to detour to avoid what appeared to be the interdiction of an entire six block square neighborhood. The guardsman who waved her around would not answer when she questioned him about it, but his face had seemed unnaturally pale in the bright sunlight.

She reached the India Point area and parked on a side street not far from the highway overpass. This had originally been an industrial area, but much of it had been cleared to accommodate the supports of the bridge which crossed the river to East Providence. There was a cluster of old factories four blocks south, most with their faces turned toward the water of Narragansett Bay. Trash covered an empty lot, and more of it pressed into the recesses of fences and up against the side of buildings, lining the gutters and blowing in the streets. A few private roads and driveways were barred by rusting gates. The parking lots adjacent to the factory buildings were almost invisible under dirt and grass. This was the closest she could legally park; she would have to walk from here.

From where she stood, Kelly could see three buildings, one of which had lost its roof in a storm. The windows gaped blankly, only a few holding any glass and most of those only fragmentary. There were a dozen or so white lumps on the ground nearby which she couldn't identify until she got closer. Dead seagulls. The first gate she came to was padlocked shut and both the lock and the chain it secured were dark with rust.

Kelly turned and walked alongside the fence until she reached the corner of a brick building. There was a small gap here that she might be able to slip through, but it was a tight fit and she decided to wait until she had explored the rest of the area. Just ahead, two smaller buildings stood close together, a small alley between them so narrow that she could stand and touch both walls at the same time. The bricks and concrete were coated with moss and attenuated vines. The opposite end of the alley seemed open, a slash of light through the gloomy shadows, so she decided to see where it might lead.

An ash tree was growing out of the cracked pavement at the far end and Kelly had to turn sideways to slip through the space that remained. She found herself in a small courtyard, bordered to her right by the earthen wall that supported the highway, to left and ahead by two buildings whose windows were boarded shut but which otherwise appeared to be in reasonably good condition. There was no obvious exit except a door to her left, but it looked as though it hadn't been opened in years and a large, unfriendly sign warned her to "KEEP OUT". Nevertheless, she walked slowly forward, and spotted a narrow stairway to her left, which ran up to a small fenced area.

The gate at the top was closed and rusted shut but not locked. Kelly placed both hands on the top rail and pushed. With a thin squeal of protest, it moved forward a short way, then stopped, immovable. But it was wide enough and she slipped through.

Two more buildings were visible from her new vantage point, both of them fairly good sized. The one to her left was speckled with broken windows, sagging gutters, and crumbling masonry. The one to the right, which extended a fair distance toward the waterfront, seemed to be in better condition, although most of its windows were similarly missing, and the exterior wall was decorated with colorful and occasionally obscene graffiti.

At the far end of the building, she found an open door. Or not exactly open, so much as broken. Splinters of wood hung from both hinges but the bulk of the door itself was lying on the floor inside. It did not appear to be recent damage. Kelly passed it by, more interested in the exterior of the buildings than the interior. There was a faint rustling sound from inside and she worried that a pack of stray dogs might be lurking in the darkness. Or rats. She reached into her pocket and closed her fingers around the Mace as she backed away around the corner of the building.

She heard the scrape of a foot on the rough surface just in time to whirl and see that she was not alone. Two men were coming toward her, unshaven and more than slightly disheveled. But it was their expression and demeanor rather than their appearance which alarmed her.

She started to run, and heard their steps immediately quicken behind her. Someone shouted and she glanced back for just long enough to see that while she was outdistancing one of the men, the other was gaining on her. She gave an involuntary cry and redoubled her efforts, so focused on the need to stay out of his reach that she ran right past the gate she'd pushed open earlier. By the time she realized her error, it was too late, and the discolored wall of the largest building in the complex was directly in front of her, cutting off further retreat in that direction.

She turned to her right and started toward the water.

Just before she reached the far end of the building, Kelly was drawn up short by a hand that grabbed her by the hair, yanking her backward. With difficulty, she kept her feet and twisted, swinging her shoulderbag in a short arc. He deflected the blow easily, but relinquished his grip in the process. Kelly managed only two quick steps before he tackled her from behind, and lost her breath as she crashed to the ground with his weight half on top of her.

"Knock it off bitch!" He struck her between the shoulderblades with his fist.

Kelly's right arm was caught under her body, but she was able to get her hand inside her pocket and grasp the can of Mace. With one hand holding her shoulder tightly, the man rose to hands and knees. "Just get up slowly and do like I tell you."

Slowly, she stood, holding the Mace pressed against the front of her body, and half turned toward her attacker. His companion was just rounding the far corner of the building, still several seconds away. Her right hand clenched, gripping the small can, and she prepared to spray it into his face. Before she could act, he grabbed her left arm and pushed her roughly forward. Kelly stumbled toward what she now saw was another cratered doorway, realized that she would have to act quickly if at all. Once the second man arrived, escape would be far more difficult. She stepped away, stumbled over the doorstep and into the shadowy interior of the abandoned factory.

She was so focused on her attacker that she never noticed the faded symbol painted on the outside wall above her head, a very ornate letter "W", trimmed with small wings.

Knowing her options were vanishing quickly, Kelly abruptly shook off the restraining hand and ran a few steps deeper into the gloomy building. He shouted and followed and almost immediately caught hold of her left arm. Almost without breaking stride, Kelly turned and raised the Mace. It wasn't as direct a hit as she might have liked, but the man released her and fell back, swearing and wiping at his streaming eyes. The second man appeared in silhouette at the entrance, but Kelly was already moving again, through a set of swinging doors and up a stairway that groaned with each step she took. She passed the second floor and continued to climb, spurred on by the sound of two sets of feet pounding upward in her wake.

The stairway ended on the third floor, and for a panicky moment, she thought the exit was locked. It gave way on her second frantic pull and she stumbled inside, dragging the door shut behind her. Off to her right was what appeared to be a series of offices, but most of this level was open space; whatever machinery had been housed here previously had now long since been removed. There was another exit at the far end, but she hadn't even reached it before the first door slammed open.

"Hold it right there, bitch!"

Kelly ignored the shout, slipped through the opposite door and climbed quickly down a short catwalk toward the ground level. It swayed threateningly but she continued without hesitation, preferring to risk inanimate over animate menace. Unfortunately, it lurched sharply when she was halfway down, rusted bolts pulling away from the wall. Kelly grabbed at the handrails desperately, losing her grip on the Mace. It fell into the darkness. At the foot of the catwalk, she found herself in a smaller room filled with wooden benches, the soggy remnants of corrugated boxes, a pile of rotting timber, and several cans of paint so elderly that dust had completely covered them.

She made her way quickly through the maze, had actually entered the next room before her pursuers reached the foot of the catwalk. There were exits to the left, right, and further forward, and a short flight of stairs directly ahead. After only a moment's hesitation, she descended again, unwilling to be cornered in one of the side rooms with no alternative escape route.

Disoriented now, she found herself in an interior room with no windows, and no idea which direction led to the outdoors. She ran around a mass of rusting, unidentifiable machinery and made her way through a series of small storage rooms, then up another flight of stairs to yet another corridor, along which she ran until she reached what appeared to be the inside of a receiving platform. The outside doors had been pulled down and chained shut, however, and she couldn't find any way out except to go back the way she had come.

Angry voices sounded from the rear, and feet began to pound their way up the stairway.

There were no windows and it was quite dark, even though there were still at least two full hours of daylight remaining outside. What little illumination penetrated this deeply was refracted from elsewhere, or seeped in through tiny cracks in the ceiling and around the edges of the overhead doors. There was evidence of water damage as well, although most of this was invisible in the shadows; the building was rapidly becoming structurally unsound, water, wind, and salt spray already having had their way with the wooden supports. There was litter on every side, refuse, piles of discarded machinery, electrical fixtures, flattened cardboard that had grown moldy and indistinct, a handful of inexpensive metal desks and broken armchairs, several stacks of wooden pallets, rotted lumber, broken boxes of nails, rubber gaskets, and other supplies. A pile of spare tires leaned against one wall, and her eyes skipped over coils of corroded wire, a disorderly row of fifty gallon drums, and a small, mesh enclosed office. Nothing suggested any escape route so her only chance was to hide.

Moving as quickly and as quietly as possible, she slipped into the narrow space behind a row of metal lockers, brushing dust webs away from her face as she retreated as far from the light as she could manage. .

She had barely settled into place when the two men entered the room, separating immediately as they crossed the threshold. The first man was clearly still incensed. "We're gonna get you, bitch, and when we do..." He left the rest unspoken. His companion remained silent, began working his way around the outside wall, limping slightly. The first man walked straight ahead toward the center of the room, his head moving slowly from left to right. From her vantage point she could see them both when they first appeared, but the limping man quickly disappeared to her right, hidden by the corner of the row of lockers.

The next few minutes were agonizing. They must have been pretty certain that she was close by because they were very thorough. She had hoped that they might believe she had escaped through one of the smaller rooms she'd passed, but obviously they hadn't been fooled. It was only going to be a matter of a few minutes before they found her, and there was no way to retreat further.

She began feeling around in the darkness for something to use as a weapon, a length of wood, a discarded tool, anything at all. The limping man was slowly making his way around the outer perimeter while the other moved from one pile of rubbish to another. Kelly figured the latter would reach her first, and wondered if she could rush forward and knock him off balance, then escape before he could recover. She was pretty sure she could outrun his companion given a few steps lead. She had just decided that this was her only possible option when the situation changed yet again.

The man furthest away was peering into a cavity in the floor which, in years past, had been the housing for an automatic scale. Bits and pieces of debris had fallen or been blown about so that it was almost entirely covered over. It was even darker there, but the man crouched and stared. "Hey, Cory. I think I've got her. C'mere and..."

Before he could finish, a hand reached up out of the darkness and closed on his throat. Kelly couldn't see the cause, but she blinked in amazement at the effect. The man's body flew up and away from the pit, slammed against a pile of machinery, and slid to the floor, motionless.

"What the fuck?" The man named Cory had been facing away, hadn't turned in time to see his friend's involuntary and very brief flight through the air. He advanced slowly, crossing through Kelly's line of sight. "Where the hell are you? Did you find the bitch?" Kelly inched forward, preparing to run, believing that this might be her best opportunity. She didn't know exactly what had just happened, but she'd figure it out later, once she was safe.

"Shit!" Cory halted in mid-step, startled as a tall figure suddenly appeared in front of him. The newcomer closed the gap quickly. At the last possible second, Cory raised his arm and partially deflected a vicious one handed blow, but he was still knocked from his feet, hit the floor hard and skidded on his back and buttocks until he became entangled in a coil of corroded cable.

Kelly stepped out from behind the locker, but froze when she saw that the newcomer was blocking her escape route. Cory managed to stand up, but his attacker had closed the distance between them, almost seeming to glide across the floor, and another blow slammed into the underside of his chin, lifting him into the air. He flew backwards and crashed into a pile of boxes.

Kelly couldn't wait any longer. She raced for the door.

Although she never exactly saw the mysterious figure move, it was suddenly directly in front of her and she skidded to a stop. Although she could barely see anything in the gloom, enough of the stranger's face was discernible to startle her. It looked like a human being, but only approximately, and she wasn't sure that she wanted to see it more clearly. She took a single step backward, caught her heel against something hard and immovable, and lost her balance. When her head fell against a cast iron bucket, she almost welcomed the retreat into unconsciousness.

The vampire stood over her limp body for a few seconds, then returned to the man named Cory. Within seconds, it had finished and rose from the motionless body, then moved to the second man, who died without ever recovering consciousness. Satisfied for the moment, it collected the bodies of its two most recent victims and dropped them unceremoniously into the dark cavity where it had been sleeping.

Although it had chafed during its imprisonment, the vampire was beginning to think that perhaps the two centuries had not been wasted after all. The people of this new time were easy prey; they didn't even seem to understand what was happening to them. It picked up Kelly's limp form effortlessly, feeling the strong beat of her heart and the steady rhythm of her blood. But it was well fed now and the compulsion to feed was almost extinguished. One of the wall lockers stood with its door open and it dumped her unceremoniously inside, twisting the metal as it closed the door so that it was jammed in place.

Then it returned to its rest.

Dan returned just before dusk, tried Kelly's apartment first, then went to his own. He found and read the note about Concord's call, which told him less than he'd hoped but more than he'd expected. He had spent the entire day reading Vera Maitlin's voluminous correspondence, skimming through her private journals, even glanced at some of the books she'd collected.

If she had had any correspondence involving Angela Harris, Timmy Blake, or the present problems besetting the city, it did not appear to be in her apartment. Some of what he read was intriguing, though irrelevant to their present problem. If the dates in her journal were to be believed, Vera had anticipated the *Challenger* disaster and the destruction of the World Trade Center, had even written several letters which had been, naturally, ignored. He found other predictions as well, crimes both petty and major, accidents, a major storm, but he wouldn't be able to confirm their accuracy without doing some research. Sometimes she tried to give warning, often she didn't bother. There was no evidence that anyone had ever taken her seriously. The few responses she had received thanked her for her concern and assured her that she had nothing to worry about.

He grew increasingly worried about Kelly as the evening progressed. Although he had managed to get through to Angela Harris by telephone, she could offer little comfort. "Missing persons are the least of our problems, Dan. I'm sorry, but for the foreseeable future she's on her own. You've got a pass, don't you? Any idea where she might have gone?."

But there was no hint of her intentions in her note. Dan managed to find Henry Concord's phone number in Kelly's address book, but the professor could offer no suggestions. "She said nothing when I talked to her earlier today. I assume she did pass on the information about the translations. Did she mention that we would very much like to examine the chest itself?"

"Yes, professor, thanks. I'll get back to you on that." He hung up quickly, even though it appeared that Concord wanted to prolong the conversation. He didn't want to stay on the phone too long, in case Kelly was trying to call.

He had a terrible feeling that something had gone very wrong. Maybe Vera Maitlin's ability was rubbing off on him.

Evan Graham's "daughter" left the house on the East Side as soon as the hated sun was safely concealed below the horizon. Like her half sibling, she had already begun to lose much of the overt reptilian appearance with which she'd been born; the scales were still visible but their edges were softening, less well defined, her breasts larger, claws shorter though no less deadly. She still walked with a slight forward cant, but her posture was less simian than it had been at birth and her musculature was quickly adapting to a full upright stance. Portions of the head had reformed, shortening the muzzle, the nose softening and becoming tubular.

Instinctively, she kept to the shadows, avoided groups of people, working her way from yard to yard, occasionally pausing at one house or another, sometimes peering in at the windows, but always moving on, barred from entering without invitation. The size of the yards declined along with the state of repair of the buildings as she headed northwest, bypassing the outer limits of the commercial district, eventually reaching an area that was a mixture of marginal businesses, dry cleaners, florists, pawn shops, used office equipment dealers, poorly lighted taverns, all sprinkled in among overcrowded multi-family houses.

She killed a dog she found chained in one yard, sneaking up as the animal dozed, taking it unawares and stealing its life with one swift strike. The blood was rich and warm but not completely satisfying, and she understood that this was not her proper prey. Three houses further along the block, she climbed a fence and peered down into a claustrophobic back yard where a toddler rode his tricycle in endless circles on a small square of paved patio. The stockade fence had been patched in places with any piece of flat wood that had come to hand and had a peculiar patchwork appearance. Inside the house, a television blared noisily but no one was watching; the boy's parents were in an upstairs bedroom, alternating between pot and cheap wine as they diffidently attempted to have sex together.

The little boy never even knew he was in danger before he was dead. He wouldn't be missed until the following morning.

Three lots further along the street stood an abandoned house. The creature dragged her prey in through a broken basement window and slaked her thirst in a corner of what had at one time been a coal bin. Satisfied, she curled up into a ball next to the small corpse and waited for the hunger to rise again.

When the bartender at *Paul's Pub* tried to close at a few minutes before nine o'clock in compliance with the curfew, several of his customers insisted on having one final round. Eric Decker was already considering quitting, having suffered too many drunken assholes for too long, and he wasn't about to take lip from anyone. When he tried to physically remove the loudest of the objectors, he was jumped from behind and stabbed in the side. More angry than hurt, he struck back but lost his footing and hit a young woman instead, which enraged her date. The pub's only waitress slipped into the back room as soon as she realized things were out of control and called the police, who eventually arrived to find the clientele had taken over the barroom and were drinking everything in sight. Decker was lying unconscious in a corner, hemorrhaging from internal injuries far more serious than the original knife wound. The waitress had used the back door to make good her escape immediately after making the call, vowing silently never to return.

The situation did not improve, and the patrolmen summoned were not experienced enough to react quickly. By the time they called for reinforcements, the disturbance had spread outside the bar and attracted many more people. Clusters of young men and not a few women were scattered along both sides of the street. One of the other bars had reopened, its owner having decided to cooperate rather than risk the destruction of his furniture.

When the police arrived, part of the crowd met them outside and a very drunk redhead began swearing loudly, staggering close enough to shout directly into a young patrolman's face, and the latter finally lost his temper and pushed her roughly up against the side of his car, planning to cuff and arrest her. Someone threw a rock through his windshield a few seconds later, and by eleven thirty the National Guard had been called in to combat an estimated three hundred rioters and protect the firefighters struggling to put out three blazes they had started.

Two of the torched buildings were completely destroyed, and one of these was an empty three family house in the basement of which the hungry flames found and devoured the body of a small boy. Although the young vampire recognized its danger and tried desperately to escape, it only managed to crawl up to the ground floor before the hungry fire found it. The flesh literally boiled off its bones, and then the bones themselves exploded into millions of tiny, rapidly dying sparks.

On the other side of the city, the original vampire raised its head and howled in frustration in the darkness, sensing that one of its children was dead.

CHAPTER ELEVEN: TUESDAY

Dan fell asleep sitting in a chair in his own apartment, waiting for a callback from Angela Harris, or preferably for Kelly to knock on the door and tell him where she'd been. He hadn't planned to spend the night that way but the sun was well up when he wakened, stiff and sore, and for the first few seconds he was disoriented. When he realized he still hadn't heard from Kelly, he stood up, ignoring the protests of cramped muscles, and rushed next door.

The apartment was empty and there was no sign that she had been there. He left another note, and told himself that it was time for both of them to stop procrastinating and get cell phones, then went back to his own apartment, reheated the previous day's leftover coffee, and drank two cups in rapid succession.

He showered and changed into fresh clothing, then finished the last of the coffee, along with two English muffins toasted and topped with cinnamon. Considerably more alert, he called Angela Harris at home and was relieved when she answered on the second ring.

Unfortunately, she had nothing to tell him. "I'm sorry, Dan, but things are just so disorganized lately, I really can't be of much help tracing your friend. I did go through the reports that were available and there is no record of anyone with her description being found dead or injured, or having been arrested. If she's been admitted to one of the field hospitals, her name hasn't gone into the computers yet. On the other hand, we're so far behind filing reports ourselves, I doubt half the calls that have been made this week have been documented. I asked around where I could, but you have no idea how exhausted and touchy everyone is."

Dan assured her that he appreciated every effort she had made. "How about her car? Any sign of it?"

"No, and if she left the city, there would probably be a record of it unless she managed to avoid the checkpoints. The perimeter isn't as secure as they would like. They log the registration number of every vehicle that passes through and hers didn't show up on the list."

"She wouldn't have left the city. We talked about it just

recently, and she was determined not to be driven out. Providence isn't that big a place. I don't understand why it's so difficult to find her car, at least. There are patrols everywhere."

"No one's looking for stolen cars; we can't even investigate all of the missing person reports. There are scores of people disappearing every day and we get constant calls demanding that we do something to find a missing child, boyfriend, husband, or employee. If you had any idea where she could have gone, something that would reduce the search area to something manageable, I might be able to arrange something. As it is..." She let her voice trail off.

"All right, I understand, I guess. Maybe I'll spend the day driving around myself."

She agreed without enthusiasm, recognizing that he needed to do something, no matter how unlikely it was that he would accomplish anything. Privately, she suspected that Kelly Marsh was dead. There had been at least twenty two people murdered the previous evening; there had been several small riots, scores of robberies, and various other incidents of random violence.

Officially, the death toll from the various diseases had dropped off, but Harris didn't believe the official line. There had been a handful of patients who had recovered, although none of them were strong enough yet to leave their beds. That much was true. There had also been an influx of expensively dressed, humorless men and women who could not have been more obviously federal agents if a label been branded onto their foreheads. None of the outsiders appeared relieved or triumphant or even hopeful, and some looked positively nervous.

"Let me know what you find out," she said at last. "In fact, if you can manage it, stop by the station downtown around one o'clock, and I might have something to show you."

Despite his preoccupation with Kelly's disappearance, Dan felt his curiosity stir. "Oh?"

"I can't promise anything, but I think I can get you in to see that box you're so concerned about. Officially, you're going to be a civilian consultant. I'd have to justify this a lot better normally, but right now there's so much confusion downtown, the rules are being interpreted pretty loosely. I got a verbal okay yesterday."

"Any chance of taking it away? I mean, the Darian case is

closed, isn't it?"

"Darian? Officially, no. And if the box is evidential at all, it's linked to the other murder, the Chin girl. And that's very much open, although no one's doing anything about it right now."

"Oh, right. What time did you say?"

"One o'clock. I officially go back on duty around then, and there are a few things I have to do at the station before I go back on the street. But come by right away if you're coming at all. The way new calls are coming in, I could be pulled out at any minute."

"All right, if I can make it, I'll see you then."

Kelly had regained consciousness less than an hour after being shut up in the metal cabinet. Her first concern was to get herself under control. When she discovered that she couldn't open the door and escape, she had nearly given in to panic. She had closed her eyes and forced herself to even out her breathing. The cabinet was tilted far enough that she couldn't stand erect, and she had lain propped up at an awkward angle long enough that her arms and legs were sore.

Despite the cramped quarters, she managed to rearrange herself into a slightly less uncomfortable position. There was no light at all, so she was forced to explore the limits of her prison with her hands. There were a few stiff rags under her feet but nothing that might help. Her shoulderbag was missing and the only things in her pocket was a ball point pen and a couple of American Express receipts.

Kelly pressed her knees against the doors and pushed, but they only moved about an inch before jamming. She leaned back, then raised her legs so that she could plant her heels firmly against the metal. Bracing herself, she tried to straighten her legs and force the door open. The metal protested and deformed, but it was wedged too securely and she made no headway. Reluctantly, she tried calling for help, but her voice echoed hollowly in the confined space, depressing rather than cheering her, and she quickly stopped. The only sound from outside was an intermittent dripping, as though rain or condensation were falling from one of the many rents in the ceiling.

Frightened, confused, and angry at herself for being so careless, she settled back to wait for the dawn.

Dan had never realized how large and convoluted the city of Providence was until he set out to search for Kelly's car. He divided his street map into sections, but the magnitude of the task discouraged him before he had even started.

He spent the morning driving up and down the streets and alleys of downtown Providence. He pulled over to the curb and walked through every parking garage and lot in the area, watching for the distinctive bright red color. Downtown traffic had dropped off by at least three quarters, and none of the lots and garages were even close to capacity. Two of them, in fact, were closed, their gates down and locked, perhaps because the people who would ordinarily have operated them were dead, sick, or had already fled the city. Or perhaps they were just hiding in their homes, waiting for the storm of disease and violence to blow over.

Military and police patrols were still active, he noticed. Mostly the former.

It took the greater part of the morning before he crossed off the first of fourteen areas he had outlined and when he returned to his apartment to find out if Kelly had returned or left a message, he was thoroughly discouraged. He made up several tuna fish sandwiches and carried them down to his car, then set off begin searching the East Side.

The collapse of much of the local infrastructure was even more obvious here in what was the most prosperous part of the city. Although some garbage trucks had been out, trash pickup was spotty and unreliable, and he passed street after street where neat plastic bags of waste waited forlornly for someone to take them away. In some places, dogs or other animals had torn them apart and scattered their contents in every direction. That puzzled him, since he hadn't seen a dog or cat in at least two days, which made him wonder if the scavengers were rats, grown more aggressive.

Most of the lawns needed cutting, and in many cases, there were piles of uncollected mail and newspapers lying on doorsteps and overflowing from mailboxes. Dan assumed people in this area had probably moved out already. It never occurred to him that some homes might still be occupied, but by people so ill they could not rise from their beds.

A gang of about a dozen teenagers blocked the road at one

point and he was forced to wait patiently while they sauntered past. One, a girl who couldn't have been much more than fourteen, picked up a stone and threw it at his windshield. It rebounded, leaving a tiny scarred crack.

"Hey!" He started to open the door, but her companions had all stopped and, rather than run for cover, were moving to her side in support. Dan decided to choose discretion over valor in this instance, pulled his door shut and accelerated down the street before their passive animosity could turn to active violence. It was an unpleasantly gut-twisting encounter, and made him all the more worried about Kelly.

Kelly was similarly concerned, and with considerably more reason. Despite her resolve to remain calm, she had given in to the temptation to call out for help, sometimes pounding against the walls until the vibrations hurt her head. Her throat was sore and her voice hoarse and unsteady, and the heat was making her dizzy.

The luminous dial of her wristwatch allowed her to keep track of the passage of time, which moved with glacial slowness. Once or twice gulls shrieked from somewhere close at hand, but she never heard anything suggesting another human presence. After a long and fruitless attempt to rock the cabinet loose from its present position, she drifted off into an uneasy sleep about noontime. Although the building was dark and she was sheltered from the sun, it provided little refuge from the hot, humid air. Her clothes were plastered to her flesh by perspiration and she was beginning to feel lightheaded and thirsty. There were two bottles of juice in her shoulderbag, wherever that was. If she had known that it was on the floor just outside the cabinet, the knowledge would only have added to her frustration.

She tried to reconstruct the physical layout of the room, and then replayed her last memories slowly so that she could understand what had happened. Two men had chased her down here, but a third had interrupted. She remembered seeing the stranger crouching over the body of the man named Cory, but she had never seen his face. There had been something odd about the way he moved, and he had smelled bad.

During the afternoon, she drifted in and out of consciousness, the soporific heat sapping her strength. She made occasional, futile attempts to force the door open when she was awake, but with little hope of accomplishing anything. And outside, the sun was once again beginning to dip toward the horizon.

Dan kept his appointment with Angela Harris, taking a break from his lonely search effort. He identified himself to a very harried front desk sergeant who begrudgingly paged the detective, then told him to take a seat while he waited. Fifteen minutes later, Harris appeared, her expression tight and strained, and gestured him through the doorway into the station interior.

Other than a terse greeting, she remained silent as she led the way down a short corridor, through an open area crowded with disorderly desks, most of which were not currently occupied, then along a second corridor to a narrow staircase. "Be careful what you say when we can be overheard," she cautioned him. "Everyone here is under a lot of pressure and tempers are frayed. We had a fist fight between two officers last night, and a couple of the desk jockeys are pissed because they've been drafted into helping with field work and they're taking it out on anyone who comes within reach."

"I'll be good." He followed her down the stairs and along another corridor that ran past a row of file rooms, some in current use, others dead storage. A handful of clerks were working at computer terminals or filing cabinets, but most of them didn't even look up as he and Harris passed.

"Heads up," she said just loud enough for him to hear. "Herman the Horrible is on duty."

The corridor opened into a larger space, bisected by a wire mesh barrier with a single wooden framed door. A rough edged desk with peeling paint stood just beyond, manned by a uniformed officer who sat, eyes downcast, studying some paperwork.

Harris cleared her throat ostentatiously, waited a second, then spoke. "Earth to Herman."

The policeman glanced up. Herman's face was round, cheeks puffy, complexion blotchy and sprinkled with spiky whiskers that had escaped the razor. His eyes were small for his face and set close together on either side of an oversized and misshapen nose. He could have been cast as Quasimodo if he'd sported a hump.

"I saw you, Harris."

"So how about opening the door?"

Herman shrugged expressively. "Who's the civilian?"

"A consultant. We need to look at some evidence, Herman. You remember evidence, don't you? The stuff we use to solve crimes."

"Nothin' doin', Harris." He tapped the paperwork on his desk. "I got nothin' here to say you can bring someone into this area. What d'you think the fence is for?"

"Come off it, Herman; you know I've got access."

"You do; he doesn't. You want in, say so; he can wait out here until you're done." Herman steadfastly refused to acknowledge Dan's presence even by so much as a direct look, and Dan was beginning to feel a deep, bright flame of anger.

"Look, Herman, sign him in and I'll countersign for you. Captain Pirelli okayed this yesterday. We're just going to look at some evidence and see if he can help me catch the bad guy. Remember, that's what police are supposed to do, catch the bad guys. Not act like them."

Harris and Herman glared at each other and the tableau held for several seconds while Dan shifted his weight restlessly from foot to foot. Ultimately, it was Herman who blinked, passing a sheet of paper and a pen out through a slot in the mesh. "You co-sign for him and initial the date and time."

Dan and Harris did as instructed and Herman grudgingly pressed the buzzer that unlocked the door. Harris led the way to a second door, then ushered Dan into a much larger room, partitioned into several walk-in cages, the largest and sturdiest of which contained an impressive collection of firearms, all neatly sorted and tagged, including at least one explosive device, currently disarmed, and other weapons including knives, machetes, hand grenades, chains, shuriken, and some things Dan couldn't identify. There was a vault at the far end of the room, closed and locked, a row of file cabinets, and two desks, one of which was occupied by an attentive looking female officer.

Harris visibly relaxed. "Elaine, how did you end up in here? I thought you were still out on disability."

The other woman rose, sketching a small smile. "The definition of disability has been narrowed a little, during the present emergency. I'm officially fit for limited duty, which means they can keep me at a desk so long as it's not for more than sixty hours a week."

"The usual crap," Harris shook her head.

"It does run downhill. What can I do for you today, Angela?"

"This is Dan Scapelli," she nodded at her companion. "He might be able to help me identify a piece of evidence that we're holding."

"Lot number?"

Harris pulled a slip of paper from her pocket and read off a short series of digits. The other woman nodded, then lifted a batch of keys from her belt and sorted through them until she found the one she wanted. "Are you going to be taking this with you?"

"Can I do that without a release?"

"No way, Angela. Sorry. It's not much of a job, but it's the only one I've got."

"I didn't really think so, but so many things are changing around here lately, you never know any more."

They were admitted to one of the larger cages, in the center of which stood a narrow table and three chairs. The woman was checking tag numbers on a row of items that included a pair of hedge clippers, a jewelry box, a briefcase with a broken handle, a dvd player, and other mundane items, but Dan and Harris both spotted the box almost immediately, tucked onto the topmost shelf in the far corner.

"That's it over there." Harris picked up a rolling stool and pushed it forward. Elaine thanked her with a nod, climbed up and confirmed the lot tag. She started to lift it down but almost lost her balance, surprised by its weight.

"Here, let me give you a hand." Dan reached up and took the box from the young woman, then carried it to the table. It was larger than he had expected, and heavier.

"I'll leave you to it. Good luck."

Once Elaine was gone, Dan reached over and gently lifted the lid of the box. Despite its age and evidence of heavy weathering, it was in excellent condition, both inside and out. Most of the discoloration was dried dirt which flaked off as soon as he touched it; some of the carvings were worn but most seemed almost new, distinct, crisp, and perfectly legible. The hinges were in remarkably good condition; the top opened easily and silently, coming to rest against its stops. The interior was spotlessly clean, and when he ran his fingers along the inside, he was surprised at how smooth and polished it felt, as though someone had taken a very fine piece of sandpaper and buffed it very carefully and thoroughly. There were no markings on the inside surfaces, no evidence of secret compartments, no hint of what might it might have contained.

One flight above, Patrolman Arthur Wiseman removed two cloth overnight bags from his locker and carried them into the men's room, locking himself inside one of the stalls. Under ordinary circumstances, Arthur would not have been expected to show up for this shift. On Saturday night, his wife had been taken to one of the field hospitals after collapsing with a very high fever, and she had not regained consciousness. On Monday afternoon, he and his partner, Del Lewis, had been called to the scene of a robbery in progress, a convenience store on the west side that had been closed since the previous evening when a suspicious fire had damaged the power lines nearby. A neighbor had reported seeing someone climb in through the rear window.

Wiseman had gone around to cover the rear while Lewis entered through the front, and had been trying the lock when he heard three shots fired inside the store. With his own weapon drawn, he had raced around to the front of the building, but by then the action had already ended. Del Lewis had been surprised by a teenaged boy, who had been hiding behind the cash register, when the unexpected figure appeared, he had reacted by raising his weapon and firing. Two of the three rounds would have been fatal by themselves.

The unexpected twist was that the dead boy had been Arthur Wiseman's only grandchild.

He had stared dumbly at the boy's motionless face and blankly staring eyes for a few seconds, then calmly emptied his own weapon into Del Lewis' back. Leaving his former partner where he lay, Wiseman calmly carried the dead boy to the squad car and drove to his home, where he laid the small body on the bed in the spare room and sat quietly in a chair until well after darkness had fallen. When neither he nor Lewis reported back during the remainder of the day or at the end of their shift, notice was taken, but there were too many more pressing matters at hand, and no one was assigned to look into their absence.

Shortly after midnight, Wiseman rose from his silent vigil and descended to the basement, whose windows he had long since painted and covered with wire mesh. He had finished the basement himself, paneling the walls, installing a drop ceiling, and covering the cement floor with indoor-outdoor carpeting. The decor was graphic and startling, consisting of framed portraits of Adolf Hitler, George Lincoln Rockwell, and others, along with both American and Nazi flags and banners. Two bookshelves were filled with publications ordered from the American Nazi Party, the John Birch Society, the White People's Party, the Aryan Nation, and kindred organizations. One wall was a locked cabinet containing various small arms, behind which a hidden compartment concealed four semi-automatic weapons, a box of hand grenades, and thirty pounds of assorted explosives.

Wiseman worked in his basement for nearly two hours, then carried two overnight bags upstairs to his bedroom, where he slept until late in the morning. Shortly after sunrise, he showered, shaved, and changed clothes, then ate a hearty meal before setting off for police headquarters.

No one paid any attention when he carried the bags into the locker room. No one who saw him there was aware of the fact that he'd been missing for the past twenty four hours. When the locker room was finally empty, he took out the devices he'd rigged the night before. Sitting in the center stall, Wiseman closed one hand over each of the two triggers he had devised, and suddenly clenched both fists.

The explosions were so close together that they were virtually indistinguishable. Wiseman died instantaneously, portions of his body blown through the adjoining walls, ceiling, and even the floor. A main support was located behind the wall to his rear, and the force of the blast was almost sufficient to shatter it completely. Part of the floor above collapsed, dumping three desks and two very startled clerks into the wreckage. The floor below imploded; plaster and fragments of wood rained down into the lower levels, followed by a rush of debris that grew for several seconds as the structure began to fall in upon itself. It took less than minute for what remained of the building to settle into an uneasy new equilibrium, but for those who were caught in the middle of it, the chaos seemed to go on forever. The locker room area was completely destroyed, and most of its mangled contents were dumped unceremoniously into the rooms directly below, which happened to be the evidence storage lockers and the adjacent waiting area.

"What the..." That was all Dan managed to say before he was forced to jump back out of the way. A thirty pound chunk of mangled wood smashed down onto the table with such force that all four legs crumpled. The chest started to slide forward and Harris instinctively reached out to hold it. A wooden beam crashed down close beside her, delivering a glancing blow to her right shoulder that knocked her off her feet.

The sound of the original double blast was replaced by a gradually diminishing rumble as the wreckage settled into its new configuration. Dan crouched with both hands raised to protect his head from the smaller debris still dropping from above, while Harris crouched in a corner, stunned and disoriented. Elaine wandered past, blood streaming from a superficial but ghastly looking scalp wound, disoriented and desperate to get out of the building. She climbed through what remained of the entrance, walked blindly past the prostrate body of Herman Raucher, who would never again bar the way to the evidence room.

When the worst of it seemed to have ended, Dan cautiously crossed the room and helped Harris to her feet. "What the hell happened?"

She brushed plaster dust and splinters from her clothing, shaking her head. "Some kind of bomb would be my guess. A pretty powerful one too. Let's get out of here before the whole thing comes down on us."

"I'm with you."

But Dan stopped first to push away some wreckage and rescue the mysterious box, which was covered with plaster dust but otherwise unharmed.

"What are you doing?"

"Taking this with us."

She shook her head. "You can't do that. It's evidence, Dan. We could both get into a lot of trouble doing that."

It was heavy, but by wrapping both arms around it, Dan was able to lift it and hold it against his chest. "Come off it, Angela." It was the first time he' had used her first name. "Look around. Do you think anyone really cares? Things are falling apart fast now, and if

Vera Maitlin was right, this might be the key to understanding what's happening and stopping it."

She still looked uneasy, but nodded and stepped past him, leading the way.

They passed several other police officers before reaching a door that led outside, but no one questioned their possession of the box, and in fact Dan suspected that no one had even really noticed them. The entire building seemed to have dissolved into chaos; people were shouting, or desperately trying to find out what had happened, or wandering aimlessly about in the initial stages of shock. A few were bleeding and one man appeared to have a broken arm, but they didn't see any other serious injuries. Dan didn't even want to guess how many bodies were buried in the rubble.

"Where are you going to take it?"

Dan hadn't really thought about it. "Back to my place, I guess. My car's only a couple of blocks away. You coming?"

"No, I've got to get back. I'm still on duty."

"You're sure?"

"Absolutely."

"All right, watch yourself. I'll be in touch as soon as I know something." He thought about it. "I guess I'll have to call you at your place."

"You do that. Take care of that chest. When things get straightened out around here, someone's going to want to know what happened to it. And Dan," she turned away for a second so that he couldn't see her eyes. "Good luck finding your friend."

"Yeah. Thanks."

The chest spent the rest of the afternoon sitting in the trunk of Dan's car while he eliminated two more of his marked search areas, with no more success than during the morning. Late that afternoon, he drove down the street where Kelly had parked her car, unfortunately turning into a side street two blocks before he would have passed it.

Kelly was woken by the sound of metal scraping against metal. A second later, the doors of her tiny prison swung open, and even the relative gloom of the room outside seemed bright. Warily, she climbed out, but her legs were so cramped and weak that she staggered and fell to her knees. Her right hand came down on a soft, yielding object, which she recognized more by touch than sight as her missing shoulderbag. Thankfully she clutched it to her, then sought desperately inside until she found the two cartons of fruit juice.

The fluid was warm, but it was tart and liquid and she consumed the first hungrily, lingering a bit longer over the second. Only when her thirst was relatively satisfied did she regain enough presence of mind to look around.

At first, she thought she was alone, but as her eyes slowly grew accustomed to the light, she saw a man standing several meters away, half obscured in the shadows. Warily, she climbed to her feet, slinging the bag over her shoulder, letting the empty carton fall to the floor.

"Who are you? What do you want?"

There was no answer. Kelly began to edge slowly to her left, trying to see more clearly. The figure was not far from the room's only exit, and was perfectly positioned to intercept her if she tried to escape. A small broken window allowed in enough of the moonlight to cast a small puddle of illumination in that part of the room, but whoever the other person was, he was standing just far enough to one side that his face remained in shadow.

In her weakened condition, Kelly wasn't sure if she could have outrun a toddler, but she sensed that her companion did not mean her well. Risky though it might be, she was about to bolt from the door when the man stirred, stepping forward so that she could see his face.

"Dan! Why didn't you say something? How did you find me?"

He remained silent, raised one finger to his lips, and Kelly nodded. They must still be danger. "Let's get out of here," she whispered urgently. "There's something very wrong here."

But Dan didn't appear to be in any hurry to leave. He came closer, raised his arms and folded them around her and she stumbled, suddenly even more lightheaded. The sour smell was back, though not as strong as before, and it made her head spin. Slowly he changed position, holding her with one arm around her shoulders while the other shifted so that he could raise his free hand to her breast. His fingers pressed against her, hard, urgent, even painful at first, but then a pleasant, all consuming heat seemed to pass from his flesh into hers. He lowered his head and his tongue was pressing between her lips. A part of her mind screamed that something was wrong, but the feeling of warmth and passion overwhelmed all rational though.

Just as she was on the verge of surrendering completely, she felt his body stiffen to steely hardness and then, before she had time to realize what was happening, he had pushed her away. She lost her balance, stumbled over her own feet, and threw her hands out to break her fall. The shoulderbag slipped free and fell to one side, the flap still open, spilling its contents.

Kelly landed jarringly and rolled over onto her back, startled and confused. Painfully, she rose onto her elbows just in time to see a second figure step through the doorway, only a meter away from Dan. The newcomer's face was silhouetted in the pallid light, distinct enough for her to recognize its alien features, the deformed nose, projecting brow ridge, smooth skull marred by only occasional tufts of coarse hair, a lower jaw just a shade too heavy to be entirely human. It was a creature of nightmare, something out of a low budget horror film, denizen of the black lagoon or the haunted cave or another planet.

But that wasn't the most startling thing. What stunned her to complete silence and immobility was that Dan stepped forward to confront the creature, and the pale finger of light touched his face as well. Except that it wasn't Dan's face at all, despite what she had seen earlier. It was coarse and malevolent looking and not entirely human either.

In fact, it looked very much like the other.

CHAPTER TWELVE: TUESDAY NIGHT TO WEDNESDAY

Even in the poor light, it was clear that while neither of these creatures was human, they were clearly two of a kind. The first resembled a cadaverously thin adult male, although all semblance to Dan Scapelli had melted away. The head was misshapen, slightly asymmetrical. The separate elements of the face were similarly irregular, the nose a shapeless mound of flesh broken by a single nostril, the lips thin and twisted and extending just a little bit too far around the sides of the face. The creature's body was sheathed in some kind of a black cloak that molded itself so closely that it was hard to tell where it ended and flesh began. Or perhaps it was itself a kind of flesh.

The newcomer was shorter, slightly heavier, and its body was canted forward, head held low against the chest. It also was cloaked in blackness, but in this case, more tenuous, unformed, as though a cloud was hovering around its torso. They faced each other warily.

They had momentarily forgotten Kelly and she took advantage of the situation to back slowly away on her hands and knees, not daring to stand up. Her left hand touched the shoulderbag and she automatically ran its strap over her shoulder. One of the vampires hissed menacing, and the taller one's amber eyes flashed as it bared its fangs. They faced each other without moving, ignoring Kelly, testing each other's will. The silent exchange resolved itself within seconds, with the younger one finally settling back, acknowledging defeat. It hadn't taken nearly long enough for her to escape.

That didn't stop her from trying. Sensing that the confrontation had ended, she stood up suddenly and ran recklessly toward the exit, one arm outstretched to ward off obstructions. She made it out of the room but she couldn't remember the route she had taken when she'd come this way before. She reached a cross corridor and turned to her right mostly because the floor seemed less cluttered in that direction. Right now the most important thing was to put some distance between herself and whatever was following.

Unfortunately, appearances are deceiving. She hadn't taken more than a half dozen steps before a piece of the flooring snapped under her weight, throwing her off balance. Her right shoulder brushed the wall and she reeled away, fighting for balance, and might have regained it if another section of flooring hadn't crumbled under her heel. Kelly fell heavily on her right hip, and that impact was sufficient to snap a rotted cross beam. Fragments of plaster and wood fell into the darkness as a meter square section of the floor slowly caved in and disintegrated, leaving her dangling on the brink of a twelve foot drop.

Moving very slowly, Kelly spread her arms and legs, trying to shift her weight onto safer ground. One hand brushed against a wooden support, but the moist wood fragmented in her hand when she tried to hold onto it. The surface beneath her began to sag and she let out a short, involuntary scream as she half slid, half fell in a shower of debris. Something cold and hard slammed against her ankle, and she kicked out, convinced that one of the creatures had grabbed her, but in fact she had caught her foot between a joist and cross beam. As the last support collapsed beneath her, she fell forward, restrained only by that pinching hold, so that she dangled upside down, her hair streaming past her head.

Smaller fragments continued to shower down and she crossed her arms over her face protectively. Something struck just behind her left ear, a glancing blow, stunningly painful, and she felt a warm wetness trickling along the side of her head. For the next few seconds she struggled to remain conscious, but it was finally too great an effort.

Kelly need not have worried about pursuit. Although the standoff had ended with a clear winner, they barely noticed when she escaped. In some silent, unimaginable way, they were directly communicating for the first time and that was much more important than the fate of one potential victim.

And there were, after all, plenty of other humans out there in the darkness.

Specialist Fourth Class Albert Rossiter was not happy. The order calling him to active duty had come just as he was in the final stages of what he hoped would be a successful campaign to convince Donna Deakins that there was no reason why they should wait until they were married before sleeping together. He had more or less proposed a month earlier and even if they had been keeping it secret for the time being, even from her parents, or perhaps especially from her parents, it was only because he couldn't afford a ring right now and the situation with his job at Eblis Manufacturing was a little bit uncertain. He wanted to wait until they could make definite long term plans before issuing an official announcement.

Donna wasn't exactly a prude but she felt constrained by the rigidly conservative standards to which she'd been raised. Albert insisted to himself and his friends that Donna was the kind of girl you married, as opposed to the kind you fooled around with, but he was hoping that she would agree to some kind of interim compromise.

Slowly but surely, he'd been chipping away at Donna's faltering resistance. She was twenty years old, hardly a kid, and entitled to make her own decisions, even if she did still live in the same bedroom where her crib had stood. Albert was careful never to test the limits of the older Deakins' patience, adhered religiously to their curfews and insistence on always knowing where the couple was going, even though he chafed at the restrictions. He made a conscious effort to cultivate their good opinion, polishing his manners in their presence, complimenting them on small things when the opportunity arose, and both Edgar and Mary Deakins seemed to view him with guarded approval, although Edgar's occasional references to "good bloodlines" and "the sins of the fathers" often made him wonder if the old man had somehow learned of his own father's youthful misadventures. Not that Sam Rossiter had been a criminal, exactly; he had never served hard time or anything. He had bent the rules but never quite broken them, or at least he'd never been caught on the wrong side of the law.

A few little bumps in the road notwithstanding, the courtship had proceeded relatively smoothly, and they had recently progressed from discussing the possibility of sex before marriage to defining the conditions under which it might take place. Albert had taken to carrying a package of condoms on his person at all times, and the single minded intensity with which he devoted himself to the campaign was as much a product of his gonads as his heart.

So the call to active duty came at just the wrong time. He'd already spent two days working fifteen hour shifts in a makeshift emergency ward at the armory, collapsing in exhaustion on a cot in the same room with several of his fellow guardsmen. He had finally been able to get a message to Donna on the third day, a very brief telephone call during a smoking break, but it seemed unlikely that they could have any real contact until the emergency was over. And as far as he could tell, that might be quite some time.

His situation was marginally improved when he was called into the colonel's makeshift office and told he was being transferred to duty at one of the traffic checkpoints. He preferred the relative freedom of patrol duty, and at least he would be away from the stink of medication and illness that pervaded the armory, now a field hospital. There was an air of hopelessness that made even the slightest setback feel like a disaster. He knew of one attempted suicide, and it had been a Guardsman, not one of the patients. Lost in his own thoughts, he climbed into the back of a jeep bound for Checkpoint Fourteen, Gano Street on the east side.

Traffic was busy on the interstate, people passing through but definitely not stopping in Providence, but almost non-existent down in the city proper. Most of those with the will and the wherewithal to leave had already gone; radio and television broadcasts continued to exhort people to remain calm, assured them that the spread of the disease had been contained and that it was only a matter of time until the situation returned to normal. Albert didn't believe it; he'd seen the volume of new patients pouring into the armory, heard enough to know the same was true of every field hospital in the city. He was also quite certain that the death toll was much higher than was being reported. The body bags were mostly taken away late at night.

His new assignment had another advantage. The Deakins house was only six blocks from the checkpoint, and he used the telephone outside a nearby drugstore to call and let Donna know where he was stationed. An hour later, he was introducing her to Scott Simonelli and Mark Cussler, the two men with whom he'd been teamed. Donna had spent most of the last two days either at the guard post or shuttling back and forth from her house. They were issued fresh rations for every meal and were supposed to avoid any local food, but the meals Donna and her mother prepared and brought to them were far more appealing. His teammates were only too willing to allow the couple some private time in return for warm, fresh cooked lunches and suppers.

She stayed quite late Tuesday night, until dusk had nearly given way to full darkness. Although she had strict orders to be home before night fell, Donna was somewhat liberal in her definition of "night". The streets of Providence had ceased to be the friendly, familiar place she'd known all her life, and even during the daylight hours, she walked directly from one place to another, eyes constantly scanning from left to right, wary of any stranger. She would have preferred go home while the sun was still up, but they'd been having such a good time, she was reluctant to break it off. Albert was actually talking about setting a date once he was released from active duty, and that meant an official announcement, of course, and an end to her uncertainty. Perhaps his having been called up was not such a tragedy after all.

When she finally took her leave, she was unsettled to see how dark it had gotten and picked up her pace, running through a selection of excuses. She was so preoccupied that she almost ran into the tall figure who stepped out into her path from behind an elderly maple. Instinctively she backed away, preparing to run, but there was just enough light for her to recognize Albert's face.

"Al, what are you doing?" She took a step toward him, but at that very moment a sports car rounded the next corner and shot down the street in her direction. Its headlights briefly outlined the figure ahead, which spun and threw both arms up to shield its eyes. As it did so, Albert's image shimmered, melting into a chaotic mix of black and chalk white. The lights swept past in an instant as the car turned onto another street with a screech of tires and brakes, and then vanished behind a row of houses. Donna blinked, trying to refocus her eyes, but Albert -- if that really had been him -- was gone. She looked all around, wondering if she'd actually seen anything or if it had just been a trick of the light.

And then a powerful blow struck the side of her head and she was falling forward into blackness. She lost consciousness before she hit the ground.

The vampire crouched over the motionless form. With skeletal fingers tipped with long black nails, it pulled open the top of her blouse, revealing her throat and chest. The scream of brakes and tortured rubber came again and the vampire jerked back with a low hiss, its amber eyes glowing with hatred. The sports car's engine was audible for a few seconds, but it did not reappear for several minutes, and by then Donna Deakins was long gone.

Kelly almost wished that she'd lost consciousness. The pain

in her left ankle was getting steadily worse. It was pitch dark and she couldn't tell how much of a drop remained if she should fall free, so she hesitated, afraid that by freeing herself she would only make things worse. Her inverted position was making her lightheaded, and she was so weak already that feared that if she didn't do something, and quickly, she might find herself unable to act at all.

She stretched her arms out slowly to either side, trying to find anything which offered firmer support. The strap of her shoulderbag, which had been tightly twisted around her upper arm, began to slide down her arm, and she bent her elbow so that she wouldn't lose it. There appeared to be nothing solid within reach.

"Wonderful," she said beneath her breath, then slipped the bag off her arm and looped the strap through her belt. Most of its contents were gone, but her hair brush and mirror were safely zippered in a side pocket, along with a few unused tissues. Scant resources, and none seemed very useful. The other zippered section held half a dozen coins, mostly pennies. Thoughtfully, she dropped two of these, listening for the sounds of impact, which came fairly quickly. She guessed she would fall no more than ten feet, but since the first impact might well be her head, she decided to forego the experience until all other alternatives proved to be even less appealing.

She tried bending at the waist and even managed to wrap her hands around her thighs for a few seconds, but the strain was too much and she fell back almost immediately. "Time to get back into shape," she whispered, but the thought occurred to her that it might well be past that time.

Her ankle and foot were starting to feel numb, but remained firmly trapped despite her gyrations. Since she could think of no other alternatives, she began pumping her arms so that she slowly swayed back and forth. At the end of each swing, she waved her hands, once brushing against a broken board which pulled free when she grabbed it. Frustrated, she let it drop into the darkness.

After rocking from side to side for several minutes, she switched to front and back, at first with no greater effect but then, just before she was about to give up the effort, her fingers brushed against something rough and unyielding. Greater exertion widened the arc of movement, but she had to grit her teeth at the growing pain in her ankle. Then one hand caught a metal pipe, corroded but intact, and after a brief moment when it began to bend under her weight, she found herself in a slightly more tenable position.

Kelly forced herself to ignore both pain and exhaustion and work her hands along the length of pipe. Slowly her body approached the horizontal, but then she discovered a new problem. The pipe extended down through a section of relatively undamaged flooring, which formed an impenetrable roof above her head. She steadied herself by wrapping the crook of her elbow around the pipe and pressing her cheek against its cold surface while she felt around with the other hand.

The flooring ended in a jagged tangle at the limit of her reach.

Kelly almost cried when she realized how close she was to safety. She stretched her arm as far as she could manage, ignoring the strain on her shoulders, trying to wrap her fingers around the far edge of the break. It was heartbreakingly close, but she couldn't quite manage it.

Then she remembered her shoulderbag. It took some effort to untie it without losing her grip on the pipe, but finally it was done. She leaned back again, the body of the bag clutched firmly, and swung the strap into the darkness. Three times she missed her mark, and on the fourth try it caught briefly, but slid off as soon as she pulled back. On the sixth try, it wrapped itself firmly around a secure anchor and she cautiously put weight on it.

The bag was not meant to withstand that much strain and the material stretched ominously. Kelly had no idea how long the stitching would survive such abuse, but lacking a better plan, she drew a deep breath, then released the pipe and let all of her weight come down on the bag.

The strap shifted slightly and for a split second, she thought she would fall free. But it held, and she pulled herself up until she could finally lift one arm above the broken flooring and anchor herself more securely. A moment later, there was a sharp crack from somewhere in the darkness and her foot was suddenly free. For a split second, she thought she'd broken her ankle, but the sound had been the last gasp of the splintered board holding her. Instinctively, she released the bag and threw her other arm up and forward, banging her elbow and just barely holding on as her legs swung under her.

Somehow she summoned the strength to pull herself up onto the more or less level surface above her, then collapsed, exhausted, bleeding from head and ankle, both hands scraped raw. For the moment at least, she was safe.

Albert knew something was wrong when Donna's father showed up at the checkpoint in defiance of the curfew. "Have you checked with her friends? Maybe she stopped somewhere on the way."

"We've already spoken to everyone in the neighborhood who might have seen her, young man." He was always "young man" or "Mr. Rossiter", never "Albert".

"Maybe you should call the police."

"I don't think we can count on much help from them right now. They're rather busy."

"Well, I'll try to get the patrols to watch for her." He hesitated. "And I'll go looking for her myself as soon as I can."

As soon as Deakins left, Albert did call in the report, but the bored voice at the other end of the line couldn't promise anything. He convinced Simonelli and Cussler to cover for him and set out on his own, using his flashlight to examine yards, side streets, abandoned lots, even parked cars.

And shortly after midnight, he saw someone stumbling along an unlighted road.

Kelly lost consciousness for a while, and even when she came to she was so groggy that she found her way out of the building more through luck than good planning. The cool breeze blowing in from Narragansett Bay restored her somewhat, and she reoriented herself and started back toward the main road, trying to remember exactly where she'd left her car. There was a purse lying on the ground nearby; it wasn't hers, but some impulse caused her to stoop and pick it up, almost losing her balance in the process. Her ankle was bothering her; it appeared to have stopped bleeding despite the deep lacerations but her sock was stiff and crusty and her toes tingled constantly. It would bear her weight but only under painful protest.

There were no lights on in any of the nearby houses, nor was there any traffic, pedestrian or vehicular, although she could hear motors growling in the distance. There was a buzzing in the back of her head telling her to find a soft place to lie down and go to sleep, but she knew she had to get as away from the abandoned buildings as quickly as possible while she still had the strength to walk.

She was so concentrated on the act of walking that she didn't hear the voice calling to her. Specialist Albert Rossiter demanded three times that she identify herself and now stood with his weapon pointed in her direction. Kelly finally realized she was no longer alone, stared at him uncomprehendingly for a few seconds, then folded up and collapsed to the sidewalk.

Albert managed to rouse her enough that she could walk, with his assistance, the several blocks back to the checkpoint. She lost consciousness again but only after they had made her comfortable in the back of their jeep. It was only then that he recognized the purse she'd been carrying and looked inside to confirm his suspicion.

It was Donna's.

Albert sat beside Kelly for almost an hour before she stirred. She would have remained asleep but he touched her shoulder and she sat up abruptly and in obvious terror. He reassured her that she was safe and, once she had calmed down, asked about the purse in as level a voice as he could manage. Kelly had no clear recollection of where she had found it, but she described the factory complex in great detail, and Albert recognized it.

"Is that where you found the purse?"

She shook her head. "I don't know. I'm sorry but I just can't remember." His companions didn't want him to leave on his own again, but he was determined, even if it meant a court martial.

He found the decaying building Kelly had described with surprising ease. The door was missing, just as she had said, but most of the rest of her story seemed improbable at best. He was perfectly prepared to accept that two or more men had abducted both women earlier in the evening, but his credulity did not extend to include inhuman creatures that looked like men.

It was very dark inside, and even his flashlight was inadequate to dispel the gloom. Kelly's description of the interior had not been particularly helpful. The building was obviously deteriorating rapidly; even within the narrow cone projected from his flashlight, Albert saw sagging walls, crumbling plaster, cracked and failing supports. The building had been stripped of any valuable contents at some point long past, but enough trash remained to make footing uncertain and accentuate the atmosphere of neglect and decay.

He began to work his way methodically from room to room, searching each perfunctorily before moving on to the next. His forward progress was arrested temporarily when he found an enormous hole in the floor, but there was enough room to bypass it, and he did so cautiously, fearing another collapse. A corridor led to his left and he followed it a short distance until it brought him to a large enclosure, apparently originally the site of some kind of small manufacturing or assembly operation. Rows of wooden benches marched off to left and right, and naked metal supports along one wall led off into the distance.

Something lay on the floor only a few meters away. Albert knew what it was even before he was close enough to see any details.

Donna's skin was chalky white in the flashlight's sterile glare; the triangular wounds in her throat still accented by tiny trails of scarlet blood.

He stood transfixed, unable to bring himself to touch her, to confirm what he already knew, that she was dead. A whisper of sound made him look up just as a dark figure emergeds from the shadows at the far edge of the room. He started to lift his weapon, but the newcomer stepped out of the shadows and he let if fall, his face relaxing.

"Donna!" he called out in surprise. It was the last word he ever spoke.

Angela Harris was fortunate in that her office was in the undamaged wing of the police station. Cleanup operations had begun but as with everything else, there were insufficient resources and it would be several days at least before the department was back to something approximating normal. Structural engineers had examined the wreckage left by the bomb and rendered their opinions, and most operations had been temporarily transferred to the public library, which had been closed to the public for the interim.

She was pleasantly surprised when Kelly Marsh's name

showed up on the ever lengthening list of people in temporary medical custody. She called Dan Scapelli's number several times during the day, finally reaching him shortly after noon, when he stopped back at his apartment for a change of clothes.

"Dan, this is Angela. I've found Kelly."

The relief and excitement in his voice was so intense that Angela felt a touch of jealousy.

"Is she all right? Where is she?"

"I've just got a preliminary report. She's in a temporary ward on Wickenden Street."

"She's where? God, don't tell me she's come down with one of these goddamned plagues."

"No, at least according to what I see here she only has superficial cuts and injuries. Maybe she was in an accident. That might explain why you couldn't find her car. She was picked up last night by a National Guard patrol."

"I'll go down right away and get her out of there."

"Wait a sec, Dan. That might not be so easy. You see, technically speaking she's under arrest."

"Under arrest? For what? Having an accident?"

"Calm down, Dan. According to the report, she was cited for being out past curfew."

"Out past curfew? You've got to be kidding. Obviously something happened to her. I'm going down there right now."

"Hold your horses, damn it! You stay right where you are, you understand?" She glanced at her watch. "Give me an hour, no, make that an hour and a half. There are some advantages of being a police officer, you know. Let me pull a few strings. I think I can claim that she's a material witness to at least one of the matters under investigation here. Let me run the paperwork past my boss and see if I can get her released in my custody. If that flies, I'll pick her up and run her back to your place. But if you run in there on your own and raise hell, it'll just piss people off and make things more difficult than they have to be."

"And if your plan doesn't work?"

"Then I'll call you and let you know and we'll figure out another plan. Keep yourself busy plotting a jailbreak or something."

As it happened, it took close to two hours to accomplish, but ultimately she was successful. She couldn't find Captain Caldwell, so she forged his signature. The officer in charge of the Wickenden Street Emergency Trauma Facility was just as happy to have one less patient to worry about. They'd already run out of beds, cots, and mattresses.

Kelly had been mildly hostile until Harris mentioned Dan's name, but they spoke very little on the way to Dan's apartment, partly because she had been pumped up with painkillers and had trouble staying awake. Harris parked, illegally, in front of the apartment building and the two walked upstairs together, Kelly wobbling slightly.

Dan greeted them both warmly but Kelly was in obvious distress and he helped her into the bedroom. Harris wondered if this should be her cue to leave, but before she could decide, Dan reappeared.

"I don't know how to thank you, Angela."

"Don't bother. It was a pleasure doing something constructive for a change."

"Well I owe you one. A big one."

They compared notes, but neither had anything new to offer and when she realized that his eyes were constantly straying toward the bedroom door, she smiled to herself and stood up, making her excuses.

Kelly's arrest report had been filled in sloppily but it included her claim that she'd been assaulted while walking near an abandoned factory building. She noted the name of the Guardsman who had found her and made a call, trying to reach him, only to discover that he'd disappeared from his post during the night.

"Possibly a desertion. We've had a few lately," a captain admitted to her with obvious reluctance. She found out where he'd been stationed and made a connection.

Vincent Marzocchi appeared in the doorway. "Time to go, Harris. We're supposed to be taking statements from the bus terminal staff about last night's shooting, remember?"

"I remember. But we're going somewhere else first." She waved the report at him for a second before dropping it to her desk and rising. "I've got a hot tip." And she wanted to act on it quickly.

CHAPTER THIRTEEN: WEDNESDAY NIGHT

Vincent Marzocchi was uncharacteristically silent on the ride to the East Side. He was older than his partner, old enough to take early retirement soon if he wanted it. Until this past week, he'd never even considered leaving the force, but he had aged a lot in a very short period, and somewhere along the line he'd decided that as soon as the present mess was cleaned up, it would be time to think about filing his papers. He hadn't mentioned it to anyone yet, not even his wife, because he felt obligated to tell his partner first, and hadn't found a way to do that just yet. He glanced at her face as she drove and knew that this wasn't the time either.

But it would have to be soon.

Marzocchi raised an eyebrow but didn't say anything when she parked under the highway, pulling up onto the shoulder and setting the parking brake. When she opened her door, he did the same, remaining silent while she took two flashlights from the trunk and handed him one. They walked side by side until their forward progress was stopped by a rusting, sagging hurricane fence.

"Might I ask what we're doing here? Just out of curiosity, you understand."

"Someone I know was attacked around here last night."

Marzocchi nodded. "People are getting attacked all over the place lately, but unless she's dead, we're talking a pretty low priority crime, Angela. Why not let the uniforms handle it?"

Harris began to walk along the side of the fence and Marzocchi followed a step or two behind. "She was chased into one of these abandoned buildings by a couple of men, but someone else showed up at the party without an invite. According to the victim, the newcomer offed the first two, then locked her in a closet of some kind until she escaped the next day."

"So we're looking for a couple of stiffs?"

"Yeah, but keep your eyes open. If her story holds up, the other guy's a rough customer."

"If he knows she got away, he's not likely to stick around waiting for us."

"Maybe. From the description, though, I'm not certain this guy thinks the same way we do." Let Marzocchi believe they were hunting a psycho; it'd keep him alert.

They found the same narrow alley that Kelly had followed, but wasted almost an hour searching the building on the court with the broken door under the mistaken impression that they'd found the right place. Harris was ready to give it up and head back for the car when Marzocchi noticed the stairway and gate. A few minutes later, they found another open door and Harris felt an electric tension stiffening the hairs on the back of her neck and along her forearms.

"Watch your step," she cautioned. The floor creaked under their feet and the wooden planks were warped and crumbling from exposure to rain and salt air. It was only a few minutes past six o'clock, but the sky was heavily overcast; what feeble light remained was unable to penetrate very far into the building, most of whose windows were boarded over. A few gaps in the roof provided glimpses of sky, but for the most part they were limited to what illumination they carried.

In one large open area, filled with rows of rough wooden tables, they found something disquieting.

They were only separated by two rows of tables when Marzocchi slipped and fell, luckily catching himself by slamming his palm down onto one of the tables. His hand came away sticky.

"Angela, come over here." He'd raised his hand to his face, and the odor of blood was quite noticeable.

"What've you got?"

He pointed the circle of light toward the table, but the stain was only slightly larger than the palm of his hand. "Well, something happened here, all right."

They searched the rest of the room thoroughly, even rechecking the areas they'd already passed over, but without finding anything else of interest.

"Let's check out the rest of the building." Harris led the way down a corridor to another, even larger enclosed space, which Marzocchi recognized as a loading dock similar to one he'd worked on during the summers back in high school.

The air smelled sour, as though something had died here.

Dan wanted very much to talk to Kelly, but she was clearly more in need of rest than conversation. He looked in on her occasionally, but spent most of his time sitting on the couch, reading and rereading Vera Maitlin's letter and Kelly's summary of Professor Concord's findings. The chest itself sat on the table in his own kitchen, where he'd carefully cleaned away all of the remaining dirt, even buffed down the metal straps, prying beneath them with a straightened paperclip to dislodge any foreign material that might have become lodged there. It was sturdily constructed, still in good condition despite having been buried in the mud, and he found it difficult to believe that it could have been there for any great length of time.

At six o'clock, he returned to his own apartment briefly to make a couple of sandwiches and retrieve a beer from the icebox. He had just re-entered Kelly's apartment when he heard her voice, rushed inside and dropped the sandwiches on an end table in his rush for the bedroom. She was still unconscious, however, twisting her head back and forth, muttering under her breath. Dan put one hand on her forehead, concerned that she was feverish, but her temperature felt normal. The contact seemed to reassure her and she grew calmer but did not waken.

He sat beside her bed so long that his beer was warm when he finally opened it.

Harris flashed her light around the inside of a metal cabinet, which matched the description of the one where Kelly had been held, but there was nothing to confirm her story except for a comb and mirror lying on the dirty floor. Marzocchi was at the opposite end of the room, poking around behind a row of lockers. A piece of pipe rolled off the top and bounced off the cement floor an arm's reach away and he jumped back in alarm. "This place is goddamned dangerous!"

Harris sensed his uneasiness, which mirrored her own. "I wish they'd just knock these things down when they abandon them," she answered. "This is an apartment building for rats, both the four legged and two legged varieties." She moved toward the far wall, picking her way carefully through the debris, almost turned back before she noticed the hatch cover. It was slightly askew, and the exposed rim was clean and shiny, not covered by the grime and dust that had settled on every other surface. She crouched and tried to lift one corner but it was heavier than she expected and she finally had to set the flashlight down and drop to one knee, using both hands to shift it a few inches to one side.

That's when the smell struck her.

"Marzocchi, get over here!" She scooped up the flashlight and directed it inside the cavity, but looked away almost immediately, biting her lip. There were at least four bodies crammed inside, their limbs all tangled together. Even after four years working homicide, it still came as a shock when she saw some of the extremes of cruelty people could inflict upon one another.

"What've you got?" Marzocchi reached her side in seconds, used his own light, and gasped. "What the fuck?"

Harris had recovered her composure and looked again, but it was impossible to determine even as simple a question as their true number. A young woman lay on top, naked to the waist, her limbs arranged so that she almost seemed to be embracing the body of the uniformed man beneath her. He in turn was supported by at least two others, both with long hair but apparently males, and there was at least one more body below them. The smell grew worse by the second.

"Christ," she whispered. "What's been going on in here?"

"I'm going back to the car to call this in." There was an audible tremor in Marzocchi's voice. "I don't care what else is going on; they've gotta come out for this one."

"Yeah, right." She leaned forward. For just a second, it had looked like... "Marzocchi, help me here! One of them's still alive!" At first, she had thought the movement to be a trick of the shadows animated by her flashlight, but now she could clearly see one hand shifting slightly, fingers starting to uncurl. "We've got to get him out of there."

"I see him." Marzocchi knelt by the open hatch and reached down with his left hand. "Let me see if I can reach his arm." Despite his revulsion, he stretched and then clamped his own fingers around the moving wrist. It felt incredibly cold and damp; the victim's body temperature must already have plummeted to near fatal levels. He tightened his grip. "Don't worry, guy, if you can hear me. We'll have you out of there in just a minute." He set his light down. "Angela, give me a hand here, will ya? This isn't gonna be too easy."

Harris moved to his side, but her assistance turned out to be unnecessary. The entire pile of bodies shifted in an unexpected parody of life as a frightening, inhuman shape erupted from beneath the corpses. Marzocchi inadvertently kicked his flashlight to one side as he was yanked forward into the hole, his own helping hand now clutched by fingers so powerful that the contact was painful.

Harris overcame her surprise in time to avoid the blow directed at her face. She stepped back and drew her weapon. "Police officers!" she shouted. "You're under arrest!"

The answer was a gargled scream, the last sound Vincent Marzocchi was ever to make. His limp body was thrown up and to one side, bleeding profusely from several deep parallel cuts across the jugular. He smashed into the metal cabinet with such force that it rose onto two legs and fell over onto its face with a resounding crash.

Harris raised her light as the figure swarmed up out of the hole, and what she saw of the creature's still vaguely reptilian face was enough to convince her that the normal rules did not apply. She managed to fire four rounds into the advancing vampire's torso before her hand was struck with such force that the bones in her wrist were shattered and she was spun halfway around. She took advantage of the momentum to jump forward and away, clutching her injured wrist tightly against her chest as she leaped over a pile of rotting corrugated boxes and staggered toward the exit.

Although she expected to feel claws ripping through her back with every step, Harris made it to the corridor. There she grew confused in the darkness and turned in the wrong direction when she reached the first intersection. Because she still held the flashlight, she was able to see the hole in the floor ahead seconds before she reached it, but despite her best efforts to maintain her balance, she toppled headlong into the shadows. The side of her head struck an old oil tank as she fell, and when she finally came to rest, her left leg was bent beneath her at an impossible angle. Despite the stunning blow and the fiery agony in her leg, she remained conscious, and through some miracle still held the intact flashlight in her left hand.

Which was unfortunate, since it provided a very good look at the face of the creature who joined her there a few seconds later.

Kelly stumbled out into the front room just before nine o'clock. Dan, who had been dozing in a chair, wakened immediately and went to her, wrapping his arms tightly around her for a few seconds without saying anything.

"I can't breathe," she whispered, and he released her.

"Sorry. How are you feeling? Do you want to sit down?"

She raised a hand to rub her forehead, smiling weakly. "Feels a little numb inside, but at least all the parts seem to be present and in working order. Is there any coffee?"

"Now I know you're feeling better. Of course there's coffee. Has the world come to an end? Hang on and I'll get you a cup."

She was ravenous as well and finished off some leftover chicken breasts, reheated chili, and a plate of Spanish rice while they talked. Slowly but with growing confidence, she told him how she had gone to investigate her hunch about the mysterious monogram, then described the encounter with the two hoodlums.

"You should have known better to wander around that part of the city alone, even under the best of conditions."

"Yeah, well, hindsight is wonderful, isn't it?" She smiled to take the sting out of it.

She explained how she had escaped into the depths of the building and then, hesitantly, her subsequent rescue and subsequent imprisonment. "I think I saw his face, but that part is all mixed up in my mind. Sometimes all I can remember is shadows." She remembered seeing Dan there as well, or something that looked like Dan, but she didn't say anything about it.

"Would you recognize him if you saw him again?"

Kelly shook her head impatiently. "Let me tell you the whole story first." He nodded and refilled both their cups. "I don't know how long I was locked up, but it had to have been close to a full day, because I lost Tuesday completely. It was dark outside again when it let me out."

"It?"

"That's right, 'it'. I'll be honest with you. I've been going along with this spooky business because you seemed to be taking it seriously, but I never really thought there was anything, well, supernatural involved. But I think I may have seen that thing's face and I don't think it was human." Her voice caught in her throat and she stopped long enough to drink half of her coffee. Dan noticed that her hand was trembling when she set the cup back down.

"Would you like something stronger than that? I have some brandy left."

Kelly shook her head. "No, I'm all right. Whatever those

things are, Dan, there are two of them."

"Are you sure about that? I mean, you hadn't had food or water for twenty hours or so and you might have been seeing things."

"I know. But Dan, those things were too horrible for me to imagine. They weren't human. I mean, they had arms and legs and a head and from a distance, they would look pretty much like people, but their faces are pasty white and disfigured." She dropped her eyes and raised the cup to her lips, then set it down determinedly. "Maybe I will take a little of that brandy."

Dan excused himself and ran next door, returning with the bottle and two glasses. They each had a double shot before she told him the rest, her escape and subsequent injury, the dazed state in which she encountered the patrol that led to her arrest. "I don't remember much of what happened after they put me in the ambulance. Somebody was asking me questions, but I don't know what I told them. They'd already given me some pills and I was pretty much out of it. I was not having a good time."

Dan suggested she go back to bed, but she resisted. "I don't know if I'll be able to sleep. I keep seeing that face." A few minutes later she stifled a yawn and decided that she might be willing to lie down for a while.

"There's one other thing I have to tell you." She was reluctant to tell him the rest, but had finally decided that it might be important. "I think this might just have been an hallucination or wishful thinking, but it seemed so real at the time. I saw you there, Dan."

"Me?" His forehead creased in confusion.

"Yes, or at least, someone who looked like you. The images are all mixed up in my mind so I don't know exactly what I saw or when, but I remember your face." Her face grew agitated with the next words. "But then everything gets kind of blurry and you weren't there anymore and that horrid face was staring at me." She stopped suddenly. "I'm sorry, I'm babbling. Like I said, that part was probably just an hallucination. But it seemed so real at the time."

Dan escorted her back to bed but declined an invitation to join her there. "I have to go out."

"Out?" Her eyes widened in alarm.

"Don't worry. I just have to run a few errands. I'll be careful."

"You do that." She was asleep before he left the room.

Dan returned to the kitchen and quickly wrote down as much of Kelly's description of the building as he could remember. He already had a pretty good idea of its location; he'd worked with a photographer for a magazine article on the Providence waterfront and they'd rented a small boat from which to photograph the coastline, which included two blocks of abandoned buildings near the highway.

After locking Kelly's door, he returned to his own apartment, where he busied himself for several minutes before emerging with his car keys, a flashlight, and a small overnight bag. In it he carried a number of seemingly unrelated items, most of them improvised. If the rest of the night went as he expected it to, he might well have need of them.

It was already after ten o'clock and the curfew was in force, though widely disregarded. He still had a valid pass, which he placed conspicuously in the corner of his windshield before driving out of the lot and turning east. Twenty minutes later, he parked less than a block away from Angela Harris' car, although he didn't recognize it.

Dan's solution to the problem posed by the hurricane fence was more direct than that of either Kelly or Harris; he tossed his bag over the top, then scrambled up its side, carefully avoiding the double strand of barbed wire at the top. He recovered the bag and started directly toward the shoreline, working his way around a collapsed storage shed and then directly toward the largest building in the complex. The faded lettering on the outside wall was impossible to read even with the flashlight, but Dan spotted the ruined doorway and guessed correctly that he'd found the place where Kelly had had her adventure.

A few steps inside, he began to have second thoughts, wondering just what the hell he was doing searching a dangerously deteriorated building in the dead of night in a city swept by plague and violence. Despite his misgivings, he didn't turn back, although his searching was considerably less thorough than that which had been conducted by Harris and Marzocchi a short time before. He limited himself to a quick flick of the flashlight from the doorway of several of the smaller rooms and skipped the side corridors, proceeding directly along the most obvious route until he reached an enormous hole in the floor. This seemed to confirm at least one part of Kelly's story, and he knelt by the hole, playing the light down through the opening, illuminating rusting machinery piled haphazardly to either side and a matched pair of oil tanks snug against an inner wall. There was a flashlight lying on the floor nearby, extinguished, but there was no way to tell how long it might have been there. The broken edges of the flooring were clean and sharp, however, proving that the damage was recent.

There was a sound from somewhere else in the building.

It was brief and muffled but distinct enough to convince him he was not alone. Dan unzipped his bag and stood up, feeling his pulse quicken, then slowly started back along the main corridor.

At the first junction, he turned to his left, peering into the inky shadows. There was no way to be sure where the sound had originated, but this direction felt right.

The shipping and receiving docks were silent, unlighted, covered by a layer of greasy dust. Dan saw the overturned cabinet, which matched Kelly's description reasonably well, and moved toward it, but stopped short when his flashlight picked out the broad smear of drying blood.

Cautiously Dan edged his way to one side, trying to look in every direction simultaneously. A few steps later, his light fell across the hatch cover, which also was streaked with blood. He crouched and pressed his palm against the cold metal, and the hatch cover rocked in place, not quite seated on its frame. Dan stood up, braced himself against the wall, and used the heel of one foot to push it aside.

When he played the flashlight inside the gap he'd created, Dan found himself staring into the dead face of Angela Harris. She'd been crammed into what little space remained in the pit, along with Vincent Marzocchi.

From somewhere close by, there was a sudden menacing hiss.

Dan whirled, sweeping the flashlight around the room, and almost immediately caught a faint movement in the far corner, something large and dark scuttling out of sight. He kept moving the light, trying to locate the elusive figure, but there were too many places to hide. Without dropping his eyes, he began fumbling in the bag, finally withdrew the cross which Kelly had given him.

"I see you there!" he shouted. "Come out into the light."

There was no answer. Dan awkwardly scooped up the bag

with the same hand that held the cross and started to move toward the exit, feeling very foolish for having come here alone in the middle of the night.

Something moved ahead and to his left, as though whatever or whoever lurked in the darkness was also trying to reach the exit. Dan tried to retreat more quickly, even though the unpredictable footing threatened to trip him up, and finally his foot did come down on a piece of loose debris and he stumbled. As he did so, there came the sound of rapid footsteps as something came at him out of the darkness.

Desperately, Dan raised the flashlight.

The light startled the younger vampire, which came to a sudden halt two meters away. Its eyes blinked rapidly and unnaturally above a lipless mouth. Dan gasped as he saw its face in detail, riddled with sores, pockmarked with bristles of short hair. The cross in his hand suddenly felt very heavy, but he raised it anyway.

The vampire stepped forward and knocked the cross from Dan's hand with an almost casual sweep of its arm. Dan leaped back, barely avoiding the backhand that was designed to rip open his throat, stumbled and nearly lost his grip on both bag and flashlight. The vampire stalked forward and Dan retreated further, realizing to his dismay that his adversary now stood between him and the only exit.

He had other religious icons and a few cloves of garlic, but since the cross had failed, he feared the worst. He stepped back quickly, one hand fumbling in his bag, ignoring the garlic, a *Bible*, a pair of sterling silver table knives, and a hand mirror, then withdrew a hammer and one of the wooden stakes he'd carved from the legs and crossbars of his easel. At least these felt like weapons.

Dan had no warning before when the vampire attacked. He threw his bag at its face and retreated but not quickly enough. One clawed hand ripped through his shirt, talons scraping shallow lines of fire across his left shoulder. Dan cried out and twisted away, then raised his hands defensively as he sensed rather than saw that it was still coming. He dropped the flashlight and the hammer but managed to hold onto the wooden stake as it caught hold of him, powerful arms wrapping around his body. He lost his balance and fell backward, still firmly in the vampire's grasp.

The wind exploded from his lungs as he fell onto a pile of

rusting pipes, and for a few seconds it was impossible even to struggle. The vampire's crushing weight lay on top of him but it was moving progressively more slowly, its arms and legs moving randomly. Dan tried to slip out from underneath, and that's when he realized that the stake he was holding had been jammed up into the vampire's torso when it fell across his body.

Bracing himself, Dan partially dislodging his attacker, then slid his legs out from beneath the dead weight and rolled away. It wasn't dead, because it began to hiss, and when Dan retrieved the flashlight, he saw that the creature had risen to its knees. Although its hands were held near the shaft protruding from its chest, they never quite touched it. The vampire's face was a twisted mask of rage, even more repulsive than before. Thick black mucous was dripping from the single nostril and the sides of its mouth.

Dan looked around for the hammer, but was unable to see where it had fallen. The vampire rose from its crouch and Dan stepped back, alarmed. Rather than dying, it seemed to be regaining its strength. It had been hurt, but apparently not fatally. Knowing that he had only a few seconds left in which to act, Dan stepped forward and swung the flashlight, smashing its head against the blunt end of the stake. The bulb and lens exploded immediately, plunging him into darkness, but the vampire screamed as the stake was driven deeper into its body. Dan grabbed the stake with his left hand and continued to pound at it until the flashlight was a shapeless mass of metal, By then the vampire had fallen to the floor and Dan was kneeling beside it, his arm rising and falling until he was too exhausted to deliver another blow. The body beneath him had stopped moving altogether, and had begun to warm up toward room temperature.

Exhausted, Dan sat on the floor, breathing heavily, feeling as though he had fallen out of the real world into a bizarre nightmare.

The flashlight was beyond repair, but he still had his cigarette lighter. The tiny flame wasn't much, but it was enough to let him confirm what he already knew. He had not just killed a human being.

His first impulse was to notify the police. "Officer, I've just killed a vampire." Sure, that would work. The only person in authority who might give him a fair hearing was lying dead only a few feet away. Remembering that, Dan felt a spike of grief; he'd liked Angela Harris.

But at least it was dead, he thought. The worst of it is over with. He had forgotten that Kelly had seen two of them.

Scott Simonelli and Mark Cussler were still manning their checkpoint, although they had yet to receive a replacement for Albert Rossiter, who was presumed AWOL. Edgar Deakins had returned twice that day, insisting that the boy had run off with his daughter and that his two "friends" must have collaborated in the "abduction".

Nor were they particularly delighted when Dan drove up and insisted that he had killed some kind of monster in an abandoned building. The smell of brandy on his breath didn't make his story any more credible and they had already been approached by several certifiable nutcases.

"Look, mister, go home and sleep it off, why don't you?" Cussler was hoping to get some rest himself; he and Simonelli had been covering for each other the past few nights, one sleeping while the other kept watch, even though they were both supposed to remain awake until they were relieved at two in the morning.

Dan's fear had morphed into anger. "Look, you idiots, call your superiors and get them down here to check this out! There are two police officers lying dead in there, and I don't know how many other people!"

Simonelli was jumpy. He had felt as though unseen eyes were watching these past few nights and it was beginning to get to him. Crazy though this guy might be, that didn't mean he hadn't seen real bodies. Or even caused them. It might be better just to humor him. "Listen, Mark, maybe we should let someone else deal with this. It's not our problem."

Cussler looked as though he wanted to argue, but he shrugged resignedly. "All right, what the fuck. But we're gonna catch hell if they send out someone on a wild goose chase because of us."

He was reaching for the field phone when a dark shape appeared out of the night, as though shadows had somehow congealed into a solid mass.

Dan blinked as something hot and wet sprayed across his face, raised one hand to wipe at the sticky substance. It was hot and smelled like blood. Cussler looked momentarily surprised as he fell backward, his jugular torn open. The streetlight provided more than enough illumination for Dan to see what had come among them, the scarred and bestial face was unmistakable, as was the butt of the makeshift wooden stake that still protruded from his chest. It wasn't dead after all.

Dan turned and ran as Simonelli raised his M16 and began firing, a staccato sound that had already turned to screams and died as Dan reached his car, got inside, and pulled away, his tires screaming as he accelerated.

CHAPTER FOURTEEN: THURSDAY MORNING

Dan was not in control when he accelerated and he
sideswiped a parked car, then overcompensated and skidded across
the road, crashing through a low picket fence. He fought the wheel
and the car slewed to one side, narrowly missing a maple tree, then
burst back out through the fence and into the street. Dan slammed
his foot down on the brakes and the car stuttered to a stop, the engine
stalling.

"Shit!" He shifted back to neutral and turned the key, and
when it didn't catch immediately, he started to panic, forced himself
to wait for several seconds, then tried again. This time it started right
up.

Just as he began to move forward, something slammed into
the back of the car. Dan glanced into the mirror, but all he could see
was that something was blocking the rear window. He wasn't sure
that he wanted to know what it was.

He pressed more firmly on the gas pedal and accelerated up
the street, which was completely empty of traffic. For a brief
moment, he thought he had successfully escaped.

Then the rear window shattered.

Dan looked back over his shoulder. The vampire was
somehow, impossibly, affixed to the rear of the car, one arm groping
in through the broken glass. Dan glanced forward, barely avoided
another glancing collision, this time with a telephone pole, then
turned toward College Hill, his wheels screeching, going the wrong
way on a one way street.

Dan swerved the car violently from side to side, but without
dislodging his pursuer. He crossed the crest of College Hill, glancing
back and forth between the road and the rear view mirror. The
vampire had pushed its head inside, was straining to fit its shoulders
through the narrow opening. Without touching the brakes, Dan eased
up on the gas pedal, letting the car slow. He was hoping to jump
from the car and let it roll forward over the edge of the bridge into
the Providence River.

His next glance into the mirror scuttled that plan. The
vampire had worked its shoulders through and was sliding forward
confidently now. Knowing he had only seconds left, Dan lifted his

foot and opened the door, gave the steering wheel a hard tug to the right, then jumped out.

He tried to break the fall with his arms, but the pavement came up fast and hard. Half rolling, half skidding across the hard surface, he protected his face as much as possible. His clothing was shredded along with some of his skin as he tried to curl into a ball. His progress stopped when he crashed into a stack of garbage bags that were mercifully filled with relatively soft trash.

Dan was bruised and battered, but he fared a lot better than did his car. It had jumped the sidewalk, smashed into the first pump of the corner gas station before coming to a stop halfway through the front window of the cashier's booth. Fuel poured from the ruptured pump, spreading quickly across the pavement. A flame flickered somewhere inside the building, providing just enough light to how him the figure that struggled to pull itself out of the wrecked car.

Dan struggled to his feet and groaned as he put his weight on his right leg. Both of his arms hurt, and he suspected there would be even more pain when the adrenaline receded. He could see that the vampire was nearly free, and experienced a sudden, chilling certainty that he was looking at his own death. But just as it started toward him, there was a flash from behind as the small fire became a larger one, then leaped out of the building and began racing across the ground. Dan had only an instant to realize what was going to happen. He turned and threw himself down behind the probably inadequate shelter of the garbage bags.

The ground and air both shuddered when the flames reached the puddle of gasoline surrounding the ruined pump. Dan screamed as flaming fragments rained down over him, sparks melting through the trash bags and setting their contents on fire, as well as his shirt. He rolled across the ground, trying to smother the flames. The noise was deafening and he crawled away, not looking back until he had reached the far end of the small parking area. Even here he could feel the heat beating against his exposed skin, and he had to shade his eyes when he turned to look back the way he had come.

Nothing moved except the dancing flames that boiled up through the ground.

Less than a mile away, in its newest lair in the darkest corner of a warehouse currently filled with electronic parts, the older vampire raised its head and bared its fangs, sensing that the second of its offspring had now also perished. In the moment of its passing, the younger passed on to its parent all that it had experienced during its brief life, including the image of its killer's face. And his scent.

There would be retribution.

There had been a time when humanity had worshipped it as a god, or more accurately as a demon. It had preyed upon the hapless humans whose only weapons were spears and arrows. From time to time it had bred others of its kind as it had tried to do here. They were creatures of pure instinct with little intelligence, although with time they developed their own personalities. For a few years, it would not be completely alone, but sooner or later its offspring had challenged their forebear's authority, and when that happened, it destroyed them as ruthlessly as if they had been merely human. From time to time, a mortal would have the audacity to bring an end to the life of one of its get, and when that happened, the one responsible and everyone around him died a horrible death.

It had thought itself beyond their reach, but it had been careless and they had trapped it and imprisoned it for countless centuries.

It would not allow that to happen again.

The fire trucks showed up eventually, but not before the conflagration had spread to both adjacent buildings and several trees. Dan concealed himself among the bushes on the opposite side of the street, waiting for the initial pain to subside, hoping he would not be too stiff to walk. He was careful to stay out of sight. The last thing he wanted right now was to be picked up for questioning or arrested as an arsonist. When he thought he could leave without attracting attention, he staggered off into the darkness.

It was hot even away from the fire, but Dan felt a chill that had nothing to do with the temperature of the air. Although it appeared that the vampire had met its end in the fire, Dan sensed that the crisis still wasn't over. Vera Maitlin had insisted that the wooden chest, the Prison Box she called it, was essential. Was this one of the cases where her intuition hadn't been right? Somehow he had no confidence in that assumption.

It took almost an hour to reach his apartment building, during which he only once saw a military patrol, and that from a distance.

His key chain had been lost when he'd thrown himself from his car, but fortunately he kept the key to Kelly's place in his wallet. Kelly was asleep when he let himself in. After reassuring himself that she was resting quietly, he retrieved his spare key from her desk and went to his own apartment and removed what remained of his clothing. Even the shoes were so badly damaged that they were unsalvageable. He carefully washed and tended to his injuries; he wasn't actively bleeding any more, but there wasn't much of his skin that wasn't bruised or scraped and it was the most painful shower he had ever taken. Some of the deeper cuts should have been stitched up, but he had no intention of going outside until the sun was up. He had to be satisfied by antiseptic spray and bandages, at least for the time being.

By the time he was done, he was stiffer than ever, and it was a considerable ordeal to dress himself. He washed down four aspirin with a mouthful of grapefruit juice, then stumbled into his bedroom and fell across the bed, intending to take a short nap and nothing more.

Kelly opened her eyes in the darkness, released from a dream in which she'd been trapped in an endless maze, pursued by a distant figure whose features were sometimes Dan's and sometimes those of the creature she'd encountered in the abandoned factory. For the first few seconds, she sat up on her elbows, blinking in the darkness, breathing quickly, trying to sort out her memories of the past two days. She was reluctant to go back to sleep, partly because of the dream, partly because she felt that she should be up and doing something positive.

She swung her legs over the side of the bed and stood up, went to the bathroom and washed her face. There were haggard lines under her eyes, and she turned away from her reflection, toweling herself dry and slipping into her robe before wandering out to the kitchen. There was coffee, but it had gone cold in the unplugged pot. Rather than reheat it, she made a fresh batch, walking idly from room to room while it perked, letting the familiar surroundings restore a sense of normality.

There was no sign that Dan had returned, although he might be back in his own apartment. She glanced at the clock and wondered if he was asleep, if she would wake him up if she called.

Dan also had vivid, enigmatic dreams. In one he was sitting in a cubical room devoid of furniture except for a small table and two chairs. Someone was knocking on the door, so he called out, "Come in." The door opened immediately, admitting an elderly woman with chalk white hair. She was carrying the chest he and Angela Harris had spirited out of the police station.

He recognized her immediately even though he hadn't seen her in years.

"Vera Maitlin! They told me you were dead!"

She crossed to the table and placed the chest carefully in its center. "They were right. You're still in danger, you know," she said calmly. "I told you that you needed this."

"Yes you did," he answered. "But I don't know what to do with it. And the monster is dead, isn't it? I saw it die."

"That which never lived cannot die." She pointed to the chest. "But it can be confined."

His eyes swiveled to the table and back. "But it was burned to ashes, Vera," he protested. Too late. She was gone and he was alone in the room. Dan placed his hands on the lid of the chest, slowly raised it so that he could stare down into its interior.

And saw a smaller version of himself standing at a table, staring down into a diminutive replica of the same chest.

Someone knocked on the door.

"Vera?" Dan sat up, found himself lying in his own bed, the remains of the dream still vivid. He thought the knocking must have been his imagination and had closed his eyes again when it was repeated.

This time he knew it was no dream.

"Just a second!" he called out, then flicked on the bedside lamp and struggled to his feet. If anything, he felt even worse than before. In addition to the stiffness and burning sensation, he had a headache. He fumbled his way into a bathrobe and plodded barefooted out into the front room. The knocking had stopped.

Dan turned the bolt and pulled the door open, and found Kelly standing in the hall, similarly dressed. Or undressed.

"Feeling better, I assume?"

She smiled slyly and nodded.

"Come on in, then. You don't have to wait for an invitation.

Want some coffee?"

Kelly entered as Dan started to turn away, but before the door was closed, she had thrown her arms around him. He staggered back a step, almost tripping over his easel, and twisted within the circle of her arms to face her. Kelly's breasts were pressed against his chest and despite his many aches and pains, he felt himself beginning to respond.

"I gather coffee isn't what you had in mind," he whispered, lowering his head, and Kelly turned her face up and met his lips with her own. The contact was electric, and he could feel the urgency. He let his hands drift down across her back to grip her buttocks, pulling her up toward him.

Dan winced but his sudden desire dwarfed his pain. Kelly twined her own legs around his, and her arms tightened until he thought his ribs might break. Slowly, Dan maneuvered the two of them down toward the floor, following her lead as Kelly moved her arms up to the back of his head and pulled him forward, her tongue inside his mouth now. He started to lean forward, but she twisted slightly, catching him by surprise. They fell onto the carpeted floor and before Dan could take the initiative, Kelly used her hands and knees to roll him over onto his back, then spread her thighs and straddled his hips.

Kelly gripped the front of his bathrobe and pulled it roughly open. Dan lifted his own arms, pushed them between their straining bodies, and her robe fell open as well, revealing breasts that seemed fuller than he remembered. Kelly sat up, her hands pressing down hard on his shoulders, and he bit back a cry of pain as she pressed against his worst injury. There was a desperate, almost violent intensity to her lovemaking and he responded in kind, reached up to grab her breasts, pressing his fingers into the soft flesh with such force that he knew he must be hurting her. But if that was true, she gave no indication that she wanted him to stop. Breathing heavily, her color high, hair damp with perspiration, she moved her hips with careful deliberation.

She kissed him again, lightly this time, then let her mouth trail down over his chin, throat, the center of his chest. Her hands left his shoulders and he breathed a sigh of relief as the pain ebbed, closed his eyes and arched his head back as she stroked his sides, her arms moving down toward his hips. He relinquished his hold on her breasts, began to massage her shoulders as she moved further back along his body, her lips marking a hot trail down his belly, her soft cheek brushing against his erection.

Dan was so caught up in the moment that he didn't realize that they were no longer alone until he felt the sudden change in Kelly's movements, sensed rather than saw her sit back, head up.

"What?" He opened his eyes, saw Kelly staring back past the top of his head, twisted his neck just enough to see that someone else had entered the apartment, someone who had just used a credit card to pop the lock.

The newcomer was Kelly Marsh. Dan blinked and wondered if he was still asleep after all. Confused, he turned toward the first Kelly to ask her what was going on.

But it was no longer Kelly Marsh who sat astride his hips; the thing that squatted there now was utterly repulsive and unquestionably inhuman, with glittering amber eyes set in a scarred and pus-streaked face, its body swathed in a dark coarseness that might almost have been clothing, or perhaps a thin coat of fur or hair, or perhaps something else entirely, darkness made solid. Its lower jaw dropped open as it hissed, exposing its fangs, and Dan was suddenly aware of his naked vulnerability.

He tried to squirm free but the vampire's knees pressed together, holding him in place. In the depths of those merciless eyes he saw his own death, but Kelly had already snatched up a chair. She swept it through the air with all the strength she could muster, and it flew to pieces when it struck the vampire's face and chest. The impact forced it to lean backwards, but it wasn't ready to relinquish its prey. Hissing, it raised its arm toward her.

Kelly retreated out of reach, but she had distracted it long enough for Dan to throw off his own paralysis. He twisted and turned frantically and squirmed out from beneath the creature, but when he rolled over and tried to get to his knees, he was struck in the small of his back with such force that he collapsed to the floor, stunned.

Screaming with rage, Kelly picked up another chair and renewed her attack, striking the vampire across the top of the head. It shrugged off this blow as well, but now its rage was directed toward Kelly and it rose from Dan's prostrate form and reached for her with both clawed hands. Kelly danced back, but not quite fast enough to escape a glancing blow that drew blood from her raised arm. She was thrown back so violently that she sent Dan's rickety wooden bookshelf crashing to the floor before stumbling and falling onto her back.

Dan knew it was now or never. He rose shakily to his feet, turning in time to see the vampire stand fully erect and turn in his direction. Frantically, he searched for something he could use as a weapon, began throwing whatever came to hand, paint brushes, his palette, cans and bottles of paint and thinner, brushes, a sketch pad. The vampire batted them aside easily and tubes of paint - red and purple and black and orange - burst and splattered across the walls, the floor, the furniture. The vampire itself was spattered, although the colors seemed to stream slowly down the length of its body without sticking anywhere. Dan picked up the can of kerosene he used to clean his brushes and raised it above his head with both hands. When he threw it the vampire punched its hand completely through the metal container, splattering liquid in every direction.

"We have to get out of here!" Kelly was back on her feet and at the door, gesturing to Dan to join her. He took a step in her direction, but the vampire was much faster. It cut off his escape route, and was almost close enough to reach Kelly as well. She shrank back against the wall, apparently paralyzed with fright.

"No!" Dan took two running steps and jumped with both hands reaching for its throat. The collision made his head swim, as both he and the vampire lost their footing. The arm of the couch hit him just below the ribcage and all of the air in his lungs exploded outward in a single gasp. He had trouble focusing his eyes, and then even more trouble breathing as something grabbed him by the throat and lifted him into the air. Then he was flying across the room and into the far wall.

Near the door, Kelly suddenly crouched, picked something up from the debris around her feet. The vampire had half turned toward her when she raised her hand and a tiny flame snapped into existence. She'd found Dan's lighter. It paused, uncertain for the first time, and Kelly stepped forward and touched the flame to its body. Kerosene still dripping from its head and shoulders and the volatile fluid ignited with a rush of flame so sudden and intense that she jerked away, her eyebrows singed.

The vampire lowered its chin, stared down into the flames

that already covered its torso, then it raised its head to stare directly at Kelly. Surprisingly enough, it made no effort to escape or douse the flames once they were started, stood almost completely motionless, accepting -- at least for the moment -- that it had been outmaneuvered. It stared at her malevolently until the amber lights of its eyes faded and the very flesh of its body began to bubble and churn.

The fire was spreading rapidly. The carpet was alight and fingers of flame were licking hungrily at the couch. Kelly ran out to the kitchen, pulled Dan's household fire extinguisher from its hook, and raced back to the front room. Dan was leaning against the far wall and when she raised the extinguisher, he spoke in almost his normal voice. "No. Let it burn for a while yet."

The vampire's bulk had already been reduced by half. It stood in a column of flame in the center of the room, as though its flesh was made of tallow. What remained bubbled and hissed as it was slowly reduced to ash, even the bones were being consumed.

Dan edged his way around to Kelly and took the extinguisher, but he waited even longer, until he was sure that the vampire's immolation was irreversible. Then he used it sparingly, preventing the fire from spreading any further, coating the walls and floor, but still doing nothing to douse the fire's boiling core. Rancid smoke was making it difficult to breathe and Kelly hastily opened the windows.

When Dan finally relented and extinguished the last of the flames, the only trace of the vampire was a featureless mass of ash and charred material.

"Is it dead?"

Dan shook his head. "I don't know. Probably not. I don't think it was every alive exactly, at least not in the sense you and I are alive. I think we're safe for the time being, but we can't waste any time."

Kelly clearly didn't understand, but she wasn't about to argue. Following Dan's lead, she helped scrape up everything that remained of the vampire and deposit it inside the wooden chest. Dan wasn't satisfied until they had even included the remnants of charred carpet that surrounded the area, and he scraped the boards beneath until new wood shone through. By the time they were finished, their fingers were cramped and sore and their lungs burned because of the lingering fumes.

Finally Dan closed the lid and engaged the lock.

"Now what?"

"Tomorrow I'm going to have this thing soldered shut and then I'm going to drive to the most remote place I can find and bury it as far down as I can dig."

Kelly found Dan's brandy, which had marvelously survived the wreck of his apartment, and poured them each a glass. "Do you think it'll be safe there? I mean, it got out this time, didn't it? Won't that just happen again?"

"Eventually, I guess." He accepted the glass, let a small portion of the liquid burn its way down his throat. "But this time I'm going to bury a clearly worded warning with it. The next people who dig it up won't have to rely on mysterious psychic predictions and dumb luck."

"But what happens if they don't believe it? I mean, would you have believed it back when this all started?"

"No, I wouldn't have. And if they don't, well, they'll just have to take their own chances."

EPILOGUE

The following morning, Dan and Kelly retrieved her car and the day after that they managed to leave Providence. They drove north, turned onto Route 13, and followed it to Managansett, then parked on Reservoir Road and carried the chest several hundred meters back into a wooded area, following an old access road that was so overgrown that even passage on foot was difficult. This was a watershed area for the reservoir and could not be developed, so there was a reasonable chance the chest would remain undisturbed for many generations to come. Dan and Kelly took turns digging until they had excavated a pit almost two meters deep, then carefully placed the box in the bottom and filled it in. A leather notebook was securely tied to the lid of the chest, and the whole package was wrapped in a thick plastic bag.

The McCandless Building, an aging and currently untenanted office building just outside downtown Providence, had seen better days. Although it was still in reasonably good repair, it was archaic enough that it was not presently an attractive alternative to the more modern buildings nearby. This part of Providence was no longer fashionable; the focus of professional business activity had shifted toward the renovated districts near the Providence River and the waterfront.

Although the upper floors were occasionally inspected by the owners, it had been years since anyone had voluntarily ventured into the clutter and gloom of the basement. Some portions were empty and relatively clean, but fully three quarters of the area was filled with abandoned filing cabinets, boxes of discarded paperwork belonging to departed tenants, and scattered mounds of old office equipment that hadn't been worth transporting to another location.

In one corner, behind a row of dust covered desks, Marie Conoyer lay on her back, in the same spot she had occupied for the past three days. The sweat suit she'd been wearing while jogging in the area had been thrown carelessly out into the center of the room. Maria was not in pain, but neither was she entirely conscious; the occasional sounds she made as she shifted slightly to ease the stresses and strains in her body went completely unheard, because no one knew she was there, and no one who missed her had thought to search this far from her apartment.

Maria's abdomen was grossly swollen, the skin stretched tightly over an enormous pregnancy, one which had very nearly come to term.

If anyone had been there to look, they would have seen the three shallow, triangular wounds that were quite visible just below her navel.

www.ingramcontent.com/pod-product-compliance
Lightning Source LLC
Chambersburg PA
CBHW072056170626
46813CB00004B/1374